HACK

AN F.X. SHEPHERD NOVEL

ALSO AVAILABLE FROM KIERAN CROWLEY AND TITAN BOOKS

Shoot (October 2016)

HACK

AN F.X. SHEPHERD NOVEL

Kieran Crowley

TITAN BOOKS

Hack
Print edition ISBN: 9781783296491
E-book edition ISBN: 9781783296507

Published by Titan Books
A division of Titan Publishing Group Ltd
144 Southwark Street, London SE1 0UP

First edition: October 2015
1 3 5 7 9 10 8 6 4 2

Did you enjoy this book? We love to hear from our readers.
Please email us at readerfeedback@titanemail.com or write to us at Reader
Feedback at the above address.

To receive advance information, news, competitions, and exclusive offers online,
please sign up for the Titan newsletter on our website:
www.titanbooks.com

FOR RIKI

1.

On my third day on the job at the tabloid *New York Mail,* I was weaving a quiet, climate-controlled cocoon of predictability inside my beige, carpeted cubicle. When I swiveled toward the window in my chair, I was rewarded with a shiny Manhattan view of the skyscraper next door, like a giant, docked cruise ship, bright with sharp spring sunlight. I watched a flock of dirty pigeons in tight formation wing up from the unseen sidewalk below, shape-shifting past my window, mounting the space between the buildings. As they rolled and climbed as one, maybe toward their never-seen nests, the space between them never changed. Until a brown blur flashed down, making a hole. The blur and the birds vanished like magic, so quickly it took me a few seconds to realize what I had seen. A hawk, probably a peregrine falcon, taking lunch. To go.

I turned back to my desk and sipped some soothing decaffeinated Earl Gray tea from my *New York Mail* mug. I glanced at my screen, where I was making headway on my second weekly feature column. Besides the computer terminal on my desk, I had a flat black letter opener for opening what little mail I got, along with some pens and thin notebooks, and a neatly folded emergency necktie for my collared shirt, in case I needed to dress up. There was a telephone and a set of three interlocked stainless-steel rings, magic rings from my early magician phase in school. As a kid, I was the pest who knew where the rabbit was hidden. That's the thing about magic, and it was a good lesson. Magic is not magic. It's misdirection. And planning.

I unwrapped my lunch, a steaming chicken souvlaki sandwich on pita bread, and was reaching for the tzatziki yogurt sauce when I was startled by my desk phone ringing. For the first time. It was loud and annoying.

I didn't answer it but it kept chirping. I had used it to phone people I needed to speak to for my column. Readers emailed and snail-mailed questions for me to answer, and my voicemail took care of the rest. Up to that point, I had been comforted by the idea that, theoretically, I would never have to communicate with anyone I didn't want to, while I worked on my other project.

The phone rang some more and I remembered I hadn't personalized my voicemail message. It might be someone important, perhaps a boss. I let it ring a while longer but it wouldn't stop. I thought about what might happen if I didn't answer it and finally decided I had no choice.

"Hello?"

"Frank Shepherd?" a young, loud female voice demanded.

"Umm... yeah. F.X. actually. Just call me Shepherd."

"Hold for Nigel Bantock on the City Desk," the voice snapped, quickly, over a noisy background of squawking police radios and more ringing phones. Damn. It *was* a boss.

"I'm sorry. Who is this?" I asked dead air. She was already gone. The City Desk. Breaking news. One floor above me and a world apart from the sleepy Features Department where I was hiding.

"Bantock here." A sharp accent. Australian? "Frank Shepherd?"

"Yeah. Call me Shepherd. I'm sorry, what did you say your name—"

"Howaya, Shep? Nice to meet ya, mate. I'm new in town, first day on the desk truth be told, but I hear you're the best. I've got what smells like a good murder uptown. Right up your alley."

"Uh, great, uh… sir," I stumbled, wondering if I was supposed to respond with enthusiasm. "What's the story? What kind of animal is involved?"

"Damn. You're bloody good. How did you know that? You listening, too?"

"Know what?"

"The pooch. Photo just heard over the cop radio a sec ago that some dog is guarding the body. Cops may have to shoot it. Top of the list right now, mate," Bantock continued without a breath. "You know, 'loyal pooch protecting slain master?' Blah blah. Got a runner from the shack on the way with Photo but I need you on this right away. I want an exclusive break on this from you or I'll know why not," he concluded in a friendly, threatening tone.

"A good murder. The shack," I repeated, trying to sound as if I knew what the hell he was talking about.

"The cop shop at police headquarters," Bantock fired back. "Looks like fun."

"A fun murder. Great. But I'm not sure why I—"

"It's a good nabe, mate, um, Clinton area, Upper East Side near Central Park, and it's indoors. Google Earth shows a bloody townhouse. Good bet it's RWPs," he assured me, rapidly reading out an address and repeating it so I could write it down. "Male dead on the scene, hacked to death. Crime Scene and Homicide are there. Get up there and get us a lead for the web, pronto, amigo. Cheers."

"Yes, sir. Have a nice day," I lied.

He was gone before I could ask him what RWPs were. Maybe this guy thought he was doing me a favor by sending me out on breaking news? Apparently, at the *New York Mail*, when they had a good murder, a fun murder, they emptied the office. I thought about it for a while. Maybe I should have told him I wasn't a reporter. Never did it once. Probably a bad idea. It was the dog. I couldn't say no to a boss on a pet story, not on my third day at work, and this might help with my little side project. My mouth was watering as I looked at my souvlaki sandwich, with its aromatic grilled chicken and shredded lettuce and tomatoes. I also had a cold can of soda, only because I figured I couldn't get away with a beer at work. I glanced at my folded tie but decided not to wear it. My lunch was too messy to take with me. I wrapped it back up and left it on my desk. Hoping to hell this was a rare thing, a quick thing.

I left my breached cocoon. It was a warm, sunny, magical day in May but I was not a butterfly. I took a cab.

It was my first time in a New York City cab, a change from the bus and subway. A bulletproof plastic barrier between me and the driver had a pay slot, a credit card machine and a flat screen TV playing lame infomercials. The last cab I was in, in another city, had none of those things and definitely wasn't bulletproof. I liked this one better. The view was also nicer. Young women in short dresses and high heels, out to lunch, laughing, gossiping in the sun. The only thing similar about this cab in this city was the Baluchistani music the driver was playing.

2.

Bantock was right. It was a good neighborhood: gourmet restaurants, boutiques and fancy townhouses with shiny brass plaques on them, a spot where people were rich enough to have lifestyles, not just lives. It even seemed sunnier. My empty stomach growled. A crowd of TV crews, photographers and reporters were hanging out behind baby-blue NYPD sawhorses on the sidewalk on East 72nd Street. I went up to two uniformed male cops, one black and one white, standing behind a tightly stretched yellow plastic CRIME SCENE DO NOT CROSS tape, which blocked the roadway. Behind them, emergency vehicles and cop cars were clustered in front of a brown townhouse in the middle of the block. As I approached, I heard the chattering of motorized camera shutters from the photographers, who were all pointing their cameras at me. They had no idea who I was and were shooting first and asking questions later. This could be useful.

"I'm Shepherd. I'm here about the dog," I told the cops.

They both giggled at my name.

"Give me a break," I said.

"No vehicle, Shepherd?" the black cop asked.

"No," I replied. "But I think our other guy, the one from

headquarters, is coming in one."

"You think?" the white cop chimed in.

"Sorry. I'm new. Third day on the job," I tried.

"Okay," the black officer said, with a shrug, lifting the tape. "I'll take you down."

As we walked, the cop, whose nametag said GUMBS, looked at my face. I got that look people gave me when they were debating whether or not to ask me about the scars on my left cheek; a dark, gnarly one, flanked by two fainter ones that missed my blue eye and vanished into my sandy sideburn and hairline. I was used to it. Everybody saw it but most people pretended they didn't. I could see the curiosity, the revulsion. The cop went for it.

"Pit bull get ya?" he asked, pointing at the claw-like lines.

"You guessed it." I smiled at him but he wasn't convinced. "You should be a detective."

"Thought you were new?" he asked.

"Happened the first day. Second day, I took off. So far, today looks okay. So, you have one dead guy inside?"

"Yeah, a homicide. Some famous fag."

I let it go.

"What are RWPs?" I asked, as we walked. The cop smirked.

"Why?"

"Something my boss said. What's it mean?"

"Rich White People," he said with a big grin.

"Oh. I just heard it today. Like I said, I'm new."

And my first assignment as a reporter would hopefully be my last. We sidestepped a dirty young Bradford Pear tree struggling out of its square hole of dirt. In the spring breeze, the tough sapling gently snowed white petals onto the filthy pavement.

"What's your first name, Shepherd?" the cop asked, smiling.

"It's not German," I countered, anticipating the joke.

"Too bad," he cackled.

As we walked up the sandstone steps and through a large antique door of dark wood, the cop talked into his portable radio. He led me down a hall toward the rear of the first floor. It was like an art gallery, with framed photographs, cookbook covers and magazine stories on both sides, a red Persian carpet underfoot. They were vanity walls for some bald fat guy with big red lips who looked like the Pillsbury Doughboy. I deduced that his name was Aubrey Forsythe and he was a food critic for the prestigious *New York Tribune*, hobnobbing with very famous people. The folks in the photographs were all eating wonderful food and smiling because it was so delicious. My stomach growled again. There were pictures of Forsythe, chowing down with an obnoxious billionaire in a cheap toupee, and with famous actors, mayors, and presidents. There was a large poster for *Food Fight*, a TV show featuring Aubrey and a lean, handsome guy with wavy hair, throwing food at each other and laughing. In some photographs, obviously personal shots, the Pillsbury Doughboy was being hugged by the same guy. One big framed photo at the end featured both men in front of a church, wearing tuxedos, holding bouquets of flowers and beaming.

At the end of the hall, several plainclothes detectives in suits waited behind a uniformed Emergency Services cop, who was pointing a black 12-gauge shotgun in the direction of a growling noise coming from the kitchen, a large, bright white and stainless-steel affair that looked like a nuclear lab. Something smelled great and something else smelled bad.

"Here he is, Lieutenant. His name is Shepherd," Officer Gumbs announced, chuckling and waiting for a reaction.

There wasn't any, except they all looked confused. "I'm Lieutenant Izzy Negron," said one of the detectives. "We got a big husky in attack mode. Guarding the boyfriend's body."

"Husband," I corrected him.

"What?" Negron asked, sounding genuinely confused.

"Husband. Looked like a wedding photo back there," I told him.

"Husband?" one detective asked. "Give me a fuckin' break." The other cops began snickering.

"Knock it off!" Negron snapped. "Okay, the husband," he said to me. "Maybe. I haven't seen a license yet. Who cares?"

"Where's your trank gun and noose?" a suddenly suspicious ESU cop demanded. "All we've got is a wire noose on a pole. We're out of trank darts."

"I don't use that stuff," I told them.

"Shit. Okay. I'll have to take the dog out," the shotgun cop said.

"Not in my crime scene," Negron said. "I don't want canine blood contaminating my body."

"Let me give it a try," I said.

They argued some more then agreed to let me try, obviously convinced I would fail—but better me than them.

"Okay, Shepherd. If he attacks you, just go down, go fetal, and we'll get close and get a better shot. Clear?" Negron said.

Yeah. I was bait. They all pulled guns and made a hole for me. I asked them to back around the corner. Negron's partner, who said his name was Detective Phil D'Amico, gave me a pair of baby-blue surgical gloves. I put them on.

"Don't let him see you," I told them, stepping into the kitchen. "I'll yell if I need you." I stopped and turned back. "What's his name?"

"Neil something," Negron answered.

"Leonardi," D'Amico said, glancing at his notebook. "Neil Leonardi, age thirty-eight."

"No, I meant the dog's name."

Now they laughed loudly. Including Negron. At me. The dog growled at the sound.

"No fucking clue," Izzy said, still laughing.

3.

I entered the kitchen with silent, baby steps. It was a large square room with a shining white marble floor and a black restaurant-style swinging door on the far side, a round window in it at eye level. There was a brick oven on one wall, a small fireplace next to it, and a huge, gleaming stainless-steel chef's stove. Above the white center island counter and sinks, suspended from a shiny oval, hung dozens of pots and pans, brilliant in the micro spotlights, like a TV set. The room cost more than I could make in ten years.

My mouth watered from the aroma of onions, garlic, parsley, sautéed butter and cheese. Someone had been making a mess, cooking, squirting oil and vinegar everywhere. A large stainless-steel frying pan was on the stovetop and various spices and other ingredients were strewn across the shiny, dark granite counter near the stove and on the center island. A white, papery garlic bulb had rolled across the floor.

As I inched forward, the low growling became louder snarling. I peeked around the island and caught a glimpse of a large white husky with glacial blue eyes, his snowy bib smeared with blood—not his own by the look of it. He snapped in my direction. Behind the dog was a pale, naked dead man, face down on the gleaming floor. The younger guy from the photographs in the hall. His head was covered in wavy hair and haloed by shiny bright red liquid on the white floor. His throat was slashed, hacked open. Something glistened in the eye I could see. I inched closer. Tears. Like he had been crying and was killed mid-sob.

Next to the body was a glazed ceramic bowl, a circular white island in the lake of crimson. The top of the dead man's right ass cheek seemed to be missing, an oval purple gash in its place. Weird. I ducked back. Did the dog maul him? It looked sliced, not chewed. It was a striking image, the china white floor, the pale corpse arrayed atop the perfect raspberry-red puddle. There was some scruffy green stuff scattered across the dead man's back. It took me a while to realize what it was.

The large expensive frying pan, splattered with burned and clotted sauce, was still on the stove. A cutting board had been used to shred lemon slices. A gouged-out wedge of Parmesan cheese had been tossed aside. Tufts of green parsley, melting butter in a glass tub, greasy knives, a cheese grater, and a smelly garlic press littered the counter. Tiny green gnarly capers were scattered about and, near the edge of the counter closest to the door, one small white pill. I looked closer at the square chalky tablet. Ecstasy? Oxycodone? I sniffed it without touching it. Mint? There was a letter A on the tablet. It was an Altoid mint. I sneaked another look at the dog and he snapped again but did not come at me. The white bowl had lettering around the rim. SKIPPY.

"Skippy!" I called out in a friendly tone. "Skippy?" The growling stopped. "Skippy, where are you?" I asked, edging toward the body.

Out of the corner of my eye I saw Izzy Negron peering

around the door at me, a confused expression on his face.

"Skippy?" I continued, getting closer. "Oh my God! What happened to Neil? Is he hurt? Skippy, what happened to Neil? What happened to Neil, Skippy?"

Skippy barked in response. I kept it up, repeating myself about a dozen times. Skippy kept up his answering barks. I opened a few cabinets until I found another bowl and half filled it with water. Wary, Skippy watched me but did not growl. I put it down in the far side of the kitchen, where Neil was hidden by the island, and sat on the floor a few feet away, next to the swinging door. I looked away. Skippy cautiously sidled over to the water, his paws leaving smeared bloody prints on the floor. He lapped up the water. When he was done, he collapsed on the floor next to me, whimpering. I petted him and told him he was a good boy. The cops peeked at us again, their guns poking into the room. Skippy howled. After a few minutes I pushed open the swinging door. Inside was a pantry and an expensive, cushioned dog bed in the corner. I held it open for several more minutes, talking to Skippy, and eventually he ambled through it and onto his bed. I went in, let the door swing shut behind us and sat with him.

Within a minute I could hear the CSI technicians entering the kitchen. I stood and looked through the door's porthole. They were beginning the process of taking photographs and processing the scene. I sat down again and googled Neil Leonardi on my iPhone and got a flood of hits. There were videos of Neil and Aubrey on their show, a website for the show and a different one for Aubrey. They were rich and famous and stars of American reality TV. There was even one episode called "Wedding."

"What happened to Neil?" I asked Skippy, who was too exhausted to bark.

"Foof," Skippy said, with a weary sigh.

"You got that right, Skippy," I told him, taking a shot of

him with my phone's camera.

I turned and took another shot through the glass porthole of Neil's body and the kitchen. I was frustrated that Skippy could not talk. Probably not as frustrated as he was. I dialed the main number for the *Mail* and asked the operator for the City Desk.

"Where the bloody hell are ya, mate?" Nigel yelled. "Nobody can find you up there. Why don't you answer your fucking phone?"

"It hasn't rung. I'm inside the townhouse, with the dog. His name is Skippy and he is a large husky. Seems to be about three or four years old. White coat, blue eyes. He is very upset but he seems unharmed. The blood on his paws and his fur is not his. He got it from the pool of blood while he was guarding his dead master. I'll send you photos. What's your email?"

"You're *inside* the bleeding townhouse?"

"Yeah. Just off the kitchen. With Skippy."

"You have pictures? Skippy? Uh… records say the building there is owned by…"

"Aubrey Forsythe, the food critic. Yeah. The blood on Skippy belongs to Neil Leonardi, Aubrey's husband. He's the one dead in their kitchen. Throat slashed."

"Bloody brilliant! Are you sure?" Nigel asked.

"I'm looking at the body. He's nude, face down and someone made a messy meal in the kitchen. Aubrey isn't here. They want to question him about—"

"Fucking fantastic! Hold the phone, Shep, let me get rewrite on the line. Give them every cough and splatter so we can toss it up on the web, and then get back to work, mate. This exclusive?"

"You mean are there other reporters in here? No. They're all a block away. Does it matter?"

"You're a pisser, Shep. I'll kiss you later," he giggled.

I wondered if Nigel was serious about the kiss. By that

time, the technicians were finished. Skippy was asleep. I stepped back into the kitchen just as Negron and D'Amico entered their crime scene.

4.

Izzy was asking questions but nobody was answering.

"So, Neil, were you cooking when this happened?" Negron asked the dead man, as he gently parted the hair on the back of the corpse's head with surgical-gloved fingers. "You were done, right? The meal is gone. What did he hit you with? Or did you get this bump when you fell?" Negron continued. "Who clipped you on the right cheek? Did Aubrey hit you? Isn't he left-handed?"

D'Amico remained silent, just looking and listening, as if this kind of behavior were normal, as if the corpse might reply. I did the same, casually glancing at the empty sinks and down into a garbage can, which had a new plastic bag in it but no garbage. One upper cabinet door was ajar. Inside I saw two stacks of fine, pure white china dinner plates, almost two dozen.

"Here we go, what's under your fingernails, Neil?" Izzy asked. "Looks like skin and blood. Alright, now we're talking. The killer hit you and you scratched him. Yes. Good man. Phil, let's get bags for his hands. So, Neil, did you cook the meal? Except for the skin under your nails, your hands are clean. Maybe you washed. Where are your clothes, buddy?"

"Upstairs on the floor in the master bedroom in a pile by the bed," Phil answered, startling me. "They don't look like they got food on them."

Izzy nodded impatiently at Phil's interruption.

"Your eyes are all bloodshot, Neil. From crying, right? Were you already unconscious when he slit your throat?" Izzy continued. "Was it your boyfriend... husband? Lady next door says she heard you two having a big fight just before Aubrey went out."

Again, Neil did not answer but Negron continued questioning the naked man, undaunted.

"So your neighbor heard you guys fighting and banging things around and then Aubrey went out. She said the TV was on very loud and the dog was barking so she eventually called 911 to complain. When the uniforms arrived, the door was unlocked. They found you and accidentally let the dog out of the pantry. Was it Aubrey? Did he do this? Why did he cut a slice out of your butt after you were dead? Fuck was that about? Trying to dismember you and he gave up? Too much work? What were you..." Negron stopped in mid-question and glared at me, like he had figured something else out.

"Ask Neil why that slice is missing," I suggested. "Where is it?"

Izzy looked at Phil and they both looked back at me. In the pantry, I heard Skippy stirring, his nails clicking on the floor. I scanned the kitchen, noticed something above the center island counter. Something not there.

"There's no real food here," I went on. "No empty meat or veggie package in the trash. If Neil cooked and ate his lunch, where's his plate, his silverware? Where's the missing butt cheek?"

"It's not here," said Phil. "But he could have eaten, cleaned up the dish and cutlery and put them away. The killer obviously removed or disposed of the missing cheek.

We'll check the garbage disposal, the plumbing traps…"

"Why leave all this mess?" I asked. "Look at this place. It's a museum. Two neat freaks live here. The knives are all in their slots but the hanging rack above the counter has something missing, something that used to hang there, maybe a meat cleaver?"

"Yeah, I noticed that." Izzy turned back to the silent victim. "Maybe you were interrupted before you could clean up? Or the killer did the cooking after you were dead and he left the mess?"

"That still leaves a pound of flesh missing," I pointed out.

Izzy scowled back at me. Then it hit him. "Shit," Izzy spat. "Why me? No way."

"Maybe," said Phil. "Hopefully not."

Izzy looked back at Neil but before he could ask him the question, a disturbance could be heard from the direction of the front door. Phil went to check it out and returned in seconds. I could hear someone shouting from the hallway. Skippy began to yip and bark from behind the pantry door.

"It's Aubrey," said Phil. "He's back from doing some restaurant review and wants to know what's happening." He raised an eyebrow. "He wants to see Neil and he will call his good friend the mayor unless we tell him right away. You have to see his face. His cheek, I mean."

"Scratches," I said.

"You got it," Phil said to me, and then realized his mistake.

"Right," Izzy said, glaring at Phil. "I'll be right there."

Skippy was scratching on the other side of the pantry door. Phil ducked out and Izzy studied me with hard, dark eyes, examining my face, my scars, my hands, my jeans, my dress shirt and sneakers. It was an uncomfortable feeling, like being measured for handcuffs or a casket. He offered his gloved hand and I shook it.

"Thanks for your help," Izzy said, like a man who detested help. "Who are you again?"

I considered giving him the same answer as Gumbs but I told him the truth.

"Shepherd. F.X. Shepherd from the *Mail*. They sent me here to get the story on the dog."

His eyes flared in anger, then narrowed. He smiled and then barked a single laugh.

"The dog? You're not Frank Shepherd. He's their police reporter. I've known him for years. Fat slob, beer sponge. A real dork."

"Well that's my name, too. I think that's what happened. Francis Xavier Shepherd. I'm new. I began my 'Dog's Breakfast' pet column this week. He and I have similar names. That would explain it. I wondered why they sent a pet columnist to cover a murder."

I laughed and Izzy joined in but stopped abruptly. A look of horror spread over his face, replaced by anger, as he realized I was telling the truth. The shouting from the hallway got closer and louder and Aubrey Forsythe burst in.

5.

The famous foodie was six feet tall and half as wide, and he was angry and scared. Aubrey Forsythe's round face was bright red. Three scarlet scratches striped his left cheek, much like mine, but his were vertical and fresh. His jowls bounced and his eyes flashed with panic as he struggled to free himself from two cops trying unsuccessfully to prevent him from entering the crime scene. He was very strong. And important. Behind the pantry door, Skippy was wailing and clawing.

"Where's Neil?" Aubrey sputtered over and over, alcohol on his breath. "I've got to talk to Neil!"

He knew. Because he did it or just because he wasn't stupid? Izzy and Phil stepped between Aubrey and the body but not before he got a glimpse.

"Mr. Forsythe, I'm very sorry for your loss," Izzy began. "Could you please tell me—"

The *New York Tribune* restaurant critic let out an anguished wail that sounded like one of Skippy's howls. He gasped for breath and stopped struggling with the officers. His legs folded under him and he crumpled like one of those buildings they rig with explosives to implode. He was consumed with wracking sobs and then rolled on his huge belly and vomited.

Skippy threw himself at the pantry door and exploded into the kitchen. He was at his master's side, yelping and licking his face, as the man hugged the dog and dripped tears onto the marble floor. Izzy was cursing under his breath in what sounded like two foreign languages and giving the stink eye to the two cops who couldn't handle the fat gourmet who was messing up his crime scene.

After Aubrey and Skippy quieted down somewhat, I found a leash for Skippy and followed Aubrey and the cops into the dining room down the hall. They sat the blubbering Aubrey down in a chair and I tied the leash to the chair leg. Skippy curled up at Aubrey's feet and I went back to the kitchen. Izzy was talking to the dead guy again but stopped when I came in.

"Please tell me you were joking when you said you were a *Mail* reporter," Izzy said.

"I'm not a reporter. I told you. I write the pet column."

"What the fuck?" Izzy said. "You came to interview the dog?"

"Actually, I think he did that," Phil interjected.

"I'm not your big problem," I told them.

They both stared at me. I looked down at the body. "Look at it. The floor is as white as a plate. The puddle of blood like raspberry sauce, the meat and the garnish on top. Like in a restaurant."

They stared at the small sprigs of green parsley scattered on the victim's pale back and then at each other.

"Fuck me," Izzy said.

"Fuck us," Phil agreed.

"And Aubrey didn't do it," I told them.

"Fuck you know that?" Izzy demanded. "You see those scratches? Victim has skin under his fingernails. It's going to be Aubrey's."

"Maybe, but you saw him, the way his knees went. If he faked that, it was great. Besides, Skippy wasn't afraid of him," I added.

"He is on TV," Izzy noted. "That reality food show. They shoot it here. He's an actor. And the dog does not enter into it."

"What we have here is Ace Ventura," Phil sneered.

"Pet Detective," chuckled Izzy.

"Easy to prove," I told them, pointing to the vomit left by Aubrey. "Or disprove."

"Oy," Izzy sighed.

He nodded at Phil, who left the room and returned with one of the CSI guys, an older detective, who collected the upchuck into a plastic bag.

"I need to know what Forsythe had in his stomach," said Izzy. "As soon as possible."

"Stomach contents of the boyfriend? Not the victim?" the CSI detective asked, confused.

"Yeah," said Izzy. "Isn't there a test to determine whether something is human or animal tissue? I mean a fast one? The M.E. will do stomach contents on the vic, as usual."

"There's the instant antibody test. That takes about ten minutes and is presumptive on that and you get a profile that's supposed to be almost as accurate as a PCR DNA test. But not on stomach contents. And it's not admissible in court yet."

"I don't care about admissible," Izzy told him. "This is just us talking. I just want human, animal, vegetable or mineral. Now. Why not stomach contents?"

"Stomach acids fuck it up," the CSI guy explained.

"Okay, if you do it on stomach contents can you still find out if it's human or animal?"

"Yeah, sure. Right away. All I need is a little pinch. How will that help?"

"We'll see. Do it."

"On the vomit. The... the meat in the vomit," Phil said.

The CSI man looked green. "Okay. You think what the big guy threw up might be... holy shit. The post-mortem slice out of the ass? Are you friggin' serious?"

"I don't know," Izzy admitted. "I'm just asking. We gotta check."

"So you're saying the food critic, chef guy—"

"I'm not saying anything," Izzy interrupted before the guy could say the word. "I'm asking the question. You tell me."

"Holy shit."

"That remains to be seen," said Izzy.

6.

While the CSI guys did their thing, I slipped into the dining room, where Aubrey was recovering. Izzy came in a minute later and began questioning him. Apparently, Izzy also questioned the living. A red-eyed Aubrey said he had lunch at a Midtown restaurant named Bistro du Bois on the Upper East Side, which he was going to review in the *New York Tribune* for next Sunday's edition. He admitted that he and Neil had an argument before he left but denied it became overly physical. He seemed confused and claimed not to remember the reason for the argument. He agreed that a stainless-steel meat cleaver seemed to be missing from the kitchen.

Izzy politely and casually locked Aubrey into specific times that he left the apartment, had lunch, left the restaurant and returned home. He wrote it all down.

"Are you absolutely sure you didn't go somewhere else, Mr. Forsythe?" Izzy asked.

He hesitated and averted his eyes. It was obvious he was lying.

"Yes, I'm sure. You're wrong about the time. Obviously some bastards broke in and... killed Neil," Aubrey blurted. "Get off your asses and go find them."

"So the folks at this restaurant can confirm you were

there and when?" Izzy asked.

"Of course," Aubrey huffed, recovering his ego. "I'm rather well known. Besides, my film crew was with me."

Izzy looked up from his notebook.

"Film crew? Was your film crew here with you before you went out?" Izzy asked.

Aubrey froze. Izzy asked the question again.

"I… don't remember," he said, another lie.

"The crew is outside," Officer Gumbs told Izzy.

"We wouldn't let them in. They're outside moaning and bitching, saying they have a contract, threatening a lawsuit."

Izzy grinned and left the room with Phil. Aubrey fidgeted and demanded to use his cell phone, which the cops had taken. A uniformed sergeant said no and would not let him use the house phone either.

"Am I under arrest?" Aubrey demanded.

"No, sir. You are being questioned and we need your cooperation. Is there something you want to tell me? Maybe you remember something?"

"No."

I left the dining room and walked into the den, toward the sound of arguing. Izzy had brought the film crew inside and was ordering them to replay their film from earlier in the day. They refused in haughty tones. Izzy and Phil handcuffed the male cameraman and female producer and told them they were under arrest for concealing evidence in a homicide. Phil recited their rights. That led to a quick improvement in attitude and an impromptu screening in the living room on the crew's small portable TV monitor. It showed a clothed, cursing Neil in the kitchen kicking Skippy, who wouldn't stop barking. The counters were clean, no cooking mess in sight when Aubrey backhanded Neil, who fell to the floor, got up and scratched his husband's face.

"If you hurt Skippy again, I'll fucking kill you," Aubrey said clearly, shoving Neil away.

I couldn't decide if Aubrey was actually upset at Neil's cruelty or was just making a show for the crew. Izzy confiscated the video camera and the producer weakly demanded a copy. They didn't get it. The TV team admitted they had filmed the domestic spat and left the townhouse before Aubrey to set up lighting at the restaurant, and the critic had arrived ten minutes before filming there began. From the timestamp on the bottom of the video it looked like Aubrey did not arrive at the Bistro du Bois until an hour after he said he left home. The crew also screened the footage from the restaurant, which was boring. It showed an imperious Aubrey holding court in the dim, crowded eatery, as waiters brought him dish after dish after dish. He would nibble at some, take notes, gobble up others, and take more notes. If he had just killed his lover, he was one cold, hungry dude. At one point, a chef, a guy with tattoos and red burn scars up and down his arms, came to Aubrey's table and just stood there, glaring at him. They looked at each other for about thirty seconds and the chef went back to the kitchen. The cameraman fast-forwarded and all we saw was Aubrey eating. He made a show of smacking his lips and inhaling aromas but he really packed it away.

The CSI detective came in, holding a small plastic kit with a colored tube. He nodded his head to Izzy, who moved him into the hallway, away from the film crew.

"Positive?" Izzy asked, his voice low.

"Yeah. It's probably the victim's muscle tissue but I won't go on the record on an ID match until we can get DNA."

"*Chingar tu madre*," Izzy moaned. "Okay, do the frying pan, the knives, everything."

"I already did. You're right. It was done there. Cut up, cooked and, obviously, then he... the sick fuck."

"Yeah. But he made it easy for us. Slam-fucking-dunk."

I kept my mouth shut. Izzy told the CSI detective to search for a meat cleaver inside or outside the house and then returned to the dining room to confront Aubrey. I followed. Izzy read the critic his rights.

"Okay, we had a fight," Aubrey said. "Obviously you saw the film. I'm sorry I didn't mention it but I did not... do that to Neil. I could never..." he trailed off.

"Mr. Forsythe, you attacked your husband. On film, you threatened to kill him. Then you lied to us about it. I can understand your anger, him hurting a helpless animal like that. Did you kill him?"

"No!"

"Hey, I can understand, in the heat of the moment, things happen, maybe accidentally," Phil said. "But why would you cook him and eat him, man?"

Aubrey's eyes popped wide, his mouth slack.

"What? What the fuck are you talking about? Are you crazy?"

"Am I crazy?" Phil shot back. "You kidding?"

"I want a lawyer," Aubrey sniffed. "You people are trying to railroad me."

"You don't want to brag about it?" Izzy asked. "Like, maybe it was the ultimate cuisine? Did it taste like chicken?"

"I didn't do anything," Aubrey protested. "Are you saying someone... dear God, no. Who would do that? No. This is not happening."

"You said on video you would kill him if he hurt the dog again. Out of your own mouth, pal." Izzy looked grim. "Out of your own mouth."

"What the hell are you talking about? I want a lawyer. I want my phone call."

"Here's how it works. You can be a mensch and tell us what you did and we can talk to the District Attorney, who is on her way. You've got the whole night to make believers out of us. Insanity would probably fly as a defense on this one. Or, you can deny everything and get a lawyer. In that case, I will arrest you for murder. After you're booked, you will get your phone call. The judge usually lets you have two. You will see your lawyer at your arraignment downtown in the morning. Which is it?"

Aubrey thought it out, anger and confusion flashing across his face.

"This is insane. I don't understand. Lies. I don't believe any of this. You're trying to trick me… Lawyer. I want a lawyer."

"Okay. Aubrey Forsythe I arrest you for the murder of Neil Leonardi."

The famous man sputtered and cried like a big pink baby.

7.

The sergeant searched Aubrey and had him sign a small, white Miranda warning acknowledgement card, which could be shown at trial to prove he had been read his rights. He had to use two pairs of linked handcuffs to manacle the celebrity's pudgy hands behind his wide ass. They took him out through the rear garden and snuck him through another townhouse to the next block, to avoid the cameras out front. They also took the film crew "witnesses" by the same route, with them complaining about the First Amendment all the way. Izzy said they would question the crew all night before releasing them, while they processed the scene. After finding some S&M bondage gear and kinky photos in the master bedroom, but no meat cleaver, Izzy, Phil and I watched the video again.

"Doesn't show him killing Neil," I said.

Izzy and Phil glared at me.

"We all saw him puke up his lunch," Izzy said. "You think the human tissue he chowed down on today is from a different guy? He's a serial cannibal?"

"Unlikely," I admitted. "But you saw him. He looks really upset, in shock. I think he loved Neil."

"If I had a buck for every killer who loved his victim

and cried after he killed them, I could buy a new car," Phil chuckled. "A nice one."

"True," I said. "But why would a neat freak clean his plate and silverware but leave the frying pan and all that mess? All that evidence? And he freaked when you mentioned the cannibalism thing. You guys are the pros but his reaction looked real to me."

"Maybe he was running late and left it for the housekeeper. We have a video of an assault and a threat to the vic. He lied about it. He's still lying about the time frame. He had plenty of time to do it. The suspect vomited ingested human flesh that is probably the dead guy. He's an actor on TV," Izzy countered.

"I never saw the show but you're probably right," I said.

"He's probably as crazy as a shithouse rat," Izzy said dismissively, shaking my hand. "Thanks for your help, Shepherd. Where were you on the job?"

"No big deal," I replied. "What job?"

"This job. The job. You're not an ex-cop?"

"Nope."

"Then I should arrest you," he said, smiling.

"What for?"

"I haven't decided yet. Trespassing? Impersonating a police officer? Obstructing governmental administration? Conspiracy to commit journalism? All of the above, maybe."

"I haven't done any of those things, although I think obstructing the government is usually a good thing."

"True. Can you give me a reason not to lock you up?" he asked.

"Nope. But you'd have to admit publicly that an inexperienced pet columnist got into your crime scene and helped you solve the murder. Quickly."

"There's that," Izzy scowled.

He looked at Phil, who shrugged.

"As far as I'm concerned," Izzy said, "you're a friend of

the family who just happened to be here and assisted us with our investigation. The dog part. You're a dog whisperer."

"Okay, thanks. By the way, I like the way you work. It was a real pleasure."

"Praise indeed from a pet columnist. Now get the fuck out of here."

"What about Skippy? What will happen to him?"

"Witness Protection Program," Phil said, with a straight face.

We all laughed. Izzy said cops would be at the crime scene for the rest of the day and all night, probably for days, and there was a housekeeper who would be there in the morning. If Aubrey didn't get out on bail, there might be relatives or the SPCA would take him. I didn't like it but they wouldn't let me take him out of there. I gave them my cell phone number and they gave me their cards.

"*Bon appétit, mon ami*," Izzy said in a passable French accent as I walked out.

I left the townhouse and began walking back down the block toward the police barricade, when I noticed the cameras and lights from the press pen on the far corner, pointing at me. They clearly thought I was *somebody*, a friend, a relative, somebody to interview. I did an about-face and headed for the other, farther end of the block, also barricaded but press-less. I stole a glance back and noticed some of the reporters and camera crews were dashing out of the pen to circle around the block and flank me. I broke into a run. By the time I hailed a cab on Lexington Avenue, a crowd of them had rounded the corner. In the lead was a hot, healthy redhead in a red top, black miniskirt and high heels, yelling her head off, jiggling nicely, as I made my escape. She was pretty enough to be on TV. You didn't have to be a lip reader to get that she was mouthing words you couldn't say on regular television.

8.

I strode into the grand lobby of the *New York Mail*, a man on a mission, past framed famous front pages, mostly giant, one-word headlines like "WAR," "CHAOS," "DOOM," and, oddly, "SPRING." There were more recent front pages, such as "MAYOR'S MAIN SQUEEZE," "FIRST LADY LEZ RAP," and "MEX STAR IN SEX BAR."

I stopped at one headline I had seen before, only two years old.

"DEATH COP SPEAKS"

The front-page story had an exclusive interview with a city police officer named Sean Joyce who had accidentally shot and killed a tall twelve-year-old boy, after the boy pointed a realistic toy gun at him in a high-crime neighborhood at night. Joyce, a white, Irish cop had been accused of racism by the *New York Mail*, which printed comments he allegedly made, calling the dead boy a "dumbass kid" for pointing a plastic automatic at him. Someone gave a civil rights activist minister Joyce's home address and the *Mail* covered the resulting ugly demonstration there, angry people holding signs reading

"RACIST MURDERER." For some reason, Joyce ignored his superiors' orders not to discuss the case and expressed his regret about the shooting to the *New York Mail* in an interview, with pictures, along with his condolences to the family of the dead boy. After the interview, Officer Joyce checked into a cheap motel and shot himself. The next day's front page was also about him:

"'DUMBASS' COP KILLS SELF"

Joyce left a widow and three young kids. A sad story.

I flashed my new photo ID card to security in the lobby and rode upstairs to the Features Department floor. I rushed to my cubicle, anticipation rising, but stopped short at my desk. My souvlaki sandwich was gone. My cold cup of tea in my *New York Mail* cup was still there, next to my black letter opener and my tie. I looked around. I asked my cubicle neighbors but no one would admit to having any information about the fate of my lunch. I decided *that* mystery would have to wait.

I rode the elevator one floor up to the City Room, with its jigsaw maze of carpeted, beige dividers and long counter desks supporting computers, and a phalanx of ceiling-mounted TV monitors. It looked like a combination of an insurance company and a sports bar. But, from what I heard, with more booze. I ambled over to the desks under the monitors and heard live police radio calls. I listened until I heard a guy with what sounded like an Australian accent and asked him if he was Nigel Bantock. He wasn't but the guy next to him was.

"Hi. I'm Shepherd," I said to Nigel, a nondescript guy in glasses, shirtsleeves, and a bow tie, with a buzz cut and dingy, crooked teeth.

"Shepherd! Mate, what the fuck are you doing here? Why aren't you in the townhouse?"

I explained that I had to leave but it was okay because I got the whole story.

"I figured we had a deadline coming up for tomorrow's paper soon and I should probably give you the rest of the story. I got it all. There was really nothing to stay for."

"Really?" Nigel asked, his voice rising. "This better be fucking great, Shep."

"Problem, Nigel?" a gentle English voice interjected.

The color drained from Nigel's face as he gaped over my shoulder. I turned and saw a round guy with a pasty pale face in a rumpled brown suit with white stripes, leaning casually against a counter with a green beer bottle in his hand. The suit looked like a Halloween costume for a gangster, minus the white tie and fedora. He was not smiling. He repeated his question softly but the tone held quiet menace. Next to him was a wiry guy in a sharp-cut three-piece suit. The thin guy had a hatchet face and dyed black hair, slicked straight back into a duck's ass over his pink collar. It was hard to tell which guy terrified Nigel. Maybe both. If Humpty Dumpty became a mobster and hired a weasel for a bodyguard, this is what they would look like, I thought.

"Hi, I'm F.X. Shepherd. Francis Xavier Shepherd," I said, to break the ice, extending my hand to the big man. "Just call me Shepherd."

"No you're not," he said, ignoring my hand.

"I was this morning," I said, attempting a chuckle.

"Who the fuck is he, Nigel?" Humpty asked.

"Uh… Shep, he gave us our web exclusive today… ah… He was inside Forsythe's townhouse. He uh…" Nigel sounded confused and was having trouble breathing.

"Frank Shepherd is on holiday," the weasel said.

"Yeah, that's the thing," I interjected. "Turns out we have the same name. I'm new. F.X. Shepherd. I do the pet column. 'Dog's Breakfast?' Nigel sent me on the fun murder."

"You sent the pet bloke on the top news story?" Humpty

snickered, taking a big swig of brew. "You're sacked, Bantock. Get out."

"What?" Nigel was suddenly unsteady on his feet, as if he was the one drinking. "I didn't know... my first day... But he was brilliant! We beat everybody! Nobody has matched us yet! I... we... he says he has more exclusive stuff... I..."

He sank back into his seat, muttering about his wife and kids and his condo lease in New Jersey. I noticed the features editor who had hired me at the edge of the small crowd, her piled hairdo bobbing and weaving. I protested that if Nigel was fired, I should also be canned. Humpty and Weasel stared at me. And then back at the quivering Nigel. It looked like they were about to agree with me.

"Bantock, you're banished to Lobster Shift until you can tell a police reporter from a pet columnist," Humpty told Nigel.

Nigel heaved a sigh of relief and faded into the background before the fat man changed his mind.

"Shouldn't I be filing the rest of the story before deadline?" I asked.

"Nobody spoke to you," Humpty snapped, tossing his empty into a trash can.

"You just did," I replied in a friendly tone.

A collective gasp of air being sucked in at the same time came from dozens of people watching surreptitiously from behind their computers. My feature editor's hairdo vanished as she fled the room. Many heads ducked for cover. Humpty put his face inches from mine, his booze breath bridging the gap, strong enough to make my eyes water.

"This better be good," he warned.

I took a step back to get some fresh air.

"Aubrey protests his innocence but he is under arrest for murder," I said. "Earlier in the day, a film crew taped Aubrey slapping Neil and threatening to kill him for kicking Skippy, their dog—the husky who was guarding the body until I got there. Cops have the video of the fight. Also, Neil scratched Aubrey's face. The killer took a slice out of Neil's ass and cooked it in their fancy kitchen in a frying pan with oil, garlic, parsley and grated Parmesan cheese." There was total silence. "And then Aubrey ate it."

I could hear muted expressions of shock, awe and disbelief. Humpty was frozen for about fifteen seconds. Then he blinked. I was afraid he was going to call me a liar, so I quickly continued.

"Aubrey lied to the cops, who have already confirmed that the food critic cannibalized his husband," I said. "A test at the scene detected human flesh in his stomach contents. Oh, and some S&M gear and pornographic photos were found in their bedroom. That's about it."

Humpty's face twitched oddly. He licked his lips and a lusty smirk appeared.

"How did they detect human flesh in his stomach?" Weasel demanded in a skeptical tone.

"He vomited when he saw Neil's corpse and they tested it. I saw it all. Aubrey had part of Neil's backside in his stomach. The frying pan in the kitchen was used to cook it."

Humpty looked at Weasel, who handed him another beer. Humpty took a deep pull, as everyone looked at him. His rosy mouth curved up in a wide leer. It looked like a smile, but sharper.

"NEIL PARMESAN!" he bellowed, so loud I jumped.

The crowd roared with laughter and then applause. Humpty did a little jig and Weasel cackled.

"NAKED LUNCH! Food Fight Ends in Gay Slay Meal!" Humpty roared, tipping his new bottle of beer toward me.

"Tubby Trib Food Critic Noshes Slain Roomie!" someone else countered.

"Big Cheese Beardsley Bites Boy Toy!"

"Top TV Chef Jailed in Gay Cannibal Feast!"

Soon everyone joined in the game, which became

increasingly raucous and obscene.

I looked around at my co-workers shouting bloodthirsty headlines and clinking beer bottles that had appeared in their hands. Where had those come from?

I had joined a tabloid death cult. There was something tribal and familiar about it.

9.

Humpty grabbed my hand with cold, wet sausage fingers.

"I'm Tal Edgar," he said, as if that explained everything. "You got The Wood, lad. Cheers. Badger, my office."

Humpty—Lucky Tal—lumbered off toward a large, glassed-in corner office. Even I had heard of the *Mail*'s British executive editor, "Lucky" Tal Edgar. Weasel slapped my back with his paw and also introduced himself.

"Good on you, my son. I'm Badger," he said, before following his boss.

I assumed it was a nickname. His smile was fake. I know envy when I smell it. I was marched to a computer station, where I typed up my notes and a rewrite reporter whipped them into titillating tabloid prose. I was told my news byline would be F.X. Shepherd, so it would be different from Frank Shepherd, who, I was assured, would shit a brick when he read it. I wondered if I could ask for a raise on my third day?

"You gave me a heart attack, mate," Nigel whispered, leaning over me. "I thought you were the crime guy. You like twisting the tiger's tail, don't you? The only reason Tal didn't sack me was you kicked bum, big time. Thanks for that. I owe you. We will kick the *Daily Press* into next week."

"What's The Wood?" I asked.

"Front page story," Nigel explained, "from the old days when they used wooden type instead of metal for the biggest headlines. In this case, that would be 'NEIL PARMESAN.'"

"Oh. Who's Edgar's sidekick?"

"Donald Badger? He specializes in... um... investigative pieces. Works the computer. I'd steer clear of him, if I were you."

"His name is really Badger? I was close."

"Sorry?"

"I thought he looked like a weasel."

"He does a bit but I wouldn't say that to anyone else, Shep. You'll be out of here like shit through a badger."

"So, he's a boss?"

"Technically? No. But yes. Have you really never done news before?"

"Nope."

"Beginner's luck, then?"

"Maybe beginner's stupidity."

"Where the fuck have you been?"

"Away."

"Only one problem, though, mate."

"Which is?"

"What do you do for an encore?"

I hadn't thought about that.

"I'll just go back to my pet column."

"Wouldn't count on it, old son. The Editor is pleased. For now."

"That was pleased?"

"Oh yes. Ecstatic. Julie Andrews. You wouldn't want to see displeased, mate. You really are new here. Wife? Family?"

"No. Not even a pet."

Nigel went back to work. I googled Tal Edgar on my iPhone and got a lot of hits about the infamous British tabloid editor whose approach to journalism seemed to be very proactive. The hard-drinking Londoner had shaken up news markets in Melbourne, Sydney, London, and Los Angeles, stomping the competition on behalf of his boss, New Zealand media billionaire Trevor Todd. One profile piece described Edgar as "The Man Who Makes News." Competing rags did hatchet jobs, claiming he threatened to fire—or did fire—one person a day, in order to terrify the non-union staff into working around the clock. There had been nervous breakdowns, suicides, newsroom fistfights. It didn't sound like *The Sound of Music* to me.

Badger intercepted me on the way to the bathroom and brought me to what he optimistically called his office, a tiny glass-walled box the size of an elevator, just off the City Room. He shut the door and I squeezed into one of two chairs on opposite sides of a small desk piled with folders and printouts. The folder closest to me had my name on the tab. My employee file. Or had he whipped one up to intimidate me?

"What happened to your face, old son? Punch-up in the pub?"

I realized he was talking about my three facial scars but it took me a few seconds to realize he was asking if I got it in a bar fight.

"Right," I agreed. "Punch-up in a pub."

"I want you to listen to something, mate," he said. The word "mate" sounded distinctly unfriendly. It was interesting how a word that sounded friendly in Neil Bantock's Australian twang could be so mangled by Badger's British consonants. His nasal voice dripped with the tone of an "I-outrank-you" school bully. Badger fiddled with his mouse and I heard the computer dialing a number. A sibilant male voice answered.

"Hello. It's Neil," the dead man said. "Aubrey and I are having a food fight right now so please leave a message. Remember what Auntie Mame said: Life is a banquet and most poor suckers are starving to death. Tally Ho!"

"You called Neil Leonardi's phone," I said, stating the obvious.

"Quiet!" he said, typing fiercely.

"Neil, I'm sorry," Aubrey's voice emerged from Badger's computer. "I love you but you made me so mad. You make me crazy. If Skippy can forgive you, I can. Call me please, sweetheart."

The message ended with a beep.

"You hacked into Neil's cell phone messages," I said, again stating the obvious.

"You reckon?" Badger sneered.

"Isn't that illegal?" I asked.

"The point is the fat man left seven messages for his boyfriend, probably after he was dead," Badger said.

"Husband."

"Pardon?"

"Husband. Aubrey and Neil were married," I told him.

"No such thing," Badger laughed.

"There is according to New York State. I thought we were supposed to be accurate?"

"I meant there is no such thing in the pages of the *New York Mail*," he explained.

"Okay, but I don't think he did it."

"Don't be a silly cunt. He's under arrest. I have all the messages, some quite naughty, what he's going to do to Neil when they make up. See if you can get your sources to say this is Aubrey's pathetic ploy to fool cops and set up a phony alibi. It's a solid follow."

"I don't have any sources," I replied, truthfully. "I just blundered in. I met a couple of guys up there but they may never talk to me again."

"You had better hope they do."

"Why?"

He looked at me with bemused pity, like he was talking to the world's dumbest bastard.

"I assume in these hard economic times you would like to continue working here?"

"Sure," I said, taking the three steps toward the door. "Nice to be appreciated. I also want a raise. Mate."

This time he blinked. I got up and walked to the door.

"Where the fuck are you going?"

"To the Greek joint. Someone stole my souvlaki. I'm hungry, mate."

In the elevator I changed my mind and went back uptown.

10.

Bistro du Bois was a converted storefront on Madison Avenue near 91st Street. The front was dark cherry wood, cut glass and shiny brass fittings. An A-frame sandwich board on the sidewalk outside said it offered "French Provincial Fusion Cuisine served dim sum style." Whatever that was, it wasn't cheap. A mesquite-grilled, truffle-infused cheeseburger special cost forty-two bucks.

Inside, it was warmly dark, with indirect honey lighting around the walls and ceiling. Waiters and waitresses in black pants and white shirts hurried among islands of white tablecloths with white plates piled high, offering them to seated customers. I realized that dim sum was like in some Chinese restaurants, where they brought you different dishes and you picked without ordering.

On the right was a small bar with more brass and a huge mirror along the wall. Set into the rear wall was a stainless-steel counter with piles of plates on one side under bright lights. The counter was flanked with walls of glass, behind which chefs in kitchen whites chopped, sliced, boiled, sautéed and argued. Some of the cooks were laughing and had champagne glasses. One of the guys celebrating was the tattooed guy from the video. The one who had glared silently at Aubrey. I walked to the bar and nodded to a female bartender, an attractive young thing with a name badge that read HEATHER, also in a white top and black pants, but tighter than the waitresses'.

"Table, sir?"

"No, thanks. You the boss?"

"Not me. He's in the back. What's this about?"

"The homicide."

"Oh yeah, some of your guys just left. Terrible. I'm Heather. This way, please."

She led me toward the glass wall and into the bright kitchen. In the kitchen she brought me to the carousing guy with the tattoos.

"He's here about the murder."

The head chef turned to me, a wide grin on his face. "The other cops told me that pig Aubrey was under arrest for murder. Please tell me that hasn't changed," he said in a voice thick with drink.

"It hasn't. He's in jail."

They all cheered and poured more bubbly.

"Thank God," he said, shaking my hand. "I'm the exec chef and owner. Maurice Verre-Montaigne."

"Sounds French. I'm Shepherd."

"Actually it's Murray Glassberg from the Bronx, but hey, French restaurant, French name, right?"

"And the best authentic Puerto Rican kitchen crew from Manhattan," laughed one cook with a crooked chef's hat, which sparked another round of drinks and cheers.

"So, what can I do for you?" Murray asked. "Need me to identify the killer out of a lineup? Number three! The fat bald guy!" He roared with laughter.

"I get the impression you did not like Aubrey very much," I observed.

"Fuck no. Everybody hates Aubrey in our business. Nasty fat fuck goes out of his way to torpedo good people. He gets off on it. He also does it on TV but now he's been harpooned. Moby Aubrey. About time. Is he eating prison food yet? Can't wait for that review."

"I don't read his reviews or watch his show so I really don't—"

"So you don't know what a colossal, candy-coated cock-gobbler he is?" Murray giggled. "He should have been the one killed but maybe it's better this way."

"Aubrey put Murray out of business years ago with a very unfair, nasty review," Heather explained. "He came here with a film crew today to do it again. He must have heard Murray was back and doing well, after ten years of working for others. Now his review won't run, thank God. We're saved."

"That crew filmed him slugging his boyfriend, Neil," I told them. "Homicide has the video. Also the footage from his meal here. I saw you glaring at Aubrey at his table but you didn't speak to him."

"No. I wanted to tell him that if he trashed me again and ruined me for a second time, I would kill him. But I was afraid if I started, I would kill him right here. Right in front of that damn camera. It was a close thing. For once he didn't bring his slimy boyfriend, the bitchy one who insults the waiters, the food, the wine, the décor—like he's some kind of expert on everything just because he's gay."

"He was the one killed," I told Murray.

"The nasty boyfriend?" Murray asked.

"Husband, I think. Yes, Neil… Leonardi." I almost said "Neil Parmesan." It was catchy. "His throat was cut."

"Gee that's too bad," Murray chuckled. "A two-for-one combination. Pig and snake."

The whole crew roared with laughter.

"And you were here all day?" I asked sharply.

"Since about eleven this morning. Ask anyone here. The other cops did."

"That's okay. I believe you. So you found out Aubrey was coming when he walked in the door?"

"No. He reserved a table in his name earlier in the week. His film crew showed up about ninety minutes before him and set up at their reserved table, so we knew it would be on TV. They even had us sign releases," Murray said.

"I thought food critics made secret visits, so they get the food everybody else eats?" I asked.

"Not Aubrey. He wants you to know he's coming for you. More fun that way."

"But isn't that corrupt? Doesn't that allow chefs to prepare and give him better dishes and service than anyone else?" I asked.

"Now you're getting the idea," Murray replied. "Welcome to Foodland. It's not about objectivity. It's about subjugation, sadism, special treatment. And then he'll piss all over whatever you do anyway, like he did the first time. I wouldn't give him the satisfaction."

Murray put down his champagne glass and embraced Heather.

"I would have, Heather," Murray told her. "I wasn't going to let him destroy us. I would have killed him. Now I don't have to."

"I know," she said, hugging him tightly.

"I'm not celebrating his boyfriend's death, even though he was a creep," Murray explained to me over her shoulder. "I'm celebrating Aubrey's arrest and especially the fact that I don't have to kill him."

"Thanks. I understand," I told him, turning to leave. "By the way, is there by any chance a chicken souvlaki sandwich on the menu?"

There wasn't. But in a few minutes I was eating the best one I'd ever tasted.

11.

My ex-boss found me a sublet on Broome Street in the TriBeCa neighborhood on the West Side downtown. It was a small, overpriced one-bedroom apartment in one of three identical six-story red-brick buildings that used to be factories. It was like living in a traffic jam. Day and night, especially during the evening rush hour, honking lines of cars filled the one-way street, bound for a nearby entrance to the Holland Tunnel. The Holland Tunnel did not go to Holland, but to New Jersey. And the rush hour was about four hours long. I have no clue what "TriBeCa" means. There were two pitiful saplings on my block and two actual trees.

Mary Catherine was waiting in my living room, her high heels off, legs tucked under a short business suit skirt on my black fake leather couch. The long, natural dirty-blonde hair she kept in a French braid during the day fell loose below her shoulders. Cold Thai food and stacks of legal documents were on the table. She was an amazing sight to come home to.

"Where the hell have you been?" she demanded.

"Working. Remind me, Mary Catherine. When did I give you a key to my apartment?"

"I gave you the key and kept a copy, and that is what's

best for our arrangement. You were writing about how to pick up dog poop until this time of night?"

"That was my first column. Now I'm working on number two. Well, the second column—whether it's right or wrong to make love in front of your pet."

"So? Which is it?" she asked, completely uninterested.

"Depends. Lots of issues. What kind of pet, the pet's reaction. All things considered, no. Especially dogs. Cats are more mature."

"Glad that's settled. Seriously, where were you? Were you with a girl?" she demanded, returning to lawyer mode, her crisp blue eyes watching me.

"No. Two gay guys."

"You're kidding."

"Yup. I'm kidding. Sort of. My new job just got more complicated."

"Is that good or bad for us?"

"Both," I told her. "We may actually have to do this."

"Okay, let's get to it," Mary Catherine said, unwinding in a way that was a pleasure to watch. "My husband hates it when I'm late."

I woke up in my rumpled bed at seven because the phones were ringing. Both my landline and my cell had the City Desk on them, telling me to go to the Criminal Courts Building at 100 Centre Street to cover Aubrey's 9:30 arraignment on a charge of murder. I tried to explain that I really wasn't a reporter and had no idea how to cover court proceedings but I was already talking to myself. I showered, threw on jeans, a clean dress shirt and black waterproof sneakers.

It was cool and hazy outside but you could tell it was going to be another nice spring day. I bought newspapers, a Danish and a coffee at the corner store. Around me, Manhattan people were buying the *Mail* and talking about my first news story—a cannibalistic murder—and laughing. It was a strange feeling. I was proud and ashamed. The emotions merged into excitement. I snagged a cab and triple-tasked in the bouncing backseat—eating, drinking, and reading. In the *Mail*, I was a superstar. Mary Catherine would freak. My name was on the front page, under the huge, screaming bold type headline:

NEIL PARMESAN
Tubby Trib Food Critic
Noshes Slain Roomie
By F.X. SHEPHERD

I had already seen the front page on the morning news shows. All of them. They held up the paper for the cameras, with my name visible. It was a national story. So much for my low-key cocoon. The front page had a shot of Aubrey stuffing his face with mysterious food and Neil's surprised face, superimposed onto a frying pan. A red banner across the top of the page said "EXCLUSIVE: Cannibalism Cuisine Confirmed by Cops." A menacing wedge of cheese was floating nearby.

> Famed *New York Tribune* food critic and author Aubrey Forsythe is today to be arraigned on charges of murder and cannibalism after he killed and dined on the naked corpse of his live-in boyfriend, Neil Leonardi, after the two had a spat at their $15 million Manhattan townhouse, the *Mail* has learned.
>
> After making a meal of his lover, Forsythe, star of TV's hit show *Food Fight*, calmly went out to review a restaurant for the Trib, gobbling up a gourmet meal, sources said. (Cont. P2, 3, 4 & 5)

The story continued on page two, surrounded by photographs of Aubrey and Neil "at happier meals," and contained everything I had absorbed at the murder scene and elsewhere. The mayor and governor both expressed shock, as did several lesser celebrities whose flagging careers probably needed a boost.

A box was inset into the type of my main story.

RECIPE FOR MURDER	
crushed garlic	parsley
½ cup of olive oil	grated Parmesan
½ stick of butter	boneless rump filet of Neil Leonardi
lemon zest	capers

Apparently alerted by me, one of our photographers got a flash shot of a dazed, sobbing Aubrey being led from a cop car at Central Booking at 1 Police Plaza, a sad Pillsbury Doughboy emerging from a red-brick oven. There were other stories by other reporters, including a review by our "Eating Out" restaurant critic, panning the deadly dish as "unimaginative and pedestrian; a strip mall entrée unworthy of a gourmet." One story, titled "FOOD FIGHT," listed Aubrey and Neil's past spats, and Neil's apparently well-known nastiness to Skippy, as documented on their TV show. It also recapped the new, unseen video I mentioned in my story. Another piece with my byline on it was headlined "LOYAL DOG GUARDS SLAIN MASTER," along with my photo of Skippy. Other stories featured a pop TV shrink speculating on Aubrey's motivations, even a real-estate piece about whether the value of the townhouse would rise or fall because of the infamous act.

Wow.

I checked the other papers. Aubrey's own newspaper, the esteemed *New York Tribune* did not cover the story at all. The *Mail*'s main competitor, the *Daily Press*, also had the story on the front page but it was very vague and contained less information than we had put on the *Mail*'s website the night before. "FOOD CRITIC NABBED. Body Found at Townhouse," by Virginia McElhone. The *Daily Press* speculated that the victim was Aubrey's companion but did not identify the corpse and said only that Aubrey was in custody. Not a word about cannibalism. Or cheese.

12.

The Manhattan Criminal Courts Building was a huge, stepped ziggurat of once-white sandstone chiseled with Art Deco designs and inspiring sayings about justice. It took me fifteen minutes and three different court officers to find the right first floor courtroom. In the hall outside, a huge crowd of TV crews and photographers strained behind barricades and began filming and shooting me as I approached. They all shouted questions at once and I couldn't understand any of them. Only one shooter wasn't firing, a female *Mail* photographer I had seen in the office, who obviously knew I wasn't worth wasting battery power on. Two court officers grabbed me by the elbows and rushed me through the double doors of the courtroom and escorted me to the front row, where I sat alone on an empty bench, a dark, dirty antique polished by a million butts since Franklin Delano Roosevelt was in the White House.

"You the other Frank Shepherd, the new guy?" a raspy voice in the row behind me asked.

I turned and saw a short, old wrinkled guy in a black rumpled suit and loose, stained red tie, his eyes watery in the morning, like a serious drinker.

"Uh, yeah," I replied. "Call me Shepherd."

"Okay, Shepherd," he said, offering his wrinkled hand for a strong clasp. "I'm Dunn. Mickey Dunn, courthouse reporter for the *Mail*. Great fuckin' yarn, pal. Is it true you're the new pet column guy? Whatya doin' here?"

"Thanks. Yes. I don't know."

"You should retire, Shepherd," Dunn said, guffawing. "Put you out to stud. You'll never top today's story, you live to be old as me."

"Yeah, really. I wouldn't know how. Never done this before. What's going to happen?"

With a smile and a shake of his white hair, Dunn explained how the prisoner would come in and plead not guilty and bail would be set or discussed. As he detailed the options, I heard a hubbub and a parade of people rushed in and surrounded me on the bench. The hot redhead who had chased me from the townhouse the night before plopped right next to me, her thigh pressing against mine. I didn't move away. Again, they all asked questions at once but I could understand her this time and caught her name.

"You're a *Daily Press* reporter?" I asked her, making her face light up.

It was a nice face and the rest was very nice, too.

"Yes, I'm Ginny McElhone," she beamed. "They call me 'Ginny Mac.' Are you a friend or family?"

"Turn it off, Ginny," Dunn interrupted. "He's with me. He's the new guy. Name's Shepherd. He kicked all of your asses."

They all groaned. Ginny's sweet look vanished and was instantly replaced with one of deep hatred. She withdrew her thigh.

"That was you?" she demanded. "And I chased you? Motherfucker!"

I thought she was going to hit me but I was saved by a

court officer who banged on a wall and yelled, "All rise!" We all rose, as a middle-aged black judge in black robes entered and took a seat at the head of the court, behind a small placard that read HON. JOSEPH BEAN, and told us to take our seats. As if on cue, a short round guy in a navy suit strode into the court. I recognized celebrity defense lawyer Roland Arbusto, who looked like a big silk bowling ball, with a purple tie and wavy black hair. Arbusto worked the room as if he were at a party, greeting the judge, shaking a court officer's hand and waving to the press corps in the front row. For a few minutes nothing happened, until a clerk called out Aubrey's name and he was led in handcuffs through a side door to one of two wooden tables in front of the judge and seated next to Arbusto. He was wearing the same clothes as the day before but the starch had gone out of them, and him. His eyes were red from crying. Arbusto slapped him on the back and whispered something in his ear.

"Well," said Dunn in his wrinkly voice. "If the trial took place on a see-saw, we know who'd win."

At the other table, two attractive women in power-dress suits were conferring over a file. One, with bright red hair and looking just as impressive as when I'd seen her on television, was the Manhattan DA, Krystal Ryan.

The clerk read out the charge of First Degree Murder and Unlawfully Dealing with Human Remains.

"How do you plead?"

"Totally, completely, without a shadow of a doubt not guilty," Arbusto bellowed.

Dunn, Ginny and the other reporters were writing down what everybody said in their notebooks. I couldn't write that fast, so I just listened.

"Is that less guilty, say, than a simple 'not guilty,' or the same?" Judge Bean asked sarcastically.

"My client is as innocent as it is possible to be," Arbusto

responded. "He has never been arrested before and I demand he be released on his own recognizance, Your Honor."

"On a First Degree Murder charge?" the judge asked, with a gentle smile. "Well, before I do that, Mr. Arbusto, if it's alright with you, I would like to hear what our distinguished District Attorney has to add on the subject. Ms. Ryan?"

Ryan stood. "Your Honor, Mr. Forsythe is charged with capital murder and one of the most repugnant acts human beings are capable of, a crime of a barbaric and inhuman nature. I would describe our case as very strong and to even suggest bail is obscene."

"What repugnant act are you referring to, Ms. Ryan? I notice you are charging him with First Degree Murder. On what grounds?"

"I would rather not disclose our entire case at this juncture, Your Honor, but we have irrefutable forensic evidence and even videotape to prove our case. Mr. Forsythe is a danger to the community and possibly to himself and The People demand he be held without bail."

"If you want me to deprive this defendant of his liberty before trial, you had better tell me on the record why he is charged with First Degree and what this barbaric and inhuman crime is."

The DA sounded reluctant. "At this point, subject to further testing and investigation we believe Mr. Forsythe is not only guilty of a senseless slaying, but of the savage crime of cannibalism, Your Honor."

A gasp of pleasure came from the hungry reporters, as they ate up every word.

"But he is not charged with that because there is no such crime in New York State," Judge Bean said.

"Correct, Your Honor," Ryan said.

You learn something every day. Manhattan was a tough town. You could eat someone in Manhattan and not even get a ticket. The judge seemed to be having fun.

"I object, Your Honor," boomed Arbusto. "If there is no such crime in this state, how can Ms. Ryan use it as sole justification to keep my client behind bars? My client is draped in the cloak of presumed innocence as he stands before this court. I demand reasonable bail."

The reporters had stopped writing for a moment, grinning at one another. I guessed that this was not the first time Arbusto had made similar arguments.

"Remand," the judge said and banged his gavel. "Return date on Friday, in this part. Court adjourned."

Some reporters stampeded from the courtroom, others were busily using their smart phones to send the news to their offices.

"What's 'remand?'" I asked Dunn.

"Remanded without bail. He stays in jail," said Dunn. "I've got to go to the press room and file this so they can get it up on the web. Can you cover anything outside, whatever Arbusto and the DA say?"

I said I would. The DA repeated almost word for word what she said in court and I wrote it down this time. She only said one thing that was different.

"This heinous crime shocks the moral conscience of our society and must be prosecuted to the fullest extent of the law—no matter how rich or powerful the defendant might be," she said.

Arbusto waited until she was done and then gave his own impromptu press conference in the hallway, with reporters shouting questions.

"Why did your client eat his victim?" a TV reporter asked.

"I assume you are referring to the fiction in today's *New York Mail*? My client did not cannibalize anyone, nor did he kill anyone, nor did he commit a crime of any kind. He is a victim, who will sue the city for a huge sum for false arrest. But that is for later. Right now, the real killer is roaming the streets of this fair city. What are the police going to do about it? We demand action. Meanwhile, I will appeal this ruling to the Appellate Division. Thank you."

Again, the reporters and photographers smiled. They had obviously heard this speech before, too. We all followed Arbusto out of the building and watched as he got into a waiting Rolls Royce limo driven by a chauffeur. As the press mob broke up, I noticed Ginny standing right in front of me, glaring.

"Thanks for not hitting me," I said to her.

"Thanks for tricking me."

"I tricked you?" I asked, amazed. "I don't even know you. How did I trick you?"

"By pretending to be a relative or something at the scene last night."

"I didn't," I replied. "I told the cops the truth and I let them believe what they wanted to believe. It was kind of tricky, I guess."

"Are you really their pet columnist?" she asked in disbelief.

"Yup. Never had a lesson."

"I reported you to DCPI," she smiled. "They'll take away your press card."

"No they won't. I don't have one. What's DCPI?"

"Deputy Commissioner of Public Information, the PR people at Police Headquarters." They were the ones who gave Ginny and her colleagues zilch while I was inside getting my big scoop.

"My boss threatened to fire me this morning if you beat me again," she told me, fixing me with a hard stare. "That's not going to happen."

"Sorry. Hey, a little friendly competition never hurt anyone, right? How about I buy you a cup of coffee?"

She ignored my peace offering. "Don't do it again. I'm warning you." Her face was completely calm, absolutely serious.

"You're warning me? Okay, forget the coffee. You are a piece of work. What's your problem?"

"You," she said, turning and walking quickly away.

13.

Aubrey's block was still closed off but, instead of dozens of reporters, photographers and video crews, today there were hundreds of them, their vehicles being held at bay by cops behind blue barricades. The clogged streets looked like an auto lot for TV satellite trucks, with microwave giraffe towers extended into the air like electronic erections. Famous faces were repeating my story into lenses, live and on tape in the warming sunlight, as I walked by. There were just as many members of the public milling around, gawking at the celebrity broadcasters and buying Mongolian barbecue sticks from a street vendor cart.

One network anchor was holding up the "NEIL PARMESAN" front page and chuckling at the tabloid tackiness, as if he was above it all. He incorrectly told his viewers that a source had told him the *Mail* reporter, meaning me, was a friend of the family—as if that explained how I got the story, instead of Mr. Famous Anchor. When he said "friend of the family" in a sarcastic tone, it sounded like he was implying I was also gay. Tacky.

As I passed the food cart, the barbecue smell hit my nose and my mouth watered. It smelled great but I was now a tabloid hack on a mission and lunch would have to wait. I found the same black cop, Officer Gumbs, at the sawhorse barrier and he let me right through, which sparked a media stampede as I walked quickly to the townhouse. Ginny Mac appeared in layers of pink and white that could have been a very short dress or a long shirt. She tried to follow me, shouting to the cop that she was with me. When Officer Gumbs looked at me for confirmation, I shook my head and shrugged. They had to carry her off, screaming and cursing like a pink lunatic.

The CSI technicians were hard at work in the mansion and ignored me. Skippy was glad to see me but was obviously still traumatized. I petted him in the hallway and told him he was a good boy. It would be nice if people were this easy. Obviously no one had walked him because there was liquid and solid proof in a corner. His bowls had not been refilled. I gave him some food and fresh water, which he inhaled. After a while, he plopped down and expressed his sadness again.

"Foof," he explained.

"I know. How about a walk, Skippy?"

The answer was an enthusiastic yes. He knew the word. I found a plastic bag and his leash and we were quickly out of the front door, Skippy pulling me down the block. He wanted to go toward the noise of the media clusterfuck at one end of the street. Some of my esteemed colleagues were actually whistling and making enticing smooching noises to lure Skippy but I was able to resist them and led him the other way. As he took care of his business, I could see they were filming me with their long lenses.

Gumbs came over. He cocked his head at the press.

"There's a back way out, through the house, if you want to avoid all that. You know. After's finished."

"Thanks."

As I stood there, a wiry woman approached me. She was sucking on a cigarette, a fuzzy little terrier by her side. The dog made a beeline for Skippy; clearly they were more than passing acquaintances.

"You're not a detective, are you?" the woman asked me.

"No. I'm just walking Skippy."

"Aubrey still in jail?" she asked.

My expression must have signaled my confusion. She cocked her head in the direction of a townhouse three doors down. "We're neighbors."

"He's being held without bail."

"Doesn't make any sense," she said, puffing away as the dogs played, faking each other out and dodging around at the ends of their leashes.

"I agree but the cops don't."

"I was walking Buster here when Aubrey left home yesterday. He didn't look like a fellow who'd just hacked up his husband." She raised an eyebrow. "What restaurant did he go to?"

I told her.

"I know that place but that's not the direction he went," she said.

"Then where?"

She explained that she had seen Aubrey get a cab but that he did not go uptown on the one-way Madison Avenue, but walked over to one-way downtown Fifth Avenue and took a cab south.

"Maybe the cab went around the block and *then* went uptown," I suggested.

She looked at me like I was a moron.

"He told the guy Times Square."

"You heard him?"

"Sure, I was right there. He waved, asked about my hip; always a gentleman, not like some jerks."

"Are you sure he said Times Square?"

Again the look.

"What am I deaf? I told you. Broadway and 43rd. Clear as a bell."

"Did you tell the cops this?"

"I don't get involved," she croaked.

She had had enough of me and jerked her nippy pet away and went down the block, trailing smoke. Skippy wanted to run, so we sprinted up and down until the media got bored and stopped filming us. Maybe they were hoping I was also going to relieve myself.

14.

Winded, I took Skippy back inside and was about to escape through the rear exit, when Izzy and Phil arrived.

"Oh Christ," Izzy groaned, when he spotted me. "Call the pound."

"Ace," was all Phil said.

I explained that I just stopped by to take care of Skippy, which no one had done. Izzy was annoyed and sent Phil off to see why the animal had been neglected. Then he thanked me.

"Did you tell the press that I'm a family friend of Aubrey's?" I asked.

"Not me," said Izzy. "A 'source' told them that. It lets us off the hook and makes the beast not so mad at us. If you don't feed the beast, it bites."

"Okay. Got anything for me to eat? I thought it was a one-day thing but my bosses expect me to stay on this story. If not, I understand."

He sighed and thought about it. "The full testing confirmed it all—Forsythe ingested and then regurgitated some of his husband's flesh. Also, the vic thought he was Elvis. Leonardi was high as a kite when he died. He had multiple drugs in his system. Marijuana, alcohol, some prescription meds, including oxycodone and even animal tranquilizer. We found some grass in the bedroom with the sex toys but we have to go through the medicine cabinets to match up the other drugs. Forsythe has at least ninety minutes unaccounted for, during which he could have sliced, diced and dined. He lied about assaulting Leonardi, he lied about where he was and he had plenty of time to dispose of the meat cleaver. We haven't found it yet. The blade is an official Aubrey Forsythe stainless-steel cleaver with a nine-inch blade that sells for almost four hundred bucks. Forsythe uses this stuff on the show to push the merchandise. That schmuck can really pack it away. He ate a chunk of Leonardi and then went out, happy-as-a-clam, and chowed down on no less than thirteen different dishes at the Bistro du Bois. The guy is a black hole."

"I know. I got a list from the restaurant last night, a dozen dim sum dishes," I said.

Phil returned from his animal-rights mission.

"Then you know it's an open mouth and an open-and-shut case."

"May I quote you on that?"

"You may not," said Izzy. "At least, not with any name attached."

"So, 'Izzy.' Is that short for Isadore or what?" I asked.

"No. Israel. Israel Negron. Puerto Rican and Jewish."

"That's so..."

"So what?"

"That's so New York," I answered.

"So are the jokes," Phil said.

"Sergeant D'Amico, don't you have medicine cabinets to search?" Izzy asked him, before turning to me. "What's your pedigree, Shepherd?"

"Mutt. My mum and dad are college professors. Actually, they met at Woodstock. I came along much later."

"Okay. I got work to do. Go out the back way before

my boss shows up. The fucking commissioner was here last night. The mayor is hiding under his desk."

I did as I was told and met the lady who lived behind Aubrey in a similar townhouse. She had a British accent, a sweet face, perfect puffy white hair, and she actually offered me tea, which I politely declined. She resembled Miss Marple the TV detective, so I asked her opinion.

"In mystery movies, when the hero gets a hot tip the police do not have, he or she keeps it a secret from the detectives and they run the clue down on their own, you know, to solve the case. What do you think about that?"

"I thought you were the police," she replied. "Well, I think that would be a bad idea. It could be dangerous. These things are best left to the professionals, young man."

To hell with Miss Marple.

15.

Outside Miss Marple's house two burly guys from the same mold blocked the sidewalk. One was big and the other was bigger. I am six foot tall and two-twenty. They were taller and looked twice as heavy. They were wearing steel-toed work boots and coveralls caked with what looked like years of black ink. Each wore a silly, small square hat made out of folded newspaper on top of their fat pink heads. The bigger guy was looking back and forth between me and a sheet of paper. I craned my neck and saw that it had a photograph printed on it. My photograph. He stuffed it into his coverall pocket.

"You Shepherd?" asked the big one in front of me, fists ready.

"Who?" I asked, trying to walk around them.

"It's him!" the bigger one on my right said, throwing his heavy left arm around my shoulder and gripping my shirt collar with his sweaty fist.

Oh man. I took a deep breath, set my feet and bent my knees. At the same time I cracked a big smile, brought my left arm up in front of me, bent at the elbow, and windmilled my right arm behind me and up between me and Bigger.

"Peace," I grinned, making the V-sign with my left fingers,

which I quickly poked firmly into Big's eyes.

I hooked my right elbow onto Bigger's arm just above his elbow and grabbed my right wrist with my left hand, as Big wailed and put his hands to his eyes. Bigger pulled on my collar, trying to lift me, which was perfect. I pulled my right arm with my left, as I jumped off the ground and twisted violently down and to the left, putting my entire weight into the move. His elbow joint gave with a pop. Bigger groaned and went down, first on his knees, then onto his right side. I followed him down and aimed my right knee and all my weight deep into his gut, letting gravity do the work. He groaned again as I rolled onto my back. A foot glanced off my foot and I saw Big above me, blinking in pain, trying to see where to punch me. I lay flat on my back, both legs out, and let him come. When he stopped at my feet, I hooked my right foot behind his left ankle and kicked him high on the same shin with my left, just under the knee, pushing through with all my strength, which whipped him backwards onto the cement with a nice thump.

I stood up, soreness beginning in my knees and elbows, and my hands had pavement scrapes on them. Big and Bigger were doing a lot worse. Big couldn't decide which to hold, his bleeding head or his eyes, as he whined on his back. Bigger was in the fetal position, cradling his dislocated elbow and muttering. I took another breath to calm down. Their paper hats had come off. They had bald spots.

I squatted next to Bigger and took his left wrist. He winced and tried to pull away but I told him to stay still. I found a good pulse in the wrist and his fingernails re-colored when I squeezed them.

"It's just dislocated. You'll be fine," I told him. "Okay, I lied. I'm Shepherd. Who are you guys?"

They just kept moaning. I noticed a lump on Bigger's butt, pulled out his dirty leather wallet and found his driver's license.

"Mickey McElhone? Are you kidding me? Ginny's your sister?"

He didn't answer until I poked his tender gut. "Uh-hunh."

"How about you?" I asked Big, dropping Mickey's wallet. "You another brother?"

"Sean," he whined.

"Mickey and Sean. Pleased to meet you guys. I gotta run. Say hi to Ginny for me. Or was there something you wanted to say to me?"

There wasn't.

16.

I walked to the end of the block but it took me a while to find a cab. As a new New Yorker, I was still figuring out how to tell which ones were available. What was clear was that whenever I needed a cab, so did everyone else. The trick was apparently to need a cab when no one else did. While I was waiting, I called my new stuff into the *Mail,* including the testing and the drugs in Neil's system, which made Nigel happy. Just as I snagged an empty yellow cab, I noticed two silhouettes sitting in a blue Honda parked down the block, looking at me. As my cab left, the car pulled away from the curb and followed. At the first traffic light I noticed the Honda had NYP plates, the same as the staff at the *Mail.* There were special free parking zones for them around Manhattan. The passenger tried to sink low in her seat but I caught the flashing eyes, the floating red hair. Beware, beware. Ginny McElhone, my favorite *Daily Press* reporter was on my tail.

Again, I recognized the Baluchistani pop music in the cab, even though it was a different cabbie. I spoke to him in a language he understood but he replied in English, suddenly nervous.

"You want me to evade someone? Where can I go that

he cannot in this traffic, sir? Who is following you, please? I want no police, no trouble, boss."

Just when it was getting to be fun. In the movies, cabbies lived to lose tails and were rewarded with big tips. Of course, an immigrant Muslim cabbie would want no trouble in post-9/11 New York. I told him to pull over and gave him a nice tip for a short trip. Behind me, I saw the Honda had also pulled over and was waiting behind an SUV. I ignored them, pretending I didn't know they were following me. I spun and walked quickly down the sidewalk toward them. When I passed, they slid down in the seats. I kept walking briskly. By the time I reached the next corner, I saw their car had done a U-turn and was heading back down the block, still on my ass. I should have done it on a one-way street. I was a new guy on their turf. This might not be so easy.

I kept walking, aware of them shadowing me at a discreet distance. I thought as I walked. Different turf but it wasn't like I didn't have experience with this. The only problem was I had no backup. No resources, no team. And no car to race away from the bad guys. There were two of them, so if I took a bus or subway, one could follow. Three blocks later, the solution presented itself.

I read the sign and took out my wallet. The price of $9.99 was a good deal for a getaway car. Well, not an actual getaway car. A bicycle. A big, blue, clunky girl's bike in fact. They were called Citi Bikes rentals and they were all over town. I swiped my new credit card and in a minute, I was off. I could see Ginny and her driver arguing. Should she rent one too or stay with the car? I spotted Ginny trying to get her own wheels but she was having trouble with the machine and gave up. I was a block away when they followed, both still in the car. Wrong move.

I let them follow me for a while as I pedaled leisurely, a slow-speed chase. I waited until I reached a block without any bike kiosk and decided to make my move. While the light was still red but cross-traffic on the avenue had thinned out, I scanned for cops. None. I floored it, sort of, through the red light. I went outlaw, weaving through the stopped traffic at the next light. A quick glance back and I saw Ginny running through the intersection, while her driver honked and tried to get through the stalled traffic. I could hear distant cursing as I cycled east. Three blocks later, no Ginny, no *Daily Press* in sight. I hung a right to the south, downtown. The sun was shining and I was enjoying my bulky blue bike in the big city. It was hard to concentrate on traffic and lights because of the distraction of the fascinating variety pack of humanity surging everywhere. It was like a zoo for every age, race, color, face and body ever invented.

When I was in the East Forties, I turned my girly bike right, towards Times Square. Half an hour later, I found another Citi Bike station near Broadway and 43rd to return my trusty wheels. I was at the Crossroads of the World, which was like being inside a giant video game, with all its lights, giant screen displays and electronic ads. I stood on the sidewalk on the east side of Broadway. Across the street was the open pedestrian area, with huge bleachers. On my side of the street were giant flashing billboards for Broadway musicals.

Why had Aubrey come here? There was the Times Square information center. Aubrey wouldn't need tourist information. There was a Body Shop store. He might have bought some toiletry items but he didn't have any purchases with him when he returned to the townhouse. There was a hotel. I asked a woman behind the desk if she knew who Aubrey was. She did know who he was but said he had not been there and thought I was nuts. By process of elimination, there was only one possible business left on the block.

I walked into the Times Square McDonald's, which was filling up with lunchtime trade, and asked for the manager in my best command voice. I used my iPhone to call it up and showed him Aubrey's photo in the *Mail*.

"I just came from the murder scene. Did this guy come in here yesterday?"

"Wow. Yeah, looks like him." The guy was young and skinny, with a buzz cut and an AIRBORNE tattoo on his arm. A name badge on his uniform shirt said EMILIANO.

"The guy was big as a house, ate like a hippo, man. Not easy to forget."

He took me into a small back room with lockers, bathroom supplies and a computerized security camera system on a shelf, topped by a small flat screen that showed eight different camera views at once. He clicked on the previous day's recordings and rewound them until he found a big white blur.

"Is that the guy?"

I watched Aubrey order a super-sized tray of a dozen Big Macs, fries and several giant chocolate shakes and then sit and methodically gobble it all down. It was impressive. A one-man eating contest. Then he went up and ordered a tray of apple pies and hot fudge sundaes and polished those off, too.

"Guy is something to watch, huh?" the manager said. "Thought the dude was going to eat the furniture."

According to the time stamp on the footage, Aubrey, the big gourmet, was loving it at Mickey D's from just after he left the townhouse until just before he rejoined his film crew at Bistro du Bois. Now I knew why he refused to tell the cops where he was. For him, the choice between a murder rap or an alibi that included a career-ending fast food pig-out might be a tough choice. I decided to come clean and told Emiliano who I was. Then I took a deep breath and really went for it. My mom always said if you don't ask, you don't get.

"Emiliano, this is very important. This footage may prove that this man is not a killer. Can I get a copy?"

"A DVD okay?"

"That would be great, thanks. Could I get two?"

"Sure."

While he made the copies, I thought it out and decided to call Izzy's cell phone.

"You again?" Izzy laughed in greeting.

"Congratulations," I told him.

"For what?"

"For great police work that led you to the McDonald's in Times Square and perhaps the prevention of a miscarriage of justice."

"The fuck you talking about?"

I told him. Izzy sounded both annoyed and suspicious but I suspected that was his normal demeanor. He and Phil got through the traffic very quickly, which is what lights and sirens are for. After viewing Aubrey's food-fest film, Izzy said something in a foreign language that sounded like German.

"*Es vaskst by mir in teller*," he groaned.

Izzy confiscated the original hard drive—along with the entire machine, which Emiliano did not like. Phil softened the blow by giving him a receipt, and explained that there were so many different video surveillance and software systems that grabbing the entire works was the only way to guarantee they could play and copy the evidence.

"So, let me get this straight," Izzy said to me. "You'll let me take credit for screwing up my own homicide case and making myself look like an asshole. Gee, thanks, amigo."

"I just get to put it in the paper first. Would you rather I took credit in the paper and didn't tell you?" I asked.

"Okay. I admit that would be much worse," Izzy agreed. "Thanks. The pooch may be screwed here but maybe I can un-screw it. But Forsythe could still have killed Leonardi before he left. This just tightens up his alibi timeframe. It could still work."

"And he still ate Neil Parmesan," Phil pointed out.

"True," I said. "And he smacked him around. But I think maybe he didn't kill Neil. I don't think he had time to do all that cooking, for one thing."

"Then who did?" Izzy demanded.

We all looked at each other for a while, clueless.

"Maybe whoever fed him Neil," I suggested.

"You'd make a great defense lawyer," Izzy said. "Nobody has proved anyone fed Leonardi to Forsythe without his knowledge."

"But now *we'll* have to eliminate that possibility," Phil sighed. "Izzy, he's right. And he did the right thing."

"Okay," Izzy said. "Sorry, Shepherd. Thanks, man."

"You're welcome."

They had investigating to do and I had another exclusive to write. I turned to leave, then paused.

"Izzy, what did you say, when you saw the footage? Sounded like German."

"Old Yiddish expression. *Es vaskst by mir in teller*," Izzy repeated. "In English it would be 'It's growing on my plate.' It means the more you eat, the more there is. Like this damn case."

17.

I went back to the *Mail* and gave them one of the DVDs so they could take stills for the morning paper and run the whole video on the paper's website. I kept the second DVD for myself. For a change, Aubrey's lawyer refused to comment. I wrote up my story about how Aubrey had lied about where he was because he did not want the world to know a haute cuisine critic had pigged-out on fast food. I did my best to write in the short, punchy *New York Mail* style, by imagining I was writing a Hallmark greeting card about murder. I made it clear that Aubrey had eaten human flesh and might still be the killer but the McDonald's footage made it possible he was innocent of the murder. Apparently, at a newspaper, when you completed a big story, they didn't congratulate or thank you. Your reward was they just stopped yelling at you to finish.

I grabbed a Dr. Pepper and a bag of pretzels from a vending machine in the lunchroom. It was after nine. I yawned. I tossed my empty soda can and plastic bag and headed home. I was too tired to walk or bicycle, so I decided to take another cab. I told the woman cabbie my memorized address in TriBeCa on Broome Street. She grunted, flipped the meter flag and sped off, punching my address into a GPS navigation unit.

"What does TriBeCa stand for?" I asked her.

"What?" she asked.

I repeated the question.

"You live there and you don't know?"

"So you don't know either?"

We both laughed.

The cab stopped in front of the wrong building, the first of three identical brick buildings on the right. My apartment was in the last one. Not wanting to lose my new friend by pointing out her mistake, I paid her and walked the fifty yards to my building. The outer door was unlocked. The inner door was supposed to be locked and opened only by key or buzzer from one of the apartments. It was closed but unlocked. So much for security. I pulled it closed behind me and, feeling lazy, took the small elevator up to the third floor. I got a glass and a cold bottle from the fridge. On the couch, I downed a full glass of icy arak, which was like getting hit over the head with a licorice stick.

How could Aubrey partake of his unholy entrée and still not be the killer? I had another blast of arak. The solution did not present itself. I had a third glass.

I was awakened at six the next morning by my doorbell ringing. It tinkled off-key like a bicycle bell, as someone pushed the mechanical doorbell button. I looked through the peephole, an ancient metal disc that swiveled over a two-inch hole in the metal door like a little porthole. It was a kid wearing a NEW YORK MAIL t-shirt, dropping off a copy of the paper. My story was page one, The Wood, again, but the copy bore no resemblance to what I'd handed in. A single word was emblazoned across the front page under a picture of Aubrey shoveling Big Macs into his face: "GLUTTON." The subtitle read: "Killer Critic Chows Down On Fast Food Fare—The Video Aubrey Did Not Want You To See."

There was also a timeline, a map of the locations involved and a profile of Aubrey's big belly, containing a list of all the food he had wolfed down that day. There was also a story with Badger's byline about Aubrey's frantic phone calls to his victim, a possible attempt to set up an alibi. Badger attributed the transcripts of the voicemails to a law enforcement source, not to illegal phone hacking. I turned on the TV and flicked through the news channels. Several anchors were holding up the *Mail* with my byline on the front.

I called Bantock. He picked up on the first ring.

"Shep! Mate! Your video's gone viral!"

"Look, I need a break. I'll call in any follow-up, okay?"

"Sure, sure. Not too long, though."

"I read The Wood. Why did you cut out the stuff about Aubrey possibly being innocent?"

Bantock laughed. "Come on, Shep. We'd never piss on our own yarn unless and until the cops drop the charges."

I ate two blueberry Pop Tarts at room temperature and crawled back into bed. My low-key cocoon at the *Mail* had been shattered. Mary Catherine would flip. I was supposed to be quietly doing my job, not being the star of my own reality show.

Aubrey's lawyer called my cell phone. How did he get my number? As he began to give me melodramatic quotes about his innocent client, I activated the recording app. He said he would ask the court to set his client free, or at least set reasonable bail, and promised I would be the first to know when it happened. When he'd hung up I typed up the transcript and emailed it to the office. I called Aubrey's townhouse and introduced myself to the housekeeper, an elderly Hispanic-sounding woman who told me her name was Adela, and that she had walked and fed Skippy. I tried to reach Izzy but got his voicemail.

I went back to sleep again, until the City Desk called

and told me to cover Neil Leonardi's funeral the following morning at St. Patrick's Cathedral. I took a shower and got dressed. The door tinkled again at noon. I looked through the peephole and cursed out loud. Obviously *anyone* could get into my building. I wasn't going to open it but I felt like a wimp so I swung the door wide to Ginny McElhone, who looked like a sexy Catholic school girl, in black stockings and a short green tartan skirt, clutching a copy of the *New York Mail*.

"Your office said you weren't in, so I came over to tell you that you won," she informed me.

I was wondering how she found out where I lived and if she had a gun. I was also wondering if Ginny's dark, curly copper hair was natural. I smiled as I thought of a way to find out.

"Won what?" I asked.

"The *Press* fired me. They saw your story today and canned me."

"Uh... Sorry. What the hell would they do that for?"

"I got beat three times in a row. Not supposed to happen."

"That's ridiculous. Don't you have a union?" I asked.

"Of course not. Neither do you."

"Right. Sorry. How are your brothers?"

"Very embarrassed. Sean has a big lump on his head and Mickey's arm is in a cast. Did you really do that yourself?"

Her tone made it clear she didn't think I could even beat *her* up.

"Why did you send them to kick my ass?"

"I'm sorry," she said. "I get... carried away. My job is very important to me."

"You're kinda crazy, aren't you?"

We gaped at each other and then she burst into tears. It was the last thing I expected. I wanted to close the door. She began sobbing, using the *Mail* as a handkerchief. It was very absorbent. Her eye makeup was smeared; she looked like a raccoon. She got control of herself and turned away, pawing at her eyes.

"Wait. Is my mascara running? I must look hideous."

"Uhm, no. I mean yes. It's all smeared. But you look great."

"Can I use a mirror for a second?"

I hesitated but let her go into my bathroom. She shut the door but I left the front door open. I heard water running. Ten full minutes later, she emerged looking terrific, as if nothing had happened. Except one more button on her creamy blouse was open, revealing a lot of cleavage. I struggled not to look. She noticed and coyly buttoned up.

"Thanks," she said in a brave voice, going up on tiptoes to kiss me on the cheek. "Sorry."

But she veered and suddenly her tongue was in my mouth, the rest of her pressing against me. I felt electricity from her chest rubbing on mine but I knew it wasn't static. She slid her manicured nails through my hair and pulled me closer, her other hand around my back, gently forcing our hips together. More electricity. I was cooked. I swung the front door shut with my free arm and put it to better use. She was making sweet whimpering noises in her throat, as we stumbled toward the bedroom. We fell in a tangle onto the unmade bed. Totally cooked.

Turns out Ginny's hair color was natural. Trust me. So was the rest of her. We spent several hours singing the body electric, taking breaks to drink arak and nibble Pop Tarts.

When I heard the key in the lock, I pulled on a pair of shorts and ran to the door. Mary Catherine stopped in the doorway, a brass key in hand, and stared at me.

"Did I wake you?"

"Yes. No. I was just…"

"Who is it, Shepherd?" Ginny called from the bed. One of Mary Catherine's eyebrows arched up. I wish I could do that. She actually blushed, her creamy cheeks going peach.

"Really?" Mary Catherine said, turning in the doorway and dropping her key on the small table there. "I didn't know you had company. I'm sorry to interrupt."

She turned to go but stopped.

"Shepherd, have you heard from Al?"

"No."

"I heard they just got home."

"That's great," I said.

"You should give Al a call."

"Sure," I said.

When I didn't say anything more, she was gone. I let her go and returned to Ginny.

"Sorry," Ginny said, with dubious sincerity. "Was that your girlfriend? I hope I haven't caused you any problems."

"No. She... she was mad at me anyway."

"Who's Al?" Ginny asked.

"Old friend. Somebody I used to work with. Nobody you know," I answered.

I excused myself and took another shower. When I got out, Ginny was gone. So was my copy of the Aubrey/McDonald's DVD and several notebooks. All the drawers in my bedroom, kitchen and desk were open, ransacked. I laughed.

"Cooked," I said out loud to no one. "Twice."

18.

The cathedral of soiled sandstone soared above Fifth Avenue but was literally overshadowed by newer, taller sectarian skyscrapers. Inside, the hiss of many voices rose in the cool echoing space between the giant marble columns and glowing stained glass, as relaxing as a fountain. It would be nice to again believe the comforting tales of my Catholic childhood; the bearded guy in the clouds and the story of immortality inside a simple cosmos centered upon me. But, after a little reading and a lot of reality, I suspected that the actual universe was vastly more complicated, mysterious and astounding.

Neil Leonardi's casket was at the end of the center aisle, in front of the altar, illuminated by the lights of the TV crews who were filming the coffin and the rich and famous mourners who sat resplendent in the rows of dark wooden pews. I found a seat and did some gawking myself. There were no politicians. The bizarre crime and Aubrey's arrest had scared away the elected officials on Aubrey's vanity wall. But the funeral for a horribly murdered man was still a wonderful photo opportunity for the power set, who may or may not have known the deceased.

I was surprised how many faces I recognized, given how

out of touch with popular culture I had become. There was the loudmouthed billionaire with a bulbous red nose and the most ridiculous, gravity-defying comb-over on the planet. Nolan Cushing's dyed blond hair was hair-sprayed into a frozen flying saucer that seemed poised for blast off. He preened pompously for the cameras, clearly unaware of how idiotic he looked. When he turned at the right angle, Cushing's pompadour looked distinctly like the tip of a dick. He probably looked in the mirror before leaving his gold-plated mansion this morning and decided he looked just marvelous. On being asked for his opinion on Neil Leonardi's death by one of the reporters, Cushing affected a serious tone.

"I'm sad to say that this is the kind of thing that happens when you slap God in the face with a degenerate lifestyle."

For a lack of something better to do, I googled Cushing on my iPhone. "Cash" Cushing was infamous for making a fortune giving blue-collar people mortgages they could not afford and somehow selling that bad debt to banks in Iceland, thereby racking up a second fortune. His third fortune was made foreclosing on the same homes, on behalf of the European banks he had cheated. When a dying woman he evicted in Queens committed suicide, *Newsweek* quoted him as saying "Losers lose. Winners win," the title of one of his ghostwritten books. He had a TV show called *You're Foreclosed*. No prizes for guessing what that was about. Next to Cushing was Julie Temple, his latest supermodel girlfriend, the best money could buy; hollow-cheeked, bored and voluptuous in a Viagra-blue dress.

A few seats from Cushing sat right-wing TV and radio commentator Harley Himmler. I googled him as well because I could not think of a reason an arch-conservative Christian would attend the funeral of a semi-famous gay man. Google found TV and radio clips in which Harley used Aubrey and Neil as signs of the decline and fall of western civilization. In the most recent, Harley gloated that perhaps some patriotic red-blooded American male had taken it upon himself "to rid the world of these simpering fags that God hates as a public service." So, Harley was here to celebrate, not to mourn.

Cameras were also swarming around a short, plump girl whose large breasts were bouncing inside a rhinestone tank top. Didn't anyone dress for funerals anymore? Some Internet stalking later I had discovered that Maria "Pookie" Piccarelli was the star of a hit reality show called *Bitch Blanket Bimbos*, airing on the Drinking Channel. Her fame seemed to revolve around her breasts, beer bongs, and blow jobs. Google found no connection between either Neil or Aubrey and this young lady.

Bored of watching Pookie hoist her impressive chest at the cameras, I scanned the other "mourners." I noticed several celebrity newspeople who hosted various talk shows and gossip websites and other once-famous faces I could not place. Amid the media elite, I spotted Don Badger and our boss, Lucky Tal Edgar. I googled Edgar again. Born in London, he had moved to New Zealand to work for the billionaire media mogul, Trevor Todd. Lucky single-handedly sensationalized the sleepy Kiwi press by covering stories that had been ignored for generations. He splashed lurid sex scandals, some of which were later revealed to be exaggerated, and gory auto accidents all over the front pages. Todd had then sent his golden boy back to the UK, and it was in London that Edgar came into his own. His formula required a constant stream of shamed celebrities to fill the paper with gossip and hijinks but there weren't enough to do the job. His brilliant solution, at least according to one website, was to simply *create* celebrities, no matter how insignificant or untalented the individuals were. He expanded the ranks of the famous by treating all TV, radio and media people, along with all rich people, public officials, models, corporate execs, and sports figures as if they were superstars. When that wasn't enough, he included their relatives, too. He also generated endless royal scandals by bribing palace servants and giving extensive coverage to the huge pool of useless aristocrats clogging the island.

I shut down the web browser. This was depressing, even for a funeral.

A group crowded into my row, jostling my elbow. I stood to let them pass, while keeping my aisle seat, and recognized Murray Glassberg, the chef from the Bistro du Bois, along with his bartender, Heather, and several other members of the restaurant staff. More people treating Neil's funeral like a party. We all shook hands. Murray introduced me to a strikingly good-looking woman in a black pants suit, with a lacy camisole just visible under the jacket, calling her "Doc." She ended up sitting next to me. I didn't mind. Her perfect oval face was framed by a curtain of blond hair that fell in gentle waves to her shoulders.

"Hi. I'm Jane. Jane Arthur."

"Shepherd." We shook. "What do you do at Bistro du Bois?"

"Eat. I live nearby, so I'm a regular customer. And a friend of Murray's. He wants to go out after this to celebrate." She raised an eyebrow. "You must be the reporter he mentioned, from the *Mail*. I've been reading your articles."

"That's me. Although they rewrote a lot of that stuff…" I paused. "I'm sort of helping the police. Were you there that day? When Aubrey Forsythe had lunch?"

"No. Well, yes, I was there earlier but I was gone by the time he arrived."

I looked along the row. Murray was deep in conversation with Heather. I kept my voice low. "Did Murray or anybody else leave and then come back?"

"I don't know," she answered in hushed tones. "Don't think so. Why? I thought Forsythe had been charged with the murder. Is Murray a suspect?"

I shrugged. "Maybe. The McDonald's video shows Aubrey may not have done it, but somebody sure did."

"This is interesting," she said. "Sounds like a mystery. I love mysteries. I'm very nosy. You got those scars on your face one or two years ago?"

She was curious but in a professional way.

"A year ago. Murray called you 'Doc.'"

"I'm a vet."

I told her about my column and how I had stumbled on the murder. She was very easy to talk to.

"You're the new pet columnist? I love it! Your pooper scooper column was hilarious."

I was captivated by her blue eyes, crystalline and sparkling.

"So you're saying Aubrey Forsythe may be innocent?"

"Maybe."

We both turned at the sound of a disturbance at the entrance of the cathedral.

A wedge of cops came in, followed by Aubrey Forsythe and his lawyer, who took seats in the front row. I emailed the fact of Aubrey's arrival to the *Mail* and they kicked back, saying Aubrey's lawyer had gotten the appellate court to order bail, which was set at $1 million and immediately posted in cash. Chicken feed. All the cameras swooped in on Aubrey, who remained mum, despite an avalanche of questions.

"Speak of the devil," Murray said.

"How can they just let him out?" Jane asked, in a disgusted tone.

Organ music began and several men in ornate religious gowns converged on the altar. The service was pretty routine, considering the sensational nature of the case. The priest did not use the words "cannibalism" or "homosexual" in his eulogy, which was of the one-size-fits-all variety. Aubrey's name was conspicuous by its absence, despite his presence. Neil, according to the priest, was devoted to God and was a wonderful man who died before his time. Pookie pretended to cry for the cameras but ruined it with a burp. Aubrey cried what seemed to be genuine tears, and the TV crews went live. The priest proceeded with the solemn service, during which they drank blood and ate flesh, at least symbolically. Food for thought.

19.

I managed to get through the crowd of mourners and out onto the steps of the cathedral in time to see Aubrey and his lawyer, Roland Arbusto, struggling through a crowd of reporters toward a black limousine at the curb.

"I am innocent. I didn't kill anyone," Aubrey protested. "A court let me out on bail because there is video proof that the case against me is falling apart."

"What's a big gourmet like you doing eating Big Macs?" one reporter asked.

He ignored the question.

"What do you think about Nolan Cushing saying that Neil's death was caused by his degenerate lifestyle?"

That made Aubrey stop, one hand on the limo's door. He turned.

"That bigot came to dance on Neil's grave and I hope he gets what he deserves," Aubrey said, as he hurried into the back seat. "Someone should hack him up, and that goes for those other media whores like Harley Himmler as well."

The door slammed shut but the limo did not move. I noticed that one of the TV crews was Aubrey's team from *Food Fight*. After a minute, the limo's tinted window slid down and Arbusto's face appeared.

"Is F.X. Shepherd from the *Mail* here?"

I walked over and Arbusto put the tinted window up. The door opened and I got in. As the limo took off, I could see Ginny McElhone and a dozen other reporters running toward the press parking area.

"I understand you were the one who uncovered the McDonald's footage," Aubrey said to me.

"The police found it. I just covered it," I said.

"I was an idiot," Aubrey said. "I tried to keep it secret, so it wouldn't damage my reputation. Rolly here tells me the cops would never have given you that video unless you had it first. He thinks you are a smooth operator."

I said nothing. Aubrey was all business. No more emotion. As long as he seemed to be grateful, I told Aubrey I needed an exclusive interview to keep my paper happy and wanted his cell phone number. He shrugged and agreed. I pulled out my notebook.

"Rolly tells me you stopped the cops from shooting Skippy. Is that true?"

"Sort of. He was scared. He was protecting Neil."

"You also came back and fed him and took him for a walk while I was in jail I hear?"

I nodded, waiting for the thank-you.

"Why?"

"Because nobody was doing it and Skippy can't do it for himself."

"Well, you don't need to do that anymore. The TV people should have taken care of that. He was their idea anyway."

I didn't hear any thank-you.

"Skippy was their idea?"

"Of course. I'm not a dog person and, as you saw on the footage, Neil absolutely detested them."

"You got a stylish dog so it would look good on TV?" I asked.

"He matched the kitchen. Obviously it was a bad idea,

considering Neil's behavior toward Skippy."

"And your behavior toward Neil. Why did you slap Neil for kicking Skippy if you don't even like Skippy?"

"Don't be so naïve, Mr. Shepherd. Reality producers encourage conflict. Good for ratings. Besides, Neil was defying me and it looked bad on film."

"As bad as you slapping *him*? So you don't abuse animals. Only people?"

"I think we've covered this, Mr. Shepherd. Your dog-walking services are no longer required. I'm going to put the dog in a kennel for a few weeks, while I hide out from the press. Bastards are camped outside my house."

"You're putting Skippy in a shelter?"

"Not a shelter. A high-end kennel and vet right in my neighborhood. I can't stay at home. Hotels won't let me bring Skippy and I don't have time to take care of him. That was Neil's job. Actually, after we're done taping this season, I may make other plans, especially now that Neil is... gone. By the way, your 'Neil Parmesan' headline was cheap, offensive, and disgusting."

"It was," I agreed. "Also accurate. I found out reporters don't write headlines."

"Have it your way," said Aubrey. "They're not dropping the case against me yet but Rolly tells me I have you to thank for getting out on bail. Of course, on the other hand, you're just a cheap, low-paid hack from a yellow rag who also wrote all those horrible things about me and Neil."

"You're welcome," I replied. "I wasn't trying to help or harm you. Just trying to get the truth. Did you kill Neil?"

"Don't answer that," Arbusto ordered.

"Of course I'll answer that," Aubrey said. "No. Of course not. I would never hurt... I could never kill Neil. I loved him, whatever his faults."

"That's what I thought."

"Why do you believe me?" Aubrey asked.

"Your reaction. It looked real. Unless you're a great actor."

"I'm not."

"You still could have done it fast, cleaned up, run to Mickey D's, then gone to Bistro du Bois."

"But I didn't."

"Okay, so who did?"

"That is not for Mr. Forsythe to discover," Arbusto objected. "That's the job of the police and prosecutors."

"Give it a rest, Rolly," Aubrey said. "It's obvious isn't it, Mr. Shepherd?"

"Just call me Shepherd. Yes. If you didn't do it, then somebody else did—and fed… it… to you at Bistro du Bois."

"Exactly," Aubrey agreed. "Murray Glassberg. He detests me and would do anything to stop me from reviewing him again. The bastard killed Neil, or had someone else do it, and… fed him to me. Then tried to pin it on me. No other solution makes sense and I think you can prove it."

"Maybe. Maybe not."

"I would like to pay you to find proof, Mr. Shepherd."

"I don't work for you."

"You're getting paid as an investigative reporter by the *Mail* anyway. Think of this as gravy, a bonus."

"I just signed an employment contract. I'm not allowed to work for anyone else. I'm new at this but isn't getting paid by someone you write about unethical?" I asked.

"Not if it's in cash," Aubrey said. "Don't tell them. It will be our little secret."

"I don't think I want a secret with you. Thanks, but I'll pass."

"So you won't take the money but you're going to continue your investigation anyway?"

"Looks that way."

"You're a hack with ethics?" he giggled.

"Funny, right?"

"Very. So, I'm rich and you have ethics and have just refused free money. Who's the schmuck?"

"If I find out you did it, you are."

"You won't. By the way, what's with the face? Someone slam a door on it?"

"You're very perceptive," I told him. "Okay. So, now that we've established I have ethics and you don't, tell me, did you intend to give Murray's restaurant a bad review again—even before you tasted the food?"

Aubrey looked at me like I was an idiot.

"Of course I did," Aubrey said proudly. "I still will, when all this is cleared up and the *Tribune* lifts my suspension. That's the whole point, to put frauds like him out of business. He should be selling used cars or maybe he could be a reporter like you. He's also a hack. One of the thirteen dishes, a chicken entrée, was far too gamey and had gone cold then been re-warmed under those damned heat lights. I can always tell. That's always a risk with dim sum style, passing all those dishes around. They get cold. I will crucify him. I will drive scum like him out of the business. His food is cheaply popular, pandering to the lowest tongues."

"You mean like McDonald's?" I asked him with a grin.

20.

"Okay," I said, before Aubrey could react. "Tell me about the day of the murder. The fight at your place, McDonald's, Bistro du Bois, all of it. By the way, do you use Altoid mints?"

"Breath mints?" Aubrey asked, in a horrified tone. "I never use mints or gum. Why would I anesthetize my taste buds? I'm a food critic, not a cheerleader. I don't even use mouthwash, only an organic baking soda tooth powder. My taste buds are my fortune."

"Did Neil use Altoids?"

"You're not listening. I don't use them. He didn't use them. They are not allowed in my home. Period," he huffed. "You might as well ask if I eat leftovers."

A guy accused of cannibalism was grossed out at the thought of reheating dinner the next day? I couldn't resist.

"Do you eat leftovers?"

Aubrey's eyes narrowed.

"No. Never. Disgusting, like eating garbage."

"Okay, so where did the Altoid on the kitchen counter come from?"

"There was a mint in my kitchen?"

"Yes."

"They're one of the sponsors of the show," Arbusto

interjected. I was surprised that the lawyer had managed to keep quiet for so long.

"Who is?" I asked.

"Altoids. They're a sponsor. You know, food show, after-dinner mints," Arbusto explained.

"So where did the mint come from?" I asked.

Aubrey shook his head. "Ask the real killer. He probably left it."

"Any idea who that might be?"

"No. Someone who hated me, obviously."

"Why? Maybe they hated Neil. I mean, he's the one who's dead."

"Yes, but it seems calculated to implicate me, to make me look bad. To ruin *me*."

"Maybe that's just gravy." I was thinking out loud now. "If someone wanted Neil dead, maybe they also wanted you to be blamed—so no one even thinks of them as a suspect. That's what feeding you… Neil… was about. You're the fall guy. They skate."

Aubrey thought about that for a bit.

"So you're saying it might have been someone from Neil's… past?"

"I'm not saying. I'm asking. I don't know. What kind of past did he have?"

Aubrey looked at Arbusto and the lawyer looked back.

Aubrey nodded.

"Mr. Leonardi had a bit of a checkered past, I'm afraid," Arbusto said. "Multiple arrests, some jail time."

"For what?" I asked.

Again, they exchanged glances and nods before Arbusto spoke.

"Various things. Kid stuff. Arrests for drugs, some vandalism, a few robberies and assaults, male prostitution and ahhh… just one child molestation."

"That's kid stuff?" I asked.

"But that was a misunderstanding and he has been relatively clean and sober for years."

I pointed out that Neil had alcohol, weed, prescription painkillers and even animal tranquilizer in his bloodstream when he died.

"I have no idea where he got any illegal drugs," Aubrey said, a bit too quickly and not too convincingly. "If any of Neil's former... associates wanted to hurt him, I had no clue. I don't know them. Maybe the police do."

"Maybe."

"Well, actually Neil testified against quite a few former associates over the years, some of them rather nasty," said Arbusto.

"But if they don't know me, why would they want to frame me?" Aubrey asked.

"Like I said, perhaps they just needed a fall guy," I suggested. "Nothing personal."

"Nothing personal?" Aubrey laughed sarcastically. "Maybe the Altoid mint people should take it personally? Maybe the killer is trying to ruin *them*."

"I don't think so," I replied. "I think the mint was a joke, to tie in with how the killer displayed Neil's body."

Both Aubrey and Arbusto looked blank.

"Displayed?" asked Arbusto.

"He was laid out like... food. Naked, on a white floor, with... garnish. That's why you were fed Neil Parmesan— sorry—the killer served him up on a platter and even left an after-dinner mint. It's a joke meant to point at you or someone in your line of work."

"Like that creep Murray Glassberg," Aubrey said.

"Maybe," I said. "But if you had just killed Neil, why go out of your way to make it obvious it was all about food? The cops are still looking at you but they're also looking at Glassberg and his people. Why make a stupid visual joke that will draw attention to a food connection? Someone with a motive?"

"You mean Glassberg's fear of Aubrey's review?" Arbusto asked.

"Yeah," I said. "If I was the killer and Neil was my real target, I would have made it look like a robbery gone bad. If Aubrey was the target, I'd make it a simple lover's quarrel. I wouldn't do hokey stuff like cannibalism or sprinkle parsley on the body and leave a mint. I'd take Neil's dead finger and have him write your name in his own blood on the floor. Open and shut—you did it. The cannibalism and the display is a show, a menu that points at you, or Murray as a backup. It's so obvious, I'm having trouble believing either one of you did it. My gut says it was somebody else."

"Someone from Neil's past?" Aubrey asked.

"I don't know. Any of them use Altoids?"

21.

They dropped me off near Aubrey's townhouse. It was lunchtime, so I found a Starbucks, got a twelve-dollar frappuccino, a twelve-dollar cheese sandwich and an eight-dollar cookie. I sat in a comfortable chair, plugged my headphones into my iPhone, and listened to my recording of the limo interview. Then I rang Badger. Badger seemed pleased when I told him it was an exclusive. I asked him to send me copies of the text and voice messages he had hacked from Aubrey's and Neil's phones.

"Why?" he asked suspiciously.

"I'm checking out the time frame and alibi and those will help a lot," I explained.

"Alright but be discreet," he said. "They're not exactly public."

"Really?"

An email with file attachments popped onto my iPhone a minute later. I emailed Badger that I was on the case and talking to the cops but I decided I had done enough work for the *New York Mail* for one day. I texted Mary Catherine at her office, using our code, and asked her to meet me at my place. She agreed and I headed downtown.

"That girl isn't here, is she?" Mary Catherine asked

nervously, standing on my threshold an hour later.

"Of course not."

"So when's the wedding?" she asked sarcastically. She seemed to be taking it well. I laughed and asked her if she wanted a drink.

"At two o'clock in the afternoon?"

"I thought you were one hundred per cent Irish. People drink at lunch."

"One of those horrible licorice things you drink?"

"Arak is delicious," I protested. "And organic."

"Arsenic is organic and I'm sure it tastes better than that candy drink from hell. Is that how you got that redhead into the sack?"

"No. And it was the other way around. Ginny practically raped me."

Mary Catherine's left eyebrow rose.

"She tried to have me beaten up but that didn't work out. Then she came over and did the job herself, using every other body part except her fists. When I took a shower, all my notes and some rather important video evidence was gone and so was she."

"That's sweet. Actually, I think I will have a drink," she grinned. "Vodka, tonic on the rocks. Lime, if you have it. I want to hear this."

Mary Catherine sipped her drink and listened to everything. I started at the beginning, with my accidental summons to a good murder. I ended with Aubrey's limo interview and Badger sending me copies of the hacked messages. She drank her V&T down to the crackling ice and put it down.

"Shepherd, you are something," Mary Catherine said. "You have done much better than I thought anyone could. But I think it's time to end our little undercover arrangement."

"Why?"

"You know why," she said. "This was a great idea and

we were doing fine but suddenly you are becoming too…
public. Front-page stories, fistfights, sexual entanglements.
Also, you're making enemies who might decide to look into
your past. Or your present. That could be embarrassing and
I can't allow that. Besides, you've done well, much sooner
than we had hoped. We actually have proof. It's time to pull
the plug. We'll find another way."

"No. What you're saying is I've been too successful. Really?
We're moving forward. We're going to call it quits just when it
starts to pay off? No one knows and they're not going to find
out. Yes, we have proof of similar behavior but not the actual
evidence we need. Sack up, Mary Catherine. We can have it
all. All you have to ask yourself is 'is it worth it?' Your call."

She regarded me silently for a full minute, thinking.

"You're right," she said. "We'll continue. I have to get
back to the office soon, so show me your stuff, soldier."

"Yes, ma'am."

I was in bed the next morning when an angry Aubrey
Forsythe woke me up on my cell phone. I let him curse
for a while to vent. Eventually, he calmed down enough to
communicate that he was peeved at my story. I asked him to
read the offensive parts to me, as I went to the front door to
retrieve my copy of the paper.

"You printed it all! Everything. You say I protest my
innocence but you also say I tried to bribe you and that I had
made up my mind about a review before I tasted the food!"

"Yup. What's the problem?"

"What's the problem? You said Skippy was the TV
producer's idea and that I was putting him in a kennel. You
make me look like a mean, pompous, unethical bastard!
They've got a cartoon of me as the Red Queen from *Alice
in Wonderland*, saying 'first the verdict, then the meal.' You
have no right!"

"I didn't see that yet," I chuckled, opening the paper. "Clever. Again, what's the problem?"

"That was all off the record!"

"No, it wasn't. You never asked for anything off the record. That's why I recorded it."

"I *assumed* it was off the record. You have to retract it. The *Tribune* has fired me. I have Rolly as a witness. I'll sue you!"

"Okay but I listened to my tape. Nobody asked for anything to be off the record. You have to ask, right? That's how it works. I'm surprised you don't know that, and you such a pro with the press."

"Tape? What tape?"

"Well, not a tape. Actually a digital recording. It's amazing the apps you can get nowadays. I had my phone under my notebook as we chatted. Didn't you notice it? I wasn't really hiding it. Hey, I'm not a real reporter. It's not like I can take shorthand or anything. You guys talk too fast for me. This way, I have a record. You know, in case there's any confusion later."

"You son of a bitch. You ruined me."

"Nah. C'mon, Aubrey, you can't be ruined. Impossible. The whole country already knows you're a nasty, pompous prick and they love you for it. You're an American idol. You'll find some way to spin this into gold. So, where are you hiding out? Aubrey? Hello? Hello?"

I was getting the hang of reporting. It was like recon sitreps but with quotations. I called in the fact that Aubrey had been fired as a result of our story and Badger was so pleased he stopped bugging me for the rest of the day.

22.

For two days, over the rainy weekend I called Aubrey on his cell phone but I kept getting his voicemail. He didn't call back. I ate, slept, walked and watched TV. Badger pestered me with calls but gave up by Sunday when I had come up with nothing.

On Monday morning it was so warm I considered renting another bicycle but I bought a Metro Card instead from a vending machine and took a bus uptown. I found Ginny outside Aubrey's townhouse but nobody was home. She and a small pod of press were staked-out, milling around with nothing to do except wait for Aubrey. The story was fading.

Looking at her was doing something to me. She was wearing one of those light translucent silky tops that ended just above her perfect butt, which was tightly outlined by black leggings that ended in black leather riding boots. The top was open and she had a lacy v-neck thing underneath that exposed enough freckled cleavage to be interesting. I remembered what she looked like without any of that on, and it was a nice image. I remembered the smell of her hair, a delicious vanilla scent.

"Hi, Ginny," I said, hoping I sounded casual.

"Hi," she said, indifferent.

"What's up?"

She looked at me with a bored expression for only a second. Her eyes were some kind of green with red flecks, like sparks. I was trying to keep my eyes on her eyes, no lower.

"Waiting for Aubrey. Nobody home," she shrugged.

So far, so good. I figured she wouldn't want to advertise our hookup to her colleagues.

"He told me he was going to hide from you guys. From us," I said.

"Where?"

"He didn't say. Then it wouldn't be hiding," I smiled. She ignored me again and it bothered me. My cell vibrated and I answered it before it rang. "Hello?"

"Shepherd? Roland Arbusto here."

"Oh, hi," I responded, not using his name in front of my competition. "What's up?"

"Oh not much... preparing for Aubrey's court date tomorrow morning... How about you? Any new leads?"

"No, not at the moment," I replied.

"Oh, too bad... hear from anybody today?"

He was fishing.

"Like who?" I asked.

He was silent for a bit.

"Off the record?" he asked.

I casually strolled slowly away from the passel of press. "I'd prefer not," I said quietly, walking down the block. "How about as a source, you know, I won't use your name?"

He thought about it.

"Okay. On the record, no source. It won't matter anyway in the morning if... I can't reach Aubrey. He missed two conferences at my office over the weekend. He won't return my calls and he never checked into the hotel he was supposed to go to. I called everyone else he might have contacted—nothing. You are the only other person he might call. I'm afraid he..."

"You're afraid he jumped bail."

"That won't be official until the judge issues a bench warrant tomorrow," Arbusto said. "I can't cover for him. I'm afraid… he may have done something stupid. He took a lot of cash and jewelry with him. I can't believe he would do this. It doesn't make any sense. I really believe he is not guilty, Shepherd. I mean no-shit innocent."

"I was beginning to think so but now I don't know. How much cash and jewelry?"

"At least half a mil total value. I won't tell anyone else. I hope to God he shows up. Call me at any time, day or night, if you hear from him."

"You want me to print it, right?"

He laughed.

"Yeah, you got me. Put it in the paper, maybe it'll scare him into coming back. Say the source said if he jumps bail, the cops will find him and he'll be in jail for two years until his trial. Also, the judge will tell the jury that fleeing the jurisdiction shows consciousness of guilt and might ensure a guilty verdict. That might do it."

"Okay, Rolly. Thanks. By the way, why am I the only other person Aubrey might call?"

"He likes you," Arbusto replied. "He told me."

"That creeps me out," I said. "His husband is barely cold."

"No, not like that," Arbusto said. "He knows you're straight. He thinks you're smart and you might help him prove he's not guilty."

"He treats people he *likes* like that? Glad he doesn't hate me."

Arbusto laughed.

"He's surprised when straight people don't hate him because he's gay," Arbusto said. "He thinks honest people are suckers but they can be useful."

"What a guy," I laughed back. "Good luck."

I hung up and dialed the office but immediately canceled

the call. Ginny was staring at me like I was lunch. What if she could read lips? I moseyed back and introduced myself to some of the reporters and camera crews, like I had nothing to do. Some were friendly, some seemed envious, others bored. I decided to hit on Ginny. That way, when she shot me down, I could leave and she wouldn't follow me.

"So, Ginny, doing anything major tonight?"

"Working. Maybe," she answered, coldly.

"How about dinner at eight? You can bring that DVD, if you're finished copying it," I said, my voice dripping with charm. "Also, my notebooks. And anything else you may have taken."

She looked at me oddly, trying to decide if I was stupid or sarcastic, but then she softened.

"You're asking me out on a date?" she smirked, making the last word sound like a turd.

"No, just dinner with a colleague. You can bring your brothers but they have to pay for their own food."

She cracked and smiled. "Where?"

I told her and she smiled again.

"Okay, it's a date," she said, extending her hand for a businesslike shake.

I detected the sweet scent of vanilla swirling in the dirty breeze. I ambled west, toward Fifth Avenue and Central Park beyond. I stopped inside the entrance, at a break in the brownstone wall surrounding the park, and looked back. Ginny wasn't following me.

23.

Walking in Central Park, I dialed the office and filed my exclusive story. Badger was ecstatic.

"He's done a bunk? Super!" Badger said. He switched to headline voice. "'FATSO FLEES!'"

"We can't say that," I pointed out. "Just that he *may* have, that he is out of touch and it's a mystery. It won't be official unless and until he does not appear in court tomorrow morning."

"I'll just add a question mark," he said. "'FATSO FLEES?'"

Murray was not at his restaurant when I called but I made my reservation and a second request of Heather the bartender, who was happy to oblige.

I hung up and dialed Izzy. He was at the precinct squad room. I told him I had some information and wanted to watch the footage of Aubrey at the Bistro du Bois on the day of the murder. He told me to come on over to East 96th Street, second floor.

"But your source isn't sure Aubrey is in the wind?" Izzy asked after I arrived by cab and gave him the news.

"Just hasn't heard from him but he is afraid Aubrey took off."

"I can't do anything until a judge issues a warrant," Izzy said.

"Right. But he missed some important meetings and no one has heard from him. Also, he took half a million in cash and jewelry with him."

"Outstanding," Izzy said. "That *schmekel* has just snatched defeat from the jaws of victory."

"What's a *schmekel*?" I asked.

"A small, shriveled penis," Izzy responded.

"Yiddish?"

"Does it sound Spanish?"

"Correct me if I'm wrong, Izzy, but Jews seem to have a lot of different names for male genitalia."

"Yah. It's like the Eskimos with snow."

"So, Aubrey taking off is an admission of guilt?"

"You got it. Who's your source?"

"I can't tell you."

"Forsythe himself?"

"No."

"Then it's Arbusto."

"I can't say. But if his own lawyer thought he'd skipped, it would carry some weight, right?"

"Yeah, maybe, but I can't do anything official until Forsythe actually fails to show up for court."

"Can you do anything *unofficially*?"

He pondered a moment.

"I can say we have a confidential informant who claims he has absconded and begin an investigation that would put his name on the Homeland Security no-fly list. That might keep him from getting on a plane to Rio."

"Is that hard to do?"

"No, it's too easy. I can label you a terrorist or arrest you for murder on anyone's alleged eyewitness statement a lot more easily than I can get a search warrant for your home."

"That doesn't sound right."

"Write your congressman."

I told Izzy my other idea and he agreed. On his desktop

computer, Izzy played the footage of Aubrey chowing down at Bistro du Bois after loading up at McDonald's. I counted the dishes. It looked like four small appetizer plates, two oval salads, and seven large entrée plates. A total of thirteen. I rewound and fast-forwarded to confirm. One dish, delivered near the end of the video, was hard to spot because the waiter or waitress—it was impossible to guess the gender—slipped it in front of Aubrey from the left, without fully entering the frame. The other servers, all in black pants and white shirts, made a big show of presentation, of smiling, giving Aubrey a plate, wishing him a hearty appetite. Probably out-of-work actors, hamming it up for the camera.

"Aubrey insists there were thirteen dishes and he's right," I told Izzy. "But the restaurant told me there were only a dozen. It was on the bill."

"So? They lost count. Forsythe got a freebie."

"Maybe. But I've found out that chefs and critics remember every part, every ingredient of every dish, like tennis champions can recall every point. I think the thirteenth dish was Neil Parmesan and the server was camera shy for a reason."

"Let me see that," Izzy said, rewinding the video. "Huh," he said, as he watched and then froze the arm proffering the extra plate. The dish bore a small, pale oval entrée sprinkled with green flecks that might have been parsley.

"He or she is wearing black pants and a white shirt," I pointed out. "But all the servers have black pants and a white shirt."

"But no face," Izzy grumbled. "No tattoo on the arm, nothing."

"Nope. But doesn't that plate look different than the others? Like maybe a different color?"

"They're all white," Izzy pointed out.

"But maybe a different shade or something, thinner?"

"Maybe," Izzy shrugged. "Too dark. So, if Forsythe is so

innocent and someone else killed Neil and slipped him Neil Parmesan, why is Forsythe making a run for it?"

"I don't know. Maybe he isn't. We'll see in the morning. Thanks for the show, Izzy. I gotta run. Got a date."

"Anybody I know?" Izzy asked.

"Ginny McElhone, the police reporter from the *Daily Press*."

He laughed long and loud. When I asked him why, he refused to say. He just kept laughing, as I walked out.

24.

The night was warm and Ginny, still wearing her diaphanous outfit, was seated at an outside table at the Bistro du Bois, behind a wooden fence on the sidewalk. The hostess, Heather, showed me to the table with a wink and Murray Glassberg, the chef, waved from the kitchen. Ginny said she was drinking Jameson Irish Whiskey on the rocks. I ordered a rum punch.

"Rum punch? Are we on a cruise?" Ginny giggled.

"They don't have my favorite drink. I did have rum punches in the islands but not on a cruise," I admitted. "Well, I guess it was a cruise. I spent a few months sailing the Caribbean alone after... after my accident. If you use over-proof 154 rum it beats pills as a painkiller."

"I'll stick with good old Irish whiskey, like God intended," she said.

"Why not Old Bushmills? I thought that was the best."

"Aren't you Irish Catholic?" she asked, shocked.

"Retired. Why?"

"Bushmills is Protestant. Everyone knows that."

"How can alcohol have a religion?" I wondered aloud.

"You're not a New Yorker. Where are you from?" she demanded.

"Kansas, sort of. Lots of other places. Now I'm a New Yorker. I moved here."

"Doesn't make you a New Yorker."

"What does? Rudeness? Dishonesty? Ruthlessness? Could we get beyond the macho city crap and just agree to be friendly competitors and maybe enjoy a meal... and maybe each other?"

She thought about it while my drink arrived. It had a small, festive, multi-colored paper parasol, chunks of fruit and a pink straw with the paper removed and curled cutely.

"Sweet," Ginny said. "Don't forget to point your pinkie."

I removed the straw and umbrella and held my glass up for a toast.

"What shall we drink to?" I asked.

"Your return to the Midwest," she beamed.

"Nope. Nothing there for me anymore."

"To the story!" she said, raising her amber glass.

"May the best man win!" I added.

She shot me an angry glance but we had a great meal, picking whatever dishes looked good and digging in. The hot shredded beef with carrots and celery was great, and so were the ginger cubes. Ginny competed at everything; drinking, eating, talking. We discussed the story but she gave up when she couldn't get anything out of me. We ordered more drinks and she told me her greatest hits, her best stories. I switched to her drink.

"I thought you didn't like whiskey?" she asked.

"I pretty much like anything with alcohol in it. I learned not to be too fussy about it."

Ginny told me about the time she dressed up as a nurse to get a bedside interview with a hero firefighter, and how she posed as a hooker to catch cops asking for free sex. Picturing her dressed up as a nurse and a hooker did not calm me.

"You always been a reporter?" I asked during the salads.

"Always. My dad was a pressman, my uncles were mailers, and my brothers are pressmen, so I grew up in newspapers."

"Mailers?"

"You really don't know anything about our business do you?"

"Nope. Don't really want to," I said. "I was writing a pet column and they sent me to Aubrey's house by mistake. I sort of stumbled into this."

"That story is true? Damn, that is so unfair," she said, glancing at her phone.

"To whom?" I asked.

"To me. It's more insulting to be beaten by... a pet columnist, a beginner."

"So, you'd feel better if I was some hotshot Pullets Prize winner?"

"Pulitzer Prize, moron. A pullet is a chicken. Yes."

"Whatever. Am I supposed to apologize? This was a mistake. I don't care about any of this. It won't last. I just got kind of... caught up in it."

As I spoke, I was caught up in watching the cute way her nose wrinkled as she spoke.

"You're hooked. I know the signs," she said, waving for more booze.

"Not the journalism stuff," I protested. "The case. I have to see how it comes out. I have to finish it. I've locked on."

"I'll finish it," she boasted. "Don't worry."

"Are you sure you haven't... done something else, another job?"

"Like what?" she asked, gulping a new drink.

"Nothing... you just remind me of some people I used to work with."

"Where?" she asked, her eyes sparkling at the prospect of new information.

"Lots of places."

She looked at me like she thought I couldn't hold my liquor.

"When did your mom die?" I asked. "Must have been hard without sisters."

She dropped her fork.

"Who have you been talking to?" she asked suspiciously.

"Nobody. Just a guess. You mentioned your dad, your brothers but no mom or sister."

"And you think I'm not feminine? Now you're a shrink?"

"No. And I think you're very feminine. And sexy. Big time."

She stared and said nothing for a moment.

"I was young when she died," she admitted after a while. "How about your parents?"

"No, they're alive and well."

"But?"

"But they don't talk to me much. Long story. Another time."

She seemed comforted by my admission and we eased back into small talk. The dessert, a chocolate mousse devil's food cake with amaretto whipped cream, was outrageous. Murray sent over snifters of Calvados, apparently some kind of fancy French brandy. I insisted on paying and Ginny did not argue. Heather brought me a large, heavy doggie bag and left it on my side of the table with another wink, as a busboy cleared. Murray stopped at the table and we complimented his food and thanked him for the Calvados. He asked what was new in the case and we each said nothing was new. We strolled outside, me carrying my white paper bag with the heavy plate hidden inside, and got into a cab without a word.

"Where to?" I asked.

"Your place, obviously," she said, kissing me.

The cab shoved us together as we kissed. I put my doggie bag behind me, out of her reach. Obviously, cabbies in New York were used to people making out in the back seat. I had never made out, drunk, in a New York cab. It was fun.

Once again, the cabbie took me to the wrong front door on Broome Street. Maybe the GPS database was off a bit. We disengaged and, as I was paying the cab driver, Ginny's phone went off with a Looney Tunes ringtone.

"Yeah?" Ginny said into her phone, as we got out onto the sidewalk. "In the *Mail*? No. What are you talking about?"

She began cursing and fiddling with the phone, reading something, her call now on speakerphone.

"Yeah, here it is. Son of a bitch! I see it. 'FATSO FLEES?'"

She ended the call. Her language got a lot worse and it was directed at me.

"You bastard. You were just babysitting me until deadline," she spat.

"I thought that's what you were doing to me."

"Screw you!" she screamed.

"Not coming up?"

She swung at me with her phone hand and I reflexively pulled my chin out of the way. She cursed again. I didn't try to explain that it would have hurt her hand more to hit my jawbone. She got back in the cab and slammed the door. In seconds, I was on the street watching the taxi speed away.

I debated my next move as I walked to my building two doors down. I couldn't face a bus or the subway or a bicycle in my condition. I hailed another taxi at the corner. I got out at Aubrey's townhouse and spoke to the cop at the door. I was pleased to see it was my friend from the day of the murder.

"Evening, Officer Gumbs. Long day?"

"Rotating night tour, Lieutenant said you might stop by," he said, opening the front door. "I hear you've got something for him."

"What's your first name?" I asked him.

"August, like the month."

"But they call you Augie?"

"You got it."

We went into the kitchen. I opened my Bistro du Bois doggie bag and took out the plate, using one of the paper napkins in the bag. The china was off-white, thin and delicate, and had a fine line of gold around the edge, obviously more expensive than the thicker plain white plates at the restaurant. I left it on the counter and opened the cabinet, where there were two stacks of plates. They matched the one I had taken from the restaurant. The left stack was one plate lower and there was a small dent in the wood of the inside rear of the cabinet, just above the top plate in the pile. I put my plate on top of the stack and the thin edge fit exactly into the groove. Now both stacks were even. I took two pictures on my iPhone, one of the plate in the stack and another of it on the counter, where I left it for Izzy.

"Probably been washed, scrubbed and sterilized a dozen times since it held Neil Parmesan," I said.

"Yeah. No prints, nothing. The killer knew that. I'll tell the lieutenant in the morning," Augie said.

"You know where Aubrey put Skippy?" I asked. "Which kennel?"

"The dog? No clue. Maybe he took the pooch with him."

"Doubt it. Would you take a dog if you were going underground?"

"Not unless he was a devil dog," he smirked. "So, you weren't on the job?"

"Not your job. Different job. Night, Augie," I said.

"Keep it up, pal," Augie said.

"Not tonight," I told him. "She ditched me."

25.

Aubrey did not show up for his court date the next day but every reporter and photographer in New York did, jostling each other, on the lookout for an Aubrey sighting outside the courthouse in the cool morning sunshine. There were more in the lobby and hallway but cameras were barred from the courtroom itself.

"Where is your client, Mr. Arbusto?" a stern Judge Bean asked inside the packed courtroom.

"I have not heard from him in several days, Your Honor. I am concerned for his safety and have filed a missing persons report with the police department."

Arbusto was clever. His client was again a victim—not a fleeing felon.

"You do not believe your client has fled the jurisdiction?" the judge asked, his voice soaked in sarcasm.

"No, of course not, Your Honor. I can't imagine Mr. Forsythe doing such a thing. He is an innocent man."

"In that case, I will do everything I can to assist the police in their search. I hereby revoke Mr. Forsythe's bail and I am signing a bench warrant for his arrest. Does the District Attorney have anything to add?"

"Without the facts? No, Your Honor, but we cannot

dismiss the possibility that the defendant has a consciousness of his own guilt and is trying to avoid justice and we will so argue at trial. Disturbing reports that the defendant fled with a substantial sum of money have reached our office and we are investigating."

She did not mention the reports had reached her office through a copy of the *New York Mail*.

"The warrant is signed. The case is adjourned until the defendant can be produced."

"All rise!" an officer shouted, as the judge left the bench.

I called the paper and filed the court session and my plate discovery from the night before and sent my phone pictures. Badger came on the line to tell me that Aubrey wasn't using his cell phone or email yet.

"How do you know he isn't using them?" I asked.

"A little bird told me," he cackled. "The same one that told me you have been leaving a lot of voice messages on his phone. The plate thing isn't bad for tomorrow—'The *Mail* Uncovers Neil Parmesan Plate,' but, mate, next time, let Photo shoot the bloody plate. We could have done a simulation, spiced it up a bit. With a lot more pixels than your flipping phone. No more flying solo."

"Okay, I'm going to nose around the neighborhood," I said, ignoring him. "I'll let you know."

I went to the Upper East Side townhouse and watched the media mob long enough to see they were getting nothing. Unless Aubrey showed up, of course. I used my iPhone to search for kennels in the area and came up with more than a dozen. I should not have been surprised. The Upper East Side had hundreds of luxury apartment buildings filled with hundreds of thousands of rich people—many with dogs and other pets. City dwellers seemed to think a dog would protect them because they could sense prowlers and could bark. Bad guys would simply rob someone with a cat.

I had almost given up when I spotted a familiar name in the Google listings. "Arthur Animal Hospital and Pet Boarding, Dr. Jane Arthur, DVM." I decided to start with a familiar face. Maybe she could help me find Skippy. Besides, she was hot.

The hospital was only three blocks away. Parked in front was a black van rigged with fake ears over the cab, painted with a faux tail and labeled CATMOBILE. It also had Jane's name on it and advertised house calls, grooming and emergency surgery on wheels. Her lobby was filled with anxious owners and their dogs and cats, the air filled with animal tension and animal smells.

Behind the counter I found Pippi Longstocking with huge boobs in a white lab coat. She had long, high, jet-black pigtails, like fluffy horns on either side of her head. She was young, slim-waisted, probably college age, with the heavy gothic eyeliner and shadow that young girls think makes them look mature. Her fingernails were glossy black. Everything she had was pierced. Her nose, lips, eyebrows, and her earlobes, which were sparkly stud farms. Her hair was so black it was obviously dyed. Under her white smock I could see a colorful MEAT IS MURDER t-shirt. Over the lab coat pocket was a nametag that said XANA.

I introduced myself and Xana gave me a nice smile after I pronounced her name correctly, as "Zana."

"You're looking for Dr. Jane," Xana said in a gentle vegetarian voice.

In a few minutes, Jane, dressed in a pink lab coat, emerged from the back with a big smile. I got a kiss on the cheek, so maybe she *had* been hitting on me at the funeral. On her coat pocket, she had a name tag, DR. JANE, flanked by a happy little dog and cat. She had a stethoscope around her neck and her pockets bulged, no doubt with lumpy animal treats. Her blond hair was pulled back in a ponytail, with a lacy pink scrunchie.

"So, Shepherd, what are you doing here? Worms? Tell me my prayer was answered and you're single."

"No and yes," I answered. "I thought you might help me. I'm trying to find out where Aubrey Forsythe kenneled Skippy before he took off."

"Oh yes, I heard he took off. Well you've come to the right place, Shepherd."

"Great. Any idea where I might find him?"

"You bet. Skippy is two blocks away. Aubrey has *always* used us. He asked us to pick up his dog on Friday night. Said he was off to hide from the media. We had to lodge Skippy at a pet hotel we use nearby. Why do you want to find him?"

I paused.

"Well, actually, I was going to find the kennel and try to B.S. them but I can't do that with you. You already know who I am."

"B.S. them to do what?" she asked.

"To get Skippy, of course. He shouldn't be in a cage."

"Hey! We are the best and so is the place we put him. That's why that jerk Aubrey used us. Skippy is fine. Go see for yourself. I'm in the middle of hydrating a cat but Xana can give you the address and a note," Jane said, gesturing to Xana.

"Actually, I wanted to ask if I could take Skippy home, you know, like foster care, until Aubrey can take him back?"

"Why?"

"Because I think Aubrey took off and if the cops find him he won't get out of jail for at least a year. He shouldn't be in a cage for a year."

"Aubrey or Skippy?" Jane asked.

"Skippy," I answered.

"He wouldn't be," she said. "If that happened, we would place Skippy, find him a new home."

"How about me? Now. Why wait?"

She looked at me, amused.

"Okay."

"Okay? That's it?"

"I think you're right. I think it would be the best thing for Skippy. If that creep Forsythe shows up, I'll just say I put his dog in temporary foster care. Can you take him now?"

"Uh... yeah. Sure."

"Okay, Xana will set you up with a collar and leash and some food and send you over with a note. You know how to take care of a dog, I suppose?"

"Yeah, I used to have one. She died."

"Okay," grinned Jane. "One condition."

"You got it."

"Dinner. Tonight. My treat. How about the Bistro du Bois at eight?"

"I just ate there last night," I explained.

"Oh. Too bad, another time," she said. "How about Kassim's, the fancy shish kabob place across the street from there? Their food is great."

"Okay. It's a deal, Doc."

"Call me Jane. See you then. Just go in the back and Xana will set you up. I have to hydrate that cat and then deal with a dachshund with a bad back."

"Okay, Jane."

Xana stepped forward. Her eyes were violet. Probably tinted contacts. I glanced at her chest and she caught me, so I tried to cover by pointing at her t-shirt.

"Tell that to dogs and cats," I told her.

"What?" Xana asked, confused.

"Tell cats and dogs that meat is murder," I said. "They eat beef, fish, all that."

"What? Oh, right, haha. You're the reporter, right? In the *Mail*? I love your stuff. Your headlines are so cool. 'Neil Parmesan,' man that is sick," she giggled. "C'mon. I'll write down the address. It's called Park Pet Services."

* * *

Park Pet Services looked like a small, exclusive hotel, but for pets. Skippy had his own room. He looked sleepy but soon perked up, sniffed me and waggled his tail. I scratched his head and he nuzzled me.

"Hi, Skippy," I said. "Remember me?"

"Wawf," he replied.

"Good."

Skippy bounced down the street, dragging me and a heavy bag containing food, bowls and dog toys. At first, he dragged me toward Aubrey's townhouse but I realized we couldn't go there. I tried three cabs but none of them would accept Skippy as a passenger unless he was in a dog carrier cage. Skippy took me to Central Park for a run instead, a real workout given how much I was carrying.

I had a brainstorm when I spotted a bike rental kiosk. In minutes, Skippy and I were breezing downtown, a white husky and a blue bike, connected by a leash. I rode to the West Side and then downtown. I was waiting for Skippy to get tired but it never happened. In my neighborhood, Skippy pulled me toward the water, and into Hudson River Park. We went out onto a long pier with a view of New Jersey—I think—and finally home. In my place, Skippy sniffed and investigated. In the bathroom, he barked at my toilet brush until I showed him it wasn't lurking vermin. His inspection done, he lapped up a bowl of cold water and some dry food. He settled down on my new couch, like he was home. It was amazing how animals could go through major trauma and bounce back. I collapsed next to Skippy and scratched his head. He fell asleep. Despite the fact that there was no one to scratch my head, I also nodded off.

26.

I got to the restaurant before Jane, and discovered it was a reasonably fancy place, with a well-dressed clientele, which didn't include me. I was wearing black pants and a black long-sleeved shirt, my all-purpose evening outfit, which covered every venue from Nathan's Famous Hot Dogs to the Four Seasons. The only necktie I owned was on my desk at the *Mail*.

It was a bit cool to eat outside. Only in New York could they take Asian peasant food, pile it on a plate like a modern sculpture and charge a fortune. Jane made a big entrance while I was chatting with a gnarly old waiter in a tux.

"Wow," I said, checking her out.

The waiter was also staring in awe. Her blond hair was feathery and straight to her naked shoulders. She had shed the lab coat and was wearing a clingy short black dress with almost invisible spaghetti straps. The V-neck of the dress revealed a lot of cleavage. Her eyes sparkled, as did dangling diamond earrings and a matching sparkler between her full breasts, which gave me an excuse to keep looking there. I could see the outline of her slinky hips through the tight velvety material. Her legs were killers; toned under smoky hose and ending in black leather pixie boots. She had just enough makeup on to draw attention to the fact that she was gorgeous.

"Nice necklace," I told her.

"It's a pendant," she smiled. "And I can tell you're not looking there."

"Typical woman. You dress like a star at the Academy Awards and then scold me for looking."

"I am not a typical woman," Jane said, sitting down, as the waiter pushed in her chair.

"You're right. I take that back," I said. "It's obvious you are something very special."

"What language were you and the waiter speaking when I came in?" she asked.

I hesitated, adopting a confused expression. "Sorry?"

"You were speaking a foreign language to him. You speak Arabic?"

"I wasn't speaking Arabic, no."

"Turkish?"

She waited me out.

"He's not Turkish," I said.

"You're cute but you're as slippery as an eel, Shepherd," she said with a smile.

"I love it when you talk dirty. Have you ever had an eel as a patient?"

"Yes. An electric one. You're doing it again. You did not answer my question. Is there some reason you don't want me to know you speak a specific foreign language?"

"The waiter and I were speaking Pashto," I told her, honestly.

"Which is what?"

"A language spoken in Eastern Afghanistan."

She looked at me, at my face, and nodded. She thought for a bit before she said anything else.

"Berlitz?" she asked casually.

"Something like that, at first."

"Nothing like immersion in the culture to pick up a language quickly."

"True."

"Want to talk about your travels? Or about your scars… lieutenant?"

"Sergeant. Not yet. Later, maybe. If that's okay?"

"Okay. Fair enough. What shall we talk about?"

"What you have on under that dress?"

"You want to talk about nothing?" she grinned.

"Definitely."

Jane ordered red wine and our waiter disappeared. "He didn't take your drink order," Jane said.

"I already ordered."

Our drinks arrived, along with an appetizer. We ripped hot pita bread and dipped it into fresh hummus and cool yogurt sauce with cucumber and dill.

"What are you drinking?" Jane asked, looking at my small glass filled with clear liquid. "Is that water?"

"It's arak," I told her. "You might not like it. It's strong."

"May I try it?"

"Do you like licorice? You know, anise?"

"When I was seven years old, yes."

"Imagine 200 proof licorice with no sugar."

She insisted on a sip and gasped.

"Oh my god! It tastes like candy-flavored gasoline."

"Pretty much. In a pinch we used it in small motors. It's very flammable. Very efficient, in terms of volume."

"You may be a strange guy," she smiled.

"I didn't start out that way."

We talked about nothing: Skippy, her practice, Aubrey, cannibalism, rabies, food, global warming, great Coen brothers movies, especially *Raising Arizona*, *Fargo* and *Miller's Crossing*. During the flaming lamb and chicken kabob entrées, we discussed electric eels, dachshund spinal columns, sex, the mayoral race, zither music in the film *The*

Third Man, how dating sucked, how we felt guilty eating animals but did it anyway, and also bad Coen brothers movies. At the end of the meal we each knew a lot about what the other person loved and hated but very little about our personal lives.

"What was her name?" Jane asked. "And don't say who. The one who burned you so bad. It takes one to know one, Shepherd."

"Fatimah," I answered after a while.

"Oh God."

"What?"

"She's dead, isn't she? I can tell by your tone."

"Yes. She is. A year ago."

"Do you want to talk about her?"

"No. Yes. Maybe sometime. Sorry."

"Damn. I like you, Shepherd."

"I like you, too, Jane. You don't have to sound so sad about it."

"No, of course not. It's just that every time I… forget it. Excuse me, I'll be right back."

As Jane returned from the bathroom, my iPhone vibrated on my hip and a little musical ring tone told me I had a text message. I was reading it as she sat back down and suggested a dessert.

"I may have to skip dessert," I told her.

"Please don't let me scare you away, Shepherd. I'm sorry I asked about Fatimah. None of my business."

"No, it's not about that. I got a text. Here, read it yourself," I said, handing her my phone.

> Need to talk to you immediately. Urgent. No police. Please come i need your help. 72 E. 72Nd. Door open, don't ring bell.

"Whose phone number is it?"

"Aubrey Forsythe. I haven't added him to my contacts yet."

"I thought he took off and the cops were looking for him?" she asked, handing the phone back.

"He did. They are."

"Shouldn't you call the police?"

"Are you kidding?"

I called the *Mail*, told Badger where I was meeting Aubrey so he could send a photographer, and hung up.

"Don't the police think he's the killer, this Hacker? It sounds very dangerous. Maybe I could come along and talk to him."

"You want to come along?"

"You'd let me?" she beamed.

"You know him. Why not? Give you a chance to catch up. Sounds more interesting than dessert. You scared?"

"No."

"Okay."

27.

Jane paid the bill and we grabbed a cab. On the way I asked if she recognized the address but she said she didn't think so. I pulled out my phone and plugged in the street and number. Google zoomed in on a townhouse in a row of brownstones.

"It figures he would hide out in an expensive townhouse. No cheap motels for Aubrey," I said, as we pulled up. "The cops aren't going door-to-door up here."

"Shepherd, I hate to interfere with your big scoop but what if Forsythe has asked you here to kill you?"

"Then you should stand behind me."

"You're not scared?"

"He's mad at me but I don't think he wants me dead. I don't think he's the killer. Either way, I'm not worried."

She stared at me with an odd expression.

"What?"

"I can't decide whether you're stupid or crazy or brave or dangerous," she explained.

"Why not all four?"

The huge five-story brownstone mansion was dark, lit only by pale street lights filtered through the trees. It was enclosed by a black wrought-iron fence and a gate that creaked like a haunted-house movie. The main steps led up to the first floor, half a story up from the street. A large shadow emerged from the basement entrance under the stairs and Jane gasped and grabbed my arm. It looked like a bear with cameras.

"Shepherd?" the bear whispered in a husky ursine voice.

"Yeah."

The shape stepped into the light, festooned with photography equipment, a tall, bulky guy with shiny dark skin, broken only by short black hair, beard and mustache.

"I'm Ernie," he said. "Badger sent me."

"You're my photographer?"

"No, pal. You're my reporter. What's the deal?"

"I got a message from Aubrey Forsythe to meet him here."

"Fuck yes!" Ernie hissed. "Does he know I'm coming?"

"No. Why are you so happy, Ernie?"

"You shittin' me? This is national. Hell, international. I'll make a fuckin' fortune on the resale pictures. I get half. I need a new car."

We mounted the steps and Ernie elbowed us aside, until he was right next to me, ready to shoot, camera up.

"I got orders to bang away so ring the bell," he said.

"No," I told him. "No bell." I turned the heavy brass door knob.

The front door was unlocked, just as Aubrey had promised. I pushed the door open. The narrow, carpeted hallway was very dark and I clipped a thin table standing against the left wall, rattling something. I went toward a door on the right, light leaking from under it. My breath became stronger, my gut and muscles tensed as I advanced. I felt unarmed. I heard faint barking from the rear of the building; maybe a neighbor's dog? Suddenly, a dim red light from behind me lit the way. Ernie was doing something with his camera, holding it over my head, pointing where I was going, lighting my way with a red beam.

I opened the door and blinked in the bright light.

He was on his back on a rug, his silent throat and mouth open wide like he had been interrupted mid-rant. Ernie was shooting frantically, his camera flashing and whirring. He was humming as he photographed the slashed throat, hacked open, echoed by the astonished rictus of the mouth. Billionaire Nolan Cushing had tears in his eyes, which had run down either cheek. Perhaps he had cried because someone had pulled his famous helmet hair comb-over aside, where it lay stiff next to his bald scalp like a dead pet. On his other side, there was a pool of sticky red blood, with silver coins and green bills congealed in the mess.

"Fuckin' great, man," Ernie muttered.

"Wait," Jane said. "Isn't that…?"

"Nolan Fucking 'Cash' Cushing," Ernie answered. "The money guy with the silly comb-over. The one Forsythe publically threatened at the funeral. Yes!"

Jane kneeled next to the body and felt for a pulse. I told her not to touch anything but she ignored me. She began compressing Cushing's chest and ordered me to call the police. She found a fancy pen inside Cushing's suit and took it apart. She took the hollow bottom half and jammed it into the bottom of the throat wound, leaving part of it sticking out. She puffed into it and Cushing's chest rose a bit. Then she returned to the chest, pressing rhythmically.

"He's fuckin' dead, lady," Ernie told her, to no avail.

"I have to try," Jane answered.

I dialed Izzy's cell phone.

"What?" Izzy said, obviously emerging from sleep.

I told him. He cursed in Spanish.

"Cushing? Like Neil?"

"Yeah, same throat wound, more posing. Scalped. This time with money all over the place. Oh, I get it. It's a sight gag, a pun. Blood money."

"Blood money?"

"You'll see."

"What do you mean *scalped*?" Izzy asked.

"Well not technically 'scalped.' They took off his wig. Or, his comb-over."

"Oh. I'll be right over. Don't touch anything."

I hung up and looked at Jane, still valiantly performing CPR. She stopped, winded, and found a tiny flashlight on her keychain, which she pointed into Nolan's glazed, lifeless eyes.

"Fixed and dilated. Okay, he's gone," Jane said, stopping.

She was smeared in blood. After hearing my "blood money" comment, Ernie worked his way around the sofa and shot the body with the currency in the foreground. Then he shot the whole room, flashing in a circle, documenting it all.

I looked around. We were in a fancy leather den with a gigantic vanity wall of Cushing posing for photographs with people more famous than he was. We were obviously in his home. One of them. I noted that the only photographs that didn't show Cushing with celebrities had him embracing a corgi with a suicidal expression. Even the dog knew he was a shit.

"Good idea calling the cops before the competition sniffs this out," Ernie said. "You need me for anything else before I go? I gotta get outta here before the boys in blue show up."

"Why?" Jane asked.

"You kiddin'? They'll take my camera. That ain't gonna happen. Besides, I gotta make the late edition. Hey, Shepherd, anytime you need a shooter, call me direct," he said, handing me his card. "Thanks, pal. With these shots, I'm gonna get me a Jag, baby."

"Take a shot of that Altoid mint on the coffee table near the body but don't give it to the office yet," I told him. "Hold it back, okay?"

He did so without question, shooting the single white mint from both sides and then he was gone. I took a quick look around the empty townhouse, looking for other surprises. I found none, returned to Jane and called the paper. When I told Badger what I had found, he seemed peeved.

"No Forsythe?"

"He's not here and won't answer his phone."

"I already wrote the bloody headline, mate."

"Bloody is right. Write another one, mate."

I told him about the blood money and the de-wigging.

"The blood money's not bad. 'Fatso strikes again.' The hair is brilliant. *That's* The Wood. I'll put you on to rewrite. You know, against my better judgment, I'm beginning to like you, Shepherd."

"Thank God for that."

"But no cannibalism this time?"

"Nope. He looks whole. Except for the hair."

"Pity."

28.

Izzy was unhappy. We were standing outside in the tiny townhouse yard inside the fence, as the CSI folks worked on the crime scene inside. Izzy became angry when Jane explained her resuscitation efforts. It was getting colder and she was shivering.

"So, you're not a doctor. You're a vet. And you just decided to roll around in my crime scene like a chocolate Lab with a bone?" Izzy accused her.

"I had a responsibility as a medical person, and just as a person, to try to preserve a life," she told him calmly.

"Bull. Look at that thickening blood. This guy has been lying there for hours. He's as dead as they come. What possessed you to shove a pen into my victim's throat?"

"You're saying I should not have tried to save this man's life? His airway was cut. That was the only way I could get air into him," she explained.

"Enough. How do I know you two didn't kill Cushing? I only have your word you didn't. Look at you—you're soaked in the victim's blood."

Jane looked down at her cocktail dress, tacky with hardening blood, and groaned.

I laughed. I showed Izzy my text from Aubrey and

explained we had another witness, my photographer, Ernie.

"Really? Terrific. So where is he? Putting pictures of my crime scene in your paper?"

"Yes. He is," I admitted.

Izzy cursed, a string of suggestions on how to insert cameras and lenses up inside the human body. I noticed he always seemed to curse in Spanish, his father's second language, not Yiddish, his mother's second tongue.

"You can't do that," Izzy protested.

"Why not? I heard you say you had notified Cushing's sister of his death."

"Yeah but she won't officially identify his body at the M.E.'s office until the morning."

"Is there any doubt?" I asked.

Izzy ignored me. "I'm too tired for this *mishegoss*. I need statements from both of you and elimination prints in the morning at the precinct."

Jane asked if she could go home and take a shower. Izzy agreed and pointed her towards a cop car for a ride. I was going to kiss her goodbye but her face was still smeared with Cushing's blood. We promised to speak in the morning.

"Thanks for an interesting evening," Jane smiled, as she closed the squad car door. "I usually don't do this on a first date."

"How do I know that?" I asked her.

"You owe me one cocktail dress," she said, waving goodbye.

I couldn't wait to pour her into a new one.

Phil appeared and I followed as he and Izzy walked back into the townhouse.

"You two got any more questions for me?"

Izzy thought about it for a while.

"Off the record, okay?" he said, turning as he opened the front door.

"You saw the Altoid?"

He grunted what might have been a *yes*.

We entered the crime scene and I shut up and watched from a discreet distance as Izzy did his thing.

"So, Cash, where did the money come from?" Izzy asked the dead man. "Your pockets are inside-out. Did he leave the bills and coins after you were dead? Why didn't you struggle? You just lay down on the floor and let him slash your throat open? Looks like it. Blood spray by the sofa. You bled out. Were your eyes open or did he open them after you were dead—for effect? Why would Aubrey Forsythe kill you? Because you insulted him at the funeral? So, he kills Neil Leonardi and eats him because he kicked the dog and talked back. He wasted you because you're against gay marriage and insulted his husband—who he also killed? Nolan, buddy, this does not make any freaking sense."

"I agree," I said.

"And what's with the mint?" Izzy continued.

"Maybe he's saying our friend also had a hint of mint?" Phil smirked.

Izzy shrugged, noncommittally.

"The mystery of the mint. It made some kind of sense when it was a food critic's husband and there was cannibalism involved. This time, it's what? Social comment on Wall Street? Now it makes no sense."

"Except as an identifier," I said. "The mint thing is not out there. Well, Aubrey knows about it but nobody else. He wants us to know it's the same guy but I don't think it's Aubrey."

"But Forsythe called you here and voila! Another body with stupid visual jokes," said Izzy. "Aubrey wanted you to find this."

"Maybe. Aubrey didn't call. He texted."

"Right," said Izzy. "Whatever."

"No," Phil pointed out. "Maybe it wasn't Forsythe."

"Just someone with his phone, maybe, I get that," Izzy said.

"Right," Phil said. "Unless Forsythe came here and found the body and then texted Shepherd."

"Maybe my photographer scared Aubrey away," I suggested.

"Hey, Cash, why would Aubrey Forsythe come to your house?" Izzy asked the corpse. "Were you boys secret pals?"

He got no answer.

"If he alerted his favorite reporter to a killing he didn't commit, how come he didn't mention the murder in the text?" Izzy demanded. "Why didn't he stick around, so we would know he was innocent?"

"I don't know," I replied.

"I wasn't talking to you," Izzy said.

29.

I was a star for another week but then it just stopped. At least the killings did. My *New York Mail* front page, with Ernie's photos of Nolan's flipped wig, went around the world, complete with a nifty nickname for the killer:

SCALPED!
Cushing Ca$hes Out
Hacker Strikes Again

Followed by Ginny and the *Daily Press*, Izzy and Phil explored every avenue of inquiry, with me occasionally tagging along. Aubrey was Public Enemy Number One and was expected to strike again at any moment. The most likely victim-to-be was Aubrey's other arch-enemy from Neil's funeral, Tea Party TV pundit Harley Himmler—who surrounded himself with armed guards, courtesy of our mutual boss, billionaire Trevor Todd. No one could find Aubrey, who didn't call me, no matter how many messages I left on his cell phone.

Every day without Aubrey, or another murder, enraged Badger and Tal Edgar, who bugged me more and more about my lack of exclusives—as if I controlled the news.

They threatened to fire me daily. Having worked at the *Mail* for two unpleasant weeks, I realized that was just their management style—threaten to fire everyone without an exclusive every day, as a motivational tool. I ignored them and went back to writing my neglected pet column. I delved into grave issues such as what to do when your female cat hisses at your beloved sister, a devoted cat-person, every time she comes over. (Have her wear freshly laundered jeans and shoes that do not smell like her male cat at home. Also, catnip on the socks is a big help.) It was relaxing and I did not care if I never saw another corpse again.

I got into a routine with Skippy, with his morning and evening walks and his new job as leftover food gobbler. It took me a while to cure him of barking every time anyone walked past the apartment door and longer to convince him that a human being could not sleep with a seventy-pound Siberian Husky on their face.

I spoke to Jane several times on the phone but she always seemed to be busy when I asked her out on a second date. It was beginning to look like events during our first encounter had put her off. Go figure. *Dear Facebook Friends, after you discover a hacked-up body on your first date, how do you get past that?*

Mary Catherine quickly bonded with Skippy and she helped me walk him every few days, so we could talk about the lack of progress on our project.

"Tell me about Tal Edgar," she said, as Skippy sniffed one of the pathetic trees on my block.

"A bully, like his hatchet man Badger, but much cooler," I told her. "Actually, he reminds me of a warlord. You know, everybody scurrying around trying to kiss his ass or hide from him while he calmly considers who his next victim will be. He obviously digs it."

"And Badger?"

"Details and dirty work."

"So you like him for this?"

"Most likely. I have the intercepts he gave me from Aubrey and Neil's phones. That's illegal."

"Yes but we have no evidence for our case?"

"Nope. Why don't I really piss them off and see what happens?"

"You're getting bored," she scolded. "That's dangerous."

"Maybe. But maybe dangerous is the only way," I suggested.

"Not officially. What did you have in mind?"

"No clue."

"Oh."

"I'll think about it," I promised her. "I'll come up with something."

It was all very relaxing until one morning, after one of our walks, Mary Catherine and I ended up on the front page of the *Daily Press*.

MASSACRE?
NY Mail star reporter is figure in shocking GI Kid Slay Shootings

A question mark. In America, you can't say someone is a child molester without proof. But, if you ask it as a question, you can call anybody anything. Is the president a traitor? The *Daily Press* had a photo of me in shorts and a t-shirt, holding Skippy's leash and Mary Catherine in one of her power-dress suits and heels, looking hot outside my apartment building. We were laughing and the competing newspaper twisted that, too.

The photo caption read "Strange Bedfellows? Intrepid *Mail* reporter Francis X. Shepherd and married Manhattan Federal Prosecutor Mary Catherine Donovan, right, share an intimate laugh outside Shepherd's Manhattan apartment, along with fugitive Aubrey Forsythe's dog, Skippy."

The words made it sound like even Skippy was involved in criminal activity. The use of the word "right" was a dig, as if readers would confuse Mary Catherine with the dog. As if. Of course, the byline was Ginny McElhone's, and the story was dripping with slime:

> *New York Mail* reporter Francis X. Shepherd seems to have experience with murder. As a U.S. Army sergeant, he commanded a gang of GIs who, some sources say, slaughtered innocent civilians in Afghanistan a year ago, in an incident those sources say may have been hushed up by Pentagon top brass.
>
> At least 11 people, including children, died during the firefight near the city of Khost but no one was ever charged in the killings.
>
> If his close personal friendship with an attractive female federal prosecutor in Manhattan, a former Army buddy of Shepherd's, had anything to do with his getting off the hook, no one is saying.

No one is saying because no one ever asked. It was like a gossip column item. The story came as a complete surprise; Ginny hadn't asked for comment before going to press. I laughed but Mary Catherine didn't.

"Didn't I warn you that raising your profile was a bad idea? This is just the beginning. Keep your head down. This is only the *Daily Press*. Now that the *Mail* knows, and Badger and his boss Edgar are on it, it's going to get busy. Keep your balls to the wall, Shepherd."

"You, too, Mary Catherine."

She paused for thought. "This is bad but it could work to our advantage."

"I told you I'd think of something."

"You gave her the story?"

"No. She must have found some paperwork from the VA

or the army when I was in the shower. When she stole that DVD of Aubrey in McDonald's."

"You were supposed to keep your place clean."

"My mail was diverted here. I get stuff from Walter Reed. My guess is she found paperwork from the hospital to get her started and the rest she googled."

"You got sloppy," she snapped.

"How did she find out we were 'Army buddies?'"

"I don't know. If you didn't tell her, it could have come from my office or my home."

"I didn't tell her."

"Okay, maybe *I* got sloppy. Could have been someone around me. My assistant maybe. I'll take care of it. Meanwhile, get ready to rumble."

"Yes, ma'am. Meanwhile, anything from your people on Aubrey Forsythe?"

"No, not a whisper. Who cares?" she asked.

"I care. Even the U.S. Marshals, with their surveillance net and flying cell tower, got nothing? No credit card use, car rental, video facial recognition, phone intercepts, cell phone chatter, cell tower hits, Netflix rental?"

"Nothing. Zip. I told you."

"That's strange."

"Duh. He's running from two murder charges. He's hiding," she pointed out.

"Yeah but you should have found him in a day or two, tops. This bozo couldn't hide in a clown convention. He has no fugitive skills and is a big, rich, nasty, spoiled baby."

"I thought you said he had a huge wad of cash to live on so he could stay off the grid?"

"True."

"He is not your problem," Mary Catherine reminded me. "Focus."

"Yes, I agree they may try to focus."

"You're not funny, Shepherd."

"How do you know?"
"I'm not laughing."
"You never laugh."
"I laugh at funny."
"Have you ever seen funny?"
"Not yet."
"Have you seen me dance?"
"That's not funny. That's just sad."

30.

"Who are you?" Tal Edgar asked me in a menacing whisper.

Three smells washed over my face with his words, in succeeding waves. The first scent was bad breath, which the other two—cheap whiskey and expensive cologne—had failed to mask. On the desk before him was the *Daily Press* "MASSACRE?" story. I politely asked Edgar to speak more loudly, which made his face go red and twitch in a weird way, like dogs do when they have nightmares.

"WHO THE FUCK *ARE* YOU?" he shrieked at the top of his lungs.

My ears hurt. My nose hurt. Out of the corner of my eye, I could see heads turn in the City Room on the other side of Edgar's glass office wall. Now I knew what the glass was for. Threat display. Next to me, in a matching visitor's chair in the big transparent corner office, Badger jumped involuntarily at his master's roar.

"Who are you working for?" he said in an almost normal voice.

"I work for you. I'm Shepherd," I answered. "Your pet columnist. Also a reporter now. We've met."

The Editor smiled but it turned into a snarl as he lifted out of his big executive chair. His boozy blue eyes bulged.

His entire body tensed, like he was going to vault over his desk and bite my face. Then he relaxed and settled back.

"Badger," he said, back in control.

Donald Badger turned to me and took the point.

"The Editor wants an explanation. In short, what are you doing with that prosecutor? Also, are you a baby killer?"

"No," I replied. "I am not a baby killer and neither were my men and women."

"That's not what it says in the *Press*," Badger countered.

"The authority of the printed word? Really?"

"I need details."

"Sorry. Classified."

"What about the fed? What are you up to with her?" Badger continued, with a smirk.

"Obviously we were walking my dog."

"You mean Aubrey Forsythe's dog, don't you?"

"You've got me there, Don."

"What are you up to with the prosecutor?" Badger demanded. "Don't tell me she's a source because you don't have any."

"I'm not going to tell you anything because it's none of your business," I said.

Edgar growled. Badger made a fake laughing noise.

"You failed to mention this massacre business on your résumé, or on your employment application," Badger actually said.

I made an actual laughing noise. If only Mary Catherine were here.

"I didn't see any box for 'never committed war crimes.' Did I miss it?" I asked.

Badger and Edgar exchanged glances. They were obviously not used to resistance. Edgar nodded encouragement. My guess was they had a signal system to manage the grillings.

"Your employment with this newspaper is hanging by a thread," Badger warned.

"Why?"

"Why what?"

"Why is it hanging by a thread? What did I do to get fired?"

"Killing children would certainly be grounds for termination," Badger said importantly.

"I already told you that was not true. Neither is any of that cover-up bullshit."

"Prove it," Badger demanded.

"I don't think it works that way," I pointed out. "You are supposed to prove it."

"We don't have to prove shit, mate," Edgar interjected.

"Okay. Am I fired now? Can I leave?"

"Do you have a sexual relationship with Mary Catherine Donovan?" Badger asked.

"Again, none of your business."

"I beg to differ. If you, as a reporter, are intimate with a possible law enforcement source, that would constitute unethical behavior."

"You just told me I didn't have any sources. And, ethics at the *New York Mail*? Seriously?"

"It's okay to fuck an elephant but not if you cover the circus," Edgar sneered.

"I'm not fucking the elephant while covering the circus. Why? What is it you're worried about?"

They said nothing but made faces at each other, apparently more signals. They were not happy.

"Somebody hired you because of some dog blog you did?" Edgar snapped in a suspicious tone, looking at printouts in front of him. "You pretended to be a dog online?"

"I wrote in the voice of a dog, yes, through her eyes."

"Why?" he demanded.

"Why not? I wanted to see if she could make more sense of the thing than I could. In a way, she did."

"What thing? Who did?" Badger asked.

"Fatimah. My dog," I explained. "The blog was called 'Fatimah's Breakfast.'"

"Why?" Edgar asked. "And don't fucking say 'why not.'"

"Something one of our British buddies said once. He said Afghanistan was a dog's breakfast. It means a big mess, a—"

"I know what it fucking means," Edgar cut me off. "So you're a leftie? A peacenik?"

"Sorry, I don't know what those words mean."

Edgar cursed and then muttered a word, possibly a name. Badger seemed surprised but he quickly suppressed it.

"You are on probation until Human Resources completes its investigation of this incident," Badger declared. "They will contact you. If you don't cooperate fully with HR, you will be summarily dismissed. Is that clear?"

"Yup. Human Resources. Got it."

We sat there for a while. They looked at me, then at each other, then back at me.

"We're done," Badger said. "Get back to work."

"Okay. Great," I replied, standing up. "Have a nice day. Oh, meanwhile, I'm going to investigate another story, an exclusive."

"What exclusive?" Badger asked.

"A follow-up story, really," I told him. "You did a lot of front pages two years ago about a cop named Sean Joyce. He accidentally killed a kid who pointed a toy gun at him."

"That story is dead," Edgar said, with the finality of a man who decided what was news and what was not.

"So is Sean Joyce," Badger chuckled.

That pissed me off.

"Yes he is. He killed himself after someone illegally hacked his phones and blackmailed him, my source told me."

"Source?" Edgar asked. "What source?"

"You know, a Deep Throat kind of source? Top secret. He said Sean was blackmailed by people who hacked his phones, took pictures of his kids and threatened to publish them in the middle of a racial witch-hunt if he didn't do what they wanted. They used his kids to screw him. He did what they wanted for his kids but he lost it. You know his wife also had a mental breakdown and tried to kill herself? The kids are still with their grandparents. Sad story. Somebody should answer for that."

"That story is dead," Edgar repeated. "It will never see the light of day."

"In the *Mail,* maybe," I replied. "I'm sure I can get big bucks for it, freelance. The *Daily Press* would love it."

"Your employment contract forbids working for anyone else," Badger said quickly.

"Not if you fire me. Or I quit."

"Get the fuck out!" Edgar bellowed, his face hot red, his fists clenched white.

As I walked out, Edgar's eyes followed me every step of the way out of his snake tank office and across the City Room. Badger's mouth was moving, obviously talking about me to his boss. Edgar's stare tracked me out of sight. I knew that look well. It was hard to turn my back on it.

31.

After my little chat with Lucky Tal and Badger I did as I was told. I got back to work. At my desk in Features, I roughed out a column on designer dogs and cats.

I admitted it was definitely cool to own a dog that looks like a wolf and very artistic to have a cat that looks like a little leopard. But the Frankenstein fashion trend was not necessarily a good thing for the actual animal.

"I don't know that I look like a cheetah and I don't care," I had one notional designer cat say. "But I do know I have trouble breathing and I have genetic problems that make me sick and will probably make me die young."

It was a very profitable business, for the people hawking the fancy animals. Same deal for puppy mills and kitten factories. Meanwhile, millions of abandoned non-designer cats and dogs languished in shelters without homes or love—if they were lucky.

When I was done I went out for lunch and kept going. I went home, took Skippy for an early unscheduled walk and we both fell asleep on the couch. Life was good.

* * *

Skippy and I woke with a bark. His, not mine. Someone was at the door. Not the doorbell. It sounded like someone was fiddling with the lock. Skippy rocketed off the couch, barking loudly at the door. The fiddling stopped. I followed and flipped the tiny door porthole aside. Two white guys in dark suits were right outside. The tall one with slick, shiny black hair was shoving something in his jacket pocket. The other one, shorter, husky, sandy-haired, with bad skin, was looking down the hall, like a lookout, a manila folder in one hand.

I pulled open the door a foot, my leg holding a snarling Skippy back, but just barely.

"You guys lost?" I asked loudly.

The short one started and stepped back. The lean one didn't flinch. He smiled and stood his ground. In the quiet that followed, I inhaled the mothball and chicken soup scent of the hallway. It looked like the guys' suits came from the same store. They weren't suits, I realized, but matching navy blazers with fake gold buttons and charcoal gray pants. Instead of dress shoes or loafers, they wore identical black sneaker-like footwear that looked sturdy and waterproof. Cop shoes. They also had cop eyes. I looked at the line of their blazers. Bulges on the right hips.

"Not sure," the slim dude finally said, his fake smile still glued on, like he was lost. "Are you Francis Xavier Shepherd?"

"I'll know when you tell me who you are," I fake-smiled back.

"Oh, sure. I'm Jack Leslie and this is Matt Molloy. We're from the *Mail*. We're here for the interview."

"What interview?"

"Human Resources," the little guy said, recovering, as if it was obvious.

I couldn't help laughing. It made them wary, as if they expected a very different reaction from me. Skippy continued growling at them. I wondered how many brothers Ginny McElhone had, even though there seemed to be no resemblance.

"Didn't they tell you we would be talking, Mr. Shepherd?" Leslie asked, his eyes darting to Skippy.

"Actually, they did. IDs please."

Molloy started to protest but Leslie touched his elbow. They both produced laminated photo ID cards with their names on them.

NEW YORK MAIL
Human Resources

They *looked* just like my ID card, although mine said FEATURES DEPARTMENT. Their smiling photographs seemed much nicer than they were in person. I nodded and they put them away.

"Why would you come to my apartment during business hours without contacting me?" I asked.

"Hold on, pal," Molloy said, pointing his finger at me. His pudgy red hands were dry, rough, the nails dark.

Again, the calmer Leslie stayed his partner's hand.

"We couldn't find you at your desk during business hours, Mr. Shepherd, so we thought we would stop by and maybe catch you in," Leslie said, a smooth reproach. "We thought you might be upset after your conference with the Editor."

"No. I was done for the day and I needed a nap."

"Okay. May we come in and talk about the issues that have been raised by your superiors?"

"No. My dog wants to attack you. Let's do this in the office. Later."

"We need to know what the hell you're doing with that fed cunt," Molloy said.

"Watch your mouth, asshole," I told him.

One leg moved back and he balled a fist, ready to rumble.

Leslie edged quickly between us.

"You have to answer these charges of unethical behavior, Mr. Shepherd," Leslie told me. "Now or later. What is it that you're concealing about her?"

"Why do you guys care so much about her? I thought the problem was that the *Daily Press* called me a baby killer. How come you're not asking about that?"

"Hey, pal, we're just doing our job," Molloy chimed in. "And if you don't do yours, you're—"

"And what is your job? Breaking and entering? Show me what you've got in that pocket, Mr. Leslie. Prove me wrong."

Leslie smiled for real this time. Game on.

"We can do this easy or rough, buddy," Molloy warned. "Don't screw with us."

"Where were you guys on the job?" I asked. "NYPD? Somewhere else, maybe? Blackwater in the Sandbox?"

"I think we got our answer," Leslie said. "We're done here. For now. We'll see you soon. Have a nice day, Mr. Shepherd."

Leslie was already on his way to the creaky elevator before Molloy realized and tagged along. I closed the door.

"Foof," Skippy huffed to me after the door was closed.

"No, Skippy. This is good," I said, petting his mane and scratching his head. "We have conferenced with Human Resources executives from the *New York Mail*. Things are moving along."

I grabbed my cell phone and dialed Mary Catherine to tell her about my new friends.

"Foof," Skippy insisted.

32.

Mary Catherine got back to me before dinner, after running the Human Resources executives through the federal government's Big Brother machine.

"This guy Jack Leslie is an ex-cop from New Jersey," she said. "You'll never guess where."

I told her I could never guess.

"Crooke Harbor," she said triumphantly.

"Really? Crook Harbor?"

"Crooke with an E on the end. You haven't heard about it," she said, disappointed with my lack of reaction.

"Nope. Been away, remember?"

"Me, too. But I read. Okay, it's a mob town. Famous. In all the papers. The wiseguys there did not bribe the cops. They *hired* the cops. The FBI came down on them years ago. Lots of cops busted, wiseguys too. There was a shootout. A few bodies turned up, some people disappeared."

"So Mr. Leslie is an ex-dirty cop?"

"Nope," she said. "Leslie was a lieutenant who retired and took his full pension before they could do anything to him. Never charged with a crime. He's one of the smart ones."

"How smart could he be?" I asked. "A cop working for mobsters?"

"College degree in Criminal Justice, a Master's degree in Public Administration."

"What about his buddy? What've you got on him?"

"That's the thing. Nothing."

"Nothing."

"Correct. Matt or Matthew Molloy is indeed an employee of the *New York Mail*, or rather, its parent company, Todd Enterprises Unlimited. He is paid a salary. He has a social security number and pays his taxes. That's it. No credit cards, no credit history, no social history, no licenses, arrests, property—nothing."

"So he pays cash. How much does he make a year?"

"You won't like it. He and Leslie each make $250,000 a year. In round numbers. No wonder they make house calls. There are no credit union deductions. The money is paid into their bank accounts at a branch in the *Mail* building and all they do is take out cash. All of it. The money goes in and right out within a day. Each account usually has a balance under $1,000."

"Maybe these guys really hate inflation caused by credit," I suggested.

"They like being off the grid, that's for sure. But that's not the most interesting thing," she said. "Go ahead, ask me."

"Okay, what?"

"Half an hour into my search, my boss, the U.S. Attorney, calls me and wants to know what I'm doing. Someone high up in the U.S. Marshal's Service wants to know the reason for my ongoing records search. They were monitoring my search in real time."

"Did you contact the marshals?"

"Nope. Since 9/11 we feds are very paranoid. State federal and local law enforcement have to explain every request for information from federal databases, with a case number and investigator's name and badge number. It's an anti-mole, anti-press thing. It's routine. But it's not routine for a big guy to call a big guy. In minutes, yet."

"Okay, so you set off a tripwire."

"Yes. I told my boss to tell the marshals it was a mistake; that I was looking for a different Matt Molloy. Then I had to go out and find a real Matt Molloy I might be interested in. Thank God for common names. I found one in Texas who's a car thief and told them *he* was my guy. Now I have to investigate that asshole for a while to keep the marshals happy."

"Why?"

"So they forget I'm interested in their guy."

"Who says he's their guy?"

"Not them. I never asked. He has to be their guy."

"You mean an undercover marshal?"

"Maybe. That's the most likely solution but I can't ask. I'm going to do more checking. Offline, outside official channels. You know, cop work."

"Mary Catherine, you're a lawyer. These two guys, Molloy and Leslie, I got bad vibes from them. Like Blackwater Security goons. Be careful."

"If one of them is an undercover marshal, I wouldn't get too worried. Besides, I'm a lawyer with a gun."

"They have guns, too. Aren't lawyers too afraid of lawsuits to use guns?"

"You know better," she said.

"Yeah, I do."

"You need to arm-up, Shepherd. This might get noisy."

"Nope. I'm done with guns. You know that."

"I understand your feelings but are they worth your life?"

"I don't know. I know they're worth a lot of other people's lives. We'll see."

"Well, on that cheerful note... I'll get back to you," Mary Catherine said, hanging up.

The phone rang two seconds later and I picked it up. "That was quick," I said.

"What was quick?" a different female voice asked.

It wasn't Mary Catherine. I needed more voice to figure out who it was. I actually knew more than three women personally now.

"Sorry, I thought you were someone else."

"I am someone else. And some*thing* else."

"Hi, Jane. Good to hear from you. How are things on the animal planet? I thought you were done with me."

"No, just a little freaked out by our last date. I... I was just calling to see how Skippy was doing."

"Would you rather speak to him?"

She laughed.

"No, I'll take your word for it. How are you doing?"

"Not good," I answered. "There's this woman I want to date but she just wants to talk about my dog."

"I know what you mean," she chuckled. "I went out on a first date with a guy and ended up at a murder scene."

"You saw the massacre story in the *Daily Press*."

"Yes," she admitted.

"You're being nice."

"I am. Sorry."

"No need. The story is bullshit."

"Okay," she replied, unconvinced.

What is it about a little ink and paper that makes people believe anything? Or, for that matter, a little video? "Maybe I can get a date out of this and we can discuss it over dinner?" I suggested.

"Maybe," she said. "But no dead bodies this time."

"What a control freak you are, Jane. No promises."

33.

Jane arrived at Bistro du Bois in casual clothes this time. Jeans, white peasant top, sneakers, pony tail. No slinky sexy cocktail dress or sparkling jewelry. She was still seriously hot.

We chatted with Murray Glassberg and the bartender, Heather, and our waitress, Ronnie, who took our orders. No one brought up the subject of a massacre and there was no foreign waiter to remind us of a war, so *I* had to.

"Can you keep a secret?" I asked Jane.

She laughed, startled, almost giddy.

"I'm a medical professional," she said with mock seriousness. "I've never revealed anything any of my patients have told me."

"The animals? That's very discreet of you." She waited, her smile slowly evaporating. "The massacre."

"Yes," she said.

"I get it you want to know if I'm a killer. That's easy. I am. But not women or kids. Came too close once, though."

"The paper said two of your men went berserk and killed civilians, kids. Then you and other soldiers killed your own guys to stop them."

"Not true. But some of the evidence makes it look that way. Our enemies are good and they're ruthless," I explained.

Jane did not ask whom I was describing.

"When they come into a village, they look like dirty bandits with weapons but they bring their whole version of society with them. One guy with an AK-47 calls himself the teacher and he drills the boys in verses from the Koran. Sometimes he drills the boys, too. Another guy with an RPG says he's a judge. He starts handing out sentences. Then the guy with the big sword gets busy. First, they try to find a thief and whack off his hand. That shows they are for law and order. Later, they behead anyone who talks to us or fails to help them spy on us. Women who don't cover up or who associate with the infidels are beaten as whores and raped. That's their favorite part. They spent a lot of time on that."

"Your point is the people in Afghanistan are afraid of them—but not of you?" Jane asked.

"Exactly. Wouldn't you be?"

"Are you explaining why, in war, some soldiers start doing bad things?"

"Like massacres? No. I'm not pleading guilty with an explanation. I'm a killer. We all were. I joined up after 9/11 to kill the bad guys, the people who attacked us, and we did. The people we killed were killers. We were the good guys and they were the bad guys. They used people as human shields. For the first time in human history, we invented smart weapons to avoid killing innocent people. *They* target innocents on purpose. What I'm saying is that the bad guys tried to make us into killers of civilians but, when that didn't work, they figured out a way to make it seem that way."

"They faked a massacre?"

"You bet. It was easy. On Tuesday, they ambush us on patrol. We kill three of their guys but two of our guys disappear. We tear the place apart looking for our people. Choppers, jets, drones, satellites, reinforcements, Stryker vehicles, the whole menu. Nothing. We stand down, they stage another ambush on Saturday but we're ready."

"Did you find your buddies?"

"Oh yeah."

"Tell me."

"We returned fire on a house, lit it up. Small arms, rockets. It was too easy. Our guys were found inside, along with a dozen *Hajis*—civilians. A man, a woman and ten fucking kids. All dead, all ripped with M4 rounds. In the back. Fresh. Make you puke."

"So your guys went crazy."

"We were all part crazy but no. Our missing guys were there, unconscious, dying. It was a mess. Mary Catherine, my captain, she called the fucking FBI to join the party. Some of the forensics seemed to support the Taliban scam—that our two guys killed civilians and we killed them because they were rogues. The bad guys were hyping that story before our ears stopped ringing, before they could possibly know. The FBI later proved the bullets fired from my missing guys' guns killed the civilians. But here's the thing—our missing guys each had enough opium in their systems to drop a camel."

"So the terrorists drugged them so it looked like they were dopers who went on a kid-killing spree?"

"Thank God they gave them too much dope. It was in their stomachs, not smoked or injected. The FBI team said my men were not conscious. Also the rounds that killed our guys were fired straight downward. They found some spent rounds in the dirt under them. The only way that could happen was if we were standing above them, which we weren't. Video to prove it. It proved they were lying on the dirt floor when they were shot from above. Also my two guys had rope burns on their wrists and ankles, and had been beaten, as had the victims."

"So they had all been held hostage."

"Yeah. Fortunately, the Taliban thinks western TV shows are Satan's tools—they missed the episodes of *CSI* that would have helped them fake their crime scene better."

"Why don't you go public with this?" Jane asked.

"Classified. My hands are tied. Mary Catherine and I signed a lot of paperwork in blood. If we blab, we go to Leavenworth."

"Leavenworth?"

"Federal prison."

"They're covering it up because it's embarrassing?"

"Sure. The Taliban faked it too good. Also, it would mean admitting that two of our guys with dope in their systems had rifles that killed kids."

"But it's not true."

"I know but they're waiting for the Taliban to release their official version and then we can counter it with the truth, the science. If anybody believes us. But I don't think that's ever going to happen."

"Why?"

"Because the Taliban commander who ordered the setup and his whole crew are dead. About two dozen of the nasty fuckers. A few weeks afterwards. It's nice when nice things happen to nice people."

"How?"

"Truck bomb."

"His own people killed him?"

"I didn't say that."

"I thought they were the ones who used car bombs. So who killed them?"

"That's also classified."

"Give me a break, Shepherd."

I thought about it for a while and then leaned closer, keeping my voice down.

"Apparently this warlord heard that a female American soldier was stranded in a broken-down Humvee. He was known to favor rape as a religious educational tool for women hostages. Especially hot infidel babes, like U.N. workers. He was a very devout guy. Liked to do the instructing himself. A female U.S. soldier would be his ultimate prize."

"What happened?"

"Apparently he heard a female voice calling for help over our radio frequency. Foolishly, she gave her location. Our friend was very eager to get there first. He and his top guys. Party time."

"And there was a bomb?"

"Big time. C-4 explosive and a lot of nails. An Improvised Explosive Device. It was a mess. Some of the bad guys lived for a few minutes but no matter how much they screamed, no one came to help."

"And the female soldier died, too?"

"Funny thing. There was only a mannequin in a uniform and blonde wig in the Hummer. The parts of the dummy were scattered all over, so the ones who took a while to die knew they had been punked."

I tried to suppress it but I couldn't help smiling. Jane stared at me with an odd expression.

"So, you did that?" she asked.

"Sorry, classified."

"That's why they shipped you home," Jane said. "You and your friend Mary Catherine? They also covered that up?"

I dug into my steak and ignored her question.

"How long has it been?" she asked.

"More than a year. It was quiet until Ginny Mac dug it up and put it in the *Daily Press*, or part of it. Haven't decided what to do about it yet."

"Remind me not to get you mad at me," Jane said. "What did your new bosses say about the story?"

"They threatened to fire me but didn't," I said. "They seemed much more interested in why I'm friends with Mary Catherine, who is a federal prosecutor. Jane, you should try this ginger steak. It's great."

Again, she looked at me oddly. I couldn't decide if she

thought I was nuts or didn't believe what I had told her. Or both.

"Tell me about your face," she said gently.

"We were on a routine patrol with Fatimah—my dog—tagging along. She sensed something. Started barking. When I kept walking, Fatimah jumped me, knocked me flat. There was an IED. She ran to it. She was a stray puppy we adopted. They set it off because they thought she was a bomb dog. She was killed and I was hurt."

"This was before the other stuff?"

"Yeah. They took me to a big F.O.B. and then to Germany and Washington. Kansas for a while. I was in the Sand, Iraq, first and then the Stan, other spots."

I paused. "I still have little pieces of her in me. Bone. It's dumb because we lost a lot more guys but one dog and... After the massacre, I decided I was done with guns and bombs and orders and crusades and here I am. Well, almost done. I've been away so long I feel like a tourist."

Jane said nothing but reached out for my hand and held it until dessert.

After dinner we walked down the sidewalk, other couples passing us in both directions. Jane took my arm. I kept searching passing faces, looking for familiar ones, judging intent, gauging threat levels. I was still not used to a world where everyone I saw was a stranger and meant me no harm. Well, most of them, anyway.

Jane's phone went off. She read a message, saying it was an animal emergency.

"But no sweat," she said, putting the phone away. "I've got a colleague covering for me."

"Are you in any hurry?" I asked.

She looked at me, cocking her head, trying to figure out my meaning.

"Do you mean do I have to get up early in the morning?"

"I'm not sure. I think so," I answered.

"No, I don't have to get up too early. You're being polite," Jane said, taking my hand. "That's sweet. You don't want to hit on me on the second date. You don't want me to think you're a slut."

"You think so? I was going to suggest a bar in my neighborhood; they have a girl who does a lot of Sheryl Crow songs."

"I can't eat any more and I definitely can't drink any more," she said. "I was going to suggest you come back to my place."

"You just want me to think you're a stud," I told her.

"You bet," she laughed. "I can't wait to tell my patients what a slut you are."

"You girls are all alike," I said.

"Not like me," she insisted. "I don't think there are too many of you, either, Shepherd."

"Good thing."

"Could you walk faster?" she asked. "We'll never get to my place at this rate."

34.

Jane opened up her townhouse, shut off the alarm and turned on the lights. My cell vibrated on my belt, making a double ding of a text message but I ignored it. I spotted a wedding photo on the mantelpiece in her living room. She was all in white, radiant, next to a handsome dark-haired guy. I stared.

"I thought you weren't married?" I said lightly.

"I used to be," she said.

I suppressed an urge to ask why her ex still held a place of honor but I didn't really care.

"Bedroom's this way," she said, gliding ahead of me.

The only way I wasn't going to follow her was if the guy in the picture was actually in the bedroom. He wasn't. Neither was his picture. Smiling, she pulled me onto the bed.

We began slowly, gently, quietly, like terrified high school kids afraid to wake the parents. But the kissing and caressing built a warm glow in my chest that spread to my throat and face. I wondered what the strange feeling was, different from the muscular lust with Ginny Mac. Jane and I pulled off our clothes and looked at every inch of one another, how we moved, how our flesh responded. She was slim, with breasts so round and perfect I wondered if they were silicone. One touch told me they were real; soft with rosy dimpled nipples. She shivered when I licked one of them. Wow. When I did it again she shook again. We locked eyes and our bodies joined and moved together. Now it was my turn.

When we were done, a warm feeling of well-being began in my chest and emanated, tingling throughout my entire body. I felt like a visitor in a strange country. Joy, I realized. This must be joy.

At last, we closed our eyes and held each other. I felt Jane shiver yet again but this time she was crying. I tried to ignore it but it built until she was sobbing against me, her tears smeared against my chest. We held tight onto each other. Fortunately, she opened her eyes first and spoke.

"I'm so sorry. I shouldn't say this but I haven't had sex in two years," she said, wiping her salty eyes and starting to laugh. "Not since my husband died. It hurts like hell but it's wonderful."

"I'm sorry but I haven't had sex for two days," I said.

She swatted me.

"Mary Catherine?"

"No. She's married. We're friends."

My phone dinged again.

"That's yours," she said.

"What?"

"I know you heard that."

"I don't care what it is," I said, kissing her. "Sorry I forgot to turn it off."

She kissed me back. The glow was still there. Weird. She kissed my shoulder and I suppressed an urge to ask her why. Then she sniffed my shoulder.

"Do I stink?"

"No, jerk. I'm just smelling you. Sorry."

"What do I smell like?"

"Lime."

"Like the stuff they throw in graves?"

"What? No. Like the fruit."

"So, I'm fruity?"

"Not limes, really. Something like that, sunshine, spring. I can't explain it. Are all these scars from the IED?"

"Most of them."

My phone made a noise again. Jane kissed me, got up and walked to the bathroom. I watched her. The light went on but the door did not close. My phone dinged again.

"Get it," she yelled from the bathroom.

There was a text.

> I've been a bad boy again. Want to see?

"Oh shit."

"What?" Jane asked over the running water.

I looked at the screen. There were five identical messages. The headers did not identify the phone as belonging to Aubrey Forsythe. It was a different, unfamiliar phone number.

I texted back.

> Who is this?

> Aubrey

> This is not his phone

> Obviously not. The cops know that one. Do you want to see or not?

> **Yes where?**

He told me.

> **On my way**

Jane emerged from the bathroom, naked, spectacular. "What did you say, Shepherd?"

"Remember when you said no more dead bodies this time?"

"Yes," she laughed.

"Funny thing. Remember what I said?"

"You said no promises."

"Exactly."

"No way."

"Yes."

I showed her the texts. She laughed.

"So it's a different phone you don't know? Don't go. It's fake."

"It makes sense he would get a new phone the cops aren't bugging. What if it isn't fake?"

"It is."

"How can you be so sure?"

"I guess I can't. Pinky bet," she giggled, grabbing me and twisting.

"Jane, I've got to go. You're probably right. Come with me. Please."

"Oh, alright but if I'm right you have to pay for it in bed."

"Deal."

"Where are we going?" she asked, throwing on her clothes.

"Central Park South, just inside the park."

"At this time of night? You're insane."

"I don't think there's any doubt about that. But I just had sex with a woman who's been horny for two years and I survived that."

"So far," she giggled. "I was just getting started."

35.

As we approached the imitation forest in the middle of Manhattan, it pushed a damp, dirty breeze in our faces. I saw bursts of light crackling amid the rustling trees as we approached on the walkway just north of the dark stone wall at Central Park South. It wasn't lightning. We ran through the deserted park in the chilly darkness, from one island of light to another, lit by shadowy lampposts. In the bushes, near the inside of the wall, there was a metal mesh trashcan, stuffed to overflowing with garbage. A large, lurking figure spun around.

"I didn't know there were bears in Central Park," I said to *Mail* photographer Ernie.

"Shit, you scared the hell out of me," Ernie gasped.

"Oh my God. There is a body," Jane said, looking at the shape on the dead grass.

A half-naked Maria "Pookie" Piccarelli was sitting in the dirt, her back against a rock outcropping, her head lolled to one side. Her large breasts were exposed, her miniskirt up around her crotch. Her throat had been slashed several times and dark, syrupy blood had cascaded down her front. Her left hand was on her bloody breast and her right was pointing at her groin, obviously posed. There were slashes on the reality show star's forearms and palms, as if she had tried to defend herself. Anger rose in my gut.

"Why would Aubrey do this?" I asked. "Okay, Neil and Cushing were dicks. Pookie was a shallow, drunken slut but why does she deserve to die? She didn't say anything about Neil at the funeral as far as I remember."

Jane stepped forward.

"What are you doing?" I asked.

"Checking for a pulse."

"Don't touch her, Jane," I warned. "She's bled out and as dead as she's ever going to be. You'll just piss Izzy off again."

She reluctantly obeyed. I texted Aubrey and asked him why he killed Pookie. No answer. I asked him to call and I tried calling *him*. No answer.

"You done?" Ernie asked. "I'm supposed to call the cops as soon as you're done—so no other press gets shots."

"Give me a sec," I replied. "Did you shoot close-ups of the wounds?"

"No."

"You should. Also, where's the Altoid? It must be here somewhere. Shoot it but don't use it. That's one of the cop hold-backs. It's too dark here. I can't see it."

"Me neither," said Ernie, taking the additional shots. "I looked for a mint but couldn't find it. Hope I didn't step on it." He peered at the corpse. "Her purse is next to her, open. Looks like a wallet and cash and some dope. Should we take out the drugs and shoot them separate?"

"No. Don't touch anything. Do the best you can. Shoot all around the body and we can look later."

I had a weird flash—what if Ernie was the killer, the Hacker? Just doing it for the money? Nah. Made no sense. I told Ernie I would call Homicide so the call would not go over the police radios until later—when our competitors would hear it. Ernie left. I took some shots with my iPhone and then called Izzy Negron's cell.

"No way," Izzy protested. "I thought we were done. Why are you calling?"

I told him where I was and what I was looking at. By the time I finished filing my story by phone, Izzy had arrived.

"Now it's official," Izzy said. "Three victims make it a serial killer. Rich, famous victims and the Hacker gives it to the *Mail* before us. My boss is apoplectic."

"Sorry," I said, as more cops arrived and began setting up a crime scene, complete with generator-powered floodlights.

"Alright, you've got a serial killer killing rich, famous assholes," I said to Izzy. "At least you know who it is."

"Yeah. A guy I can't find, even though everyone in the country knows what he looks like," Izzy said.

"What about the new phone he used to text me?" I asked hopefully.

"Already checked it out," Izzy answered. "A pre-paid throwaway, bought in Times Square right near his favorite McDonald's. We're up on it now but he'll probably never use it again. Don't print that part, about us being on the number."

"Okay," I said. "This murder seems different from the others."

"Maybe," Izzy agreed. "Look, I have no problem with you sticking around but your girlfriend has to get back behind the tape."

Jane looked hurt but agreed.

"Sorry," I whispered to her. "I'll tell you everything later, anyway."

"Good," she said, giving me a quick kiss before walking toward the yellow crime scene tape.

I turned back to watch Izzy work, sidling close in the hope of hearing his chat with the newest corpse, but we had to wait for CSI photographers and a video guy to document the murder scene. While they did that, Izzy conferred with a uniformed sergeant, whose men had been literally beating the bushes around the body and looking for any witnesses, hoping to find a sleeping drunk. The sergeant shrugged and Izzy plodded back. After walking around the reality star's body, Izzy stared at her for several minutes before he began asking the dead girl questions in a soft voice.

"Why outside?" Izzy wondered. "How come nobody saw anything, Pookie? Did Forsythe talk you into coming here? Why would you do that? Don't you read the papers?"

She did not respond.

"How'd you get those bruises on your arms, Pookie? He dragged you here, right? Why didn't you scream? We all know you got a good set of lungs. Then he exposed your boobs. No, then he started slashing and you tried to defend yourself. That's how you got the defensive wounds on your hands. *Then* he exposed you. The other killings were peaceful. No muss, no fuss. This was slashing. In real time. Why? Did you piss him off, Pookie?"

Izzy moved around the body, crouching, leaning close, using gloved hands to lift the victim's hands and examine them.

"He exposed your breasts and crotch after you collapsed," Izzy told his subject. "That's why he couldn't get your skirt all the way up, right? Why? Just to show you off as a slut? No offense, Pookie."

"Maybe that's just the theme of this one," I suggested.

"Yeah, maybe," said Izzy. "The victims are a gay man, a straight man, and a straight woman. Food. Money. Sex."

"Right," I said. "No more cannibalism."

"Small favors," Izzy smirked.

"But no Altoid," I pointed out. "Maybe we've got a—"

"Too soon," Izzy said, cutting me off before I could say the word. "Gotta wait until daylight. If the mint's here, we'll find it. We'll sift the dirt. Also the autopsy. Let's see what we find in her system. The other two, Neil Leonardi and Cash Cushing, both had drugs in their systems, including animal trank. She's got weed and coke and pills in her purse. Let's see if her pills match up with the others."

"So… you're not thinking copycat?" I asked.

"Bite your tongue," Izzy said. "That's all I need. Two of them. And none of this makes any sense, other than some vague 'I-hate-reality-TV-stars' motive. Makes no sense—Aubrey was one of those assholes himself."

"True. Maybe this is it," I suggested, hopefully. "Maybe he's done."

"With my luck? No way. This is Manhattan," Izzy countered. "More rich, famous assholes here than in Hell."

36.

The next morning my name and picture—along with a photo of the bloody horror of the slaughtered girl—were on the front page under the giant nasty headline:

SLIT
Hottie Hacker Victim

My exclusive story—which I didn't have to leave my building to read, thanks to the copy of the *Mail* left outside my apartment door—contained the information I had filed from Central Park the night before but it was rewritten as an open challenge to the Hacker.

"You are a degenerate coward not fit to breathe the same air as decent human beings," said the story with my name on it. "I challenge you, man-to-man, to come out from the shadows," I read out loud to Skippy at the breakfast table, after he took his usual seat opposite me, his head cocked to one side.

It went on like that, weaving in the details of the murder among the insults. It read like *Gone With The Wind* or some dumb dueling movie. I called Badger and he pretended to be both surprised and insulted.

"But, mate, we put your byline and face on the front page. It's being picked up nationwide, around the world. You're a star."

"No, you're a star. You totally rewrote everything I filed."

"As is our right, amigo. Check your contract. The Editor felt it was time for us to move it to a higher level. We're upping the game."

"Yes, I believe you are. Did it occur to you that the tone of the story might piss off the killer?"

"Who cares?" he said in a disgusted tone. "That could be good for us. You're not scared are you? Of Aubrey Forsythe?"

"You have me challenging a demented serial killer to… some kind of vague showdown. Why would I be concerned? I don't suppose you care that Aubrey will probably never call me again now that you've called him every name in the tabloid cliché book. He'll probably call the *Daily Press*."

"Nonsense, dear boy. I'm sure you'll smooth it all over."

"Right. I'll just take him out for a few drinks on the expense account."

"Don't forget to take photos if you do," Badger said, breaking the connection.

While I was on with Badger, Izzy and Jane had called. I called Izzy first.

"You got some kind of death wish, pal?" he asked me.

"I didn't write that crap," I told him. "That was my bosses' brilliant idea."

"Don't they get that if you become victim number four it will make it kinda hard for you to cover the story?"

"I think they see me as expendable. Also, I'm beginning to think they want me dead. Maybe this is normal in the newspaper business."

"Really. Your story is addressed to 'The Killer,' like they were covering the bases, so, if there's a copycat, he'll want to knock you off, too."

"Looks that way."

"You'd think they would want to keep the guy who's giving them all these exclusives alive."

"You'd think."

"What's going on?" Izzy asked. "What's with you and this prosecutor?"

"I'll tell you as soon as I can, Izzy."

"Okay. By the way, the autopsy only found alcohol in Pookie Piccarelli's blood, plus THC. Beer and grass. No animal tranquilizers, unlike Leonardi and Cushing. But she had Vicodin in her bag. Her throat was slashed at least eighteen times, as opposed to once."

"Sloppy," I said. "Or angry."

"Yeah. No mint, either. We dug up the dirt and sifted it through a screen. No Altoid. Unless she ate it."

"Maybe the killer ran out of mints and drugs. Maybe the killer is their drug dealer? Maybe the Altoid didn't fit in with the slut theme. It wasn't about food."

"Uh-huh. Then why did he leave a mint at the money murder?"

"Right," I said. "So, either he's doing it differently or it's a different guy."

"Yeah," Izzy sighed. "And now they both hate your guts."

"Comforting."

"Are you listed in the phone book?"

I told my new detective friend that I was a new listing, but I did not request an unlisted home number. He told me that meant that anybody could get my number and home address. He asked how security was at my building. I just laughed.

Izzy told me that Pookie was very drunk and was last seen at a bar called the Tiki-Peekie, where she was ejected after doing some kind of trick that involved dancing with beer bottles tucked under her breasts. Apparently it was a big hit on her reality show. Then he made me an offer.

"If we do have a copycat, you won't see him coming,"

Izzy said. "Want protection? I think I can arrange it."

I thought about it. My apartment windows were open and I could hear a bird twittering through the screen before an accelerating bus drowned it out.

"Nah."

"Don't be stupid," Izzy said. "You're beginning to grow on me."

"Thanks, Izzy, but I'm not that easy to kill."

"Everybody is easy to kill," Izzy countered. "From what I hear, you've seen enough killing to know that."

I thanked Izzy and said we would chat soon. When I called Jane, she was also worried about the ridiculous challenge to the Hacker.

"Why would your own people do that to you?" she asked.

"They're not my people," I answered. "I just work for them."

I told her about all the differences between the first two killings and the third in the park.

"Whether it's Aubrey or someone else, you are probably in danger," she said.

"Maybe."

"What kind of sick person reads about murders and decides it would be a great thing to imitate?"

"The same kind of person who sees planes crashing into buildings and decides to blow up a truck in Times Square," I told her.

I told her about the huge number of emails and letters I was getting from readers, all with solutions to the crimes. "Most people want to play Sherlock Holmes," I said. "It's fun. A few decide it's an interactive game, I guess."

"It's insane," she said.

"So are the first two killings but at least the killer thought he had some kind of motive. A copycat is just a ham."

"I'm worried about you," she said.

"Want to protect me?" I asked.

"Yes."

"When?"

"Lunchtime?" she asked.

"Where?"

"My place?"

"I feel safer already."

37.

Skippy and I went out for his morning walk. Going down in the elevator, I went through the case with him.

"I'm not afraid of Aubrey, physically, even though he's a suspected serial killer. He has weight on me but doesn't look like he knows how to use it. Just because he and Neil were into S&M doesn't mean Aubrey is an accomplished assassin. Or does it?"

Skippy looked thoughtful.

"I can't really see him killing Neil—his shock and grief seemed so real. I can only picture Aubrey killing Neil in a fit of rage, not coldly, methodically. Or is Aubrey a very good actor? But why would he kill Nolan Cushing? Or Pookie? He probably didn't have lovers' quarrels with them." I shook my head. "So a world-renowned food critic just decides to throw away his fame and fortune and become a fugitive for the sheer fun of slaughtering other celebrities? It makes zero sense!"

Skippy chewed his leash a little.

"Fear of a second possible killer is more abstract. It's easy to fear an unknown—because it's unknown. If Aubrey isn't the killer, then someone else is. Who? If the unknown killer or killers did all three victims it makes more sense.

A psychopath bent on sensational serial slayings. Well, not sense, but it seems more consistent. Right?"

Skippy did not agree or disagree but he was a good listener.

As soon as we emerged from my building, I spotted my armed pals from Human Resources. They were sitting in a cop-style unmarked Ford Taurus at the curb, looking right at me. They weren't trying to hide. In one pocket of my brown shorts, I had my house keys. They were my only weapon. In the other pocket, I had a crumpled plastic bag, for Skippy's anticipated activity. I could smother one of them with it if he stood still. They started to open their doors but quickly closed them when Skippy began barking at the car, tugging on his leash. Correction. *Skippy* was my only weapon. I noticed movement out of the corner of my eye and saw more silhouettes, one small and two large, in a Honda parked down the block. Ginny Mac and her brothers tried to hide by sliding down in their seats. Ginny vanished from sight behind the wheel but her hulking siblings just wiggled, unable to hide their bulk, rocking the car on its suspension.

I held up my palm and yelled at Skippy to stop barking. Amazingly, he stopped.

"Good morning," I said to Jack Leslie through his slightly open driver's window. "Is there a Human Resources problem in front of my building?"

"You're the fucking problem," his partner Matt Molloy snapped.

"What Matt means is we have been asked to keep an eye on you, a little special attention," Leslie smiled flatly.

I smiled flatly back.

"You're too late," I told them, jerking my thumb towards the packed Honda. "I already have bodyguards. Their Human Resources are much larger."

Skippy and I walked away from their confused expressions

and strolled across the street a few hundred feet to Ginny's car. She magically rose up in the driver's seat. Skippy barked again and I told him a second time to stop. He did. Incredible. Who had trained him? I rapped on Ginny's window and it rolled down a bit.

"My armed bodyguards from the *Mail* told me they don't like you hanging around," I told her with a straight face, using my thumb to point out the Human Resources dynamic duo. "They don't like you. I had to convince them not to attack you."

"Bodyguards?" Ginny asked. "I thought they were cops."

"Don't worry, I told them not to shoot you. So, Ginny, you here to steal another story or are you just here for more sex?"

Her face frosted over. The brothers looked at Ginny and each other and scrambled to open their doors to get at me. Skippy began barking again. They closed the doors. For the third time I told Skippy to stop. He stopped. Totally cool.

"Good boy," I told him, patting his head.

Skippy sat on the pavement, alert, watching the occupants of the stuffed car, as I scratched his fluffy neck.

"If it's for sex, that's great, I just need to finish walking Skippy," I told an infuriated Ginny. "But your bros have to stay down here. That would be awkward."

She rolled up her window. All three McElhones began yelling at each other, arguing and pointing at the Human Resources execs down the street—who were both watching, both parties convinced the others were my protectors.

Skippy and I moved on. He pulled me west, toward the sparkling river a few blocks away, and I began to jog to keep up with him. My fan club stayed in their cars.

"Who taught you to do that?" I asked Skippy. "Who taught you to stop barking when I say 'stop?'"

He ignored my question and took care of business, which I deposited inside the plastic bag and then into a trash can.

We ran out to Hudson River Park again and admired the Manhattan and Jersey City skylines. We ran along the river some more before slowly working our way home. On the way back into my building, I gave friendly waves to both cars. As we walked inside, I glanced back to see the two sets of angry people glaring at each other as if I did not exist.

Back in the elevator, I began laughing and the dog joined in, jumping and yipping, which was probably the closest Skippy got to laughing.

38.

When I got out of the shower and got dressed in my black pants and black shirt, there was a text on my phone from another number I did not recognize.

> Aren't u naughty? Let's get together to discuss latest developments. 12 Midnight tonight at central park scene. No cops.

The only developments were the new murder and "my" letter to the killer. He seemed to be taking the insults in his stride. I texted back.

> I'll be there. You know my paper wrote that stuff.

He did not reply. I tried several messages but there was no response. Obviously Aubrey, or whoever it was, had switched phones again because he knew the cops would be monitoring the one he used previously—waiting to pounce.

Izzy had refused to be specific but I assumed they would trace the cell towers to pinpoint a location if the previous phone was used and rush police to the spot. Neither Izzy nor the *Mail* would know about the new phone unless I told them. I didn't know whether Badger had the ability to tap my phone and any phone that called me. With the cops, it would probably take time and involve a subpoena. That meant I was the only one who knew about the new message. So far.

I left Skippy chewing one of my sneakers on the couch and went to Jane's place for lunch. She produced fresh hummus with tahini, yogurt sauce with cucumber and dill and hot pita bread to dip in it. Also feta cheese, seedless red grapes, wine and sparkling water.

"This is great," I told her.

"I got it because I know you liked it at the restaurant the other night. It's ancient. People have been eating this meal for thousands of years. Helen of Troy, Aristotle, Alexander the Great."

"That's what I said—it's great. How about Aristotle Onassis? Or Pita the Great?"

She threw a grape at me and I caught it in my mouth. It was delicious.

"Wow. You're fast. How did you do that?" she asked.

"The seeds are the problem," I said.

"What?"

"I'm not sure how long ago they figured out how to grow seedless grapes. Maybe not that long ago."

"Don't ruin it. I was feeling romantic," Jane said, dipping her bread.

"Sorry."

"And don't look it up on your phone. I hate that. My husband used to do that."

"I'm not your husband," I pointed out.

"I know that."

"Sorry, Jane. Okay, even if there were seeds, it's the same thing. It was a nice thought. I like your brain."

"Pig. I want to be loved for my body, too."

"And that."

We ate in silence for a few minutes. I smiled at her and she smiled back.

"Aubrey sent me another text," I said, between bites. "I'm going to meet him alone."

"What?" she asked, her mouth stunned open.

I showed her the message. She shut her mouth.

"I hope you told the cops all this," Jane said.

"Nope. So far, just you."

For some reason she looked at me like I was a crazy man.

"But you're telling your paper. What's-his-name, that big photographer will be there."

"Nope. I'm not telling them anything."

"Oh, I get it," Jane said, dropping her pita. "You're the brave guy, going out to meet the Hacker alone but telling the little lady, so when this guy kills you, I'll be able to tell the police where to pick up your body. So I'll feed Skippy."

"I wasn't going to tell you either, but I just decided to—not so they find my body—but because I trust you," I told her.

Her angry expression softened. She picked up her pita.

"Do you want me to come?"

"No. It'll be fine. Trust me."

"I... I do trust you but you're crazy. Why are you doing all of this?"

"You mean why am I meeting Aubrey, or whoever it is, alone, or why am I working on the case, or why am I at the *Mail* in the first place?"

"All of the above," she said.

"Well, I'm meeting the guy because I'm curious and I've got to keep going until it's done. I'm working on the case because... because it's fun."

"Fun?" she asked, with a laugh.

"Yeah. The reason I'm at the *Mail* is something else entirely."

She waited.

I said nothing.

She waited some more, eating grapes, enjoying the ancient, eternal meal.

I told her.

"So, you're undercover?" Jane asked, when I was done. "The only reason you got a job at the *Mail* was to try to prove they blackmailed some cop, who killed himself?"

"Well, yeah. His brother was one of our team. But I'm not undercover anymore. I told them I was working on a story about the Sean Joyce case."

"But you're not. You're trying to find evidence that will prove they did something wrong. Why tell them what you're doing?"

"Because I have evidence they do this kind of thing, but not evidence they blackmailed the dead cop. I know they did it but I can't prove it. I figured if I told them I was onto them, I would draw fire, you know, get them to react, show themselves."

"And they have."

"Yeah," I agreed. "I assume most corporations in New York do not have Human Resources people who carry guns and threaten employees."

"These days, who knows?" Jane laughed. "So your definition of success for your not-so-secret mission would be if they started shooting at you?"

"Well, as my friend Al would say, it would be a start."

"Have you considered the possibility that you may be insane?"

"Everything about my life proves that is true."

She laughed and took me by the hand, leading me toward her bedroom.

"Where are we going?" I asked her.

"To do something I want to do again before the murderer or your employers kill you."

39.

After lunch, I went back to my desk at the newspaper with a smile on my face. I called Mary Catherine on my iPhone to update her, while opening a small pile of snail mail with my black letter opener. At least a few readers had liked my column. I looked up and spotted Jack Leslie and Matt Molloy watching me from across the room for a bit before drifting away.

"This is your plan?" Mary Catherine asked sarcastically. "Blab the mission to the bad guys to piss them off and then go to meet a killer alone?"

"Best plan I've got," I told her.

"It sucks," she concluded.

"It does. But I won't be alone. I'm open to suggestions."

"Let's just let them incriminate themselves with an electronic trail," she suggested.

"There won't be one."

"Shit. We can't use a dummy and a wig this time."

"I'm the dummy."

"Yes, you are, Shepherd."

"Just be there."

"Okay. I'm praying for you, Shepherd."

"Don't do that. Do your job."

"Okay, I will."

"I mean it, Mary Catherine. No praying. Didn't you read that scientific study they did about praying for sick people?"

"No. Who wasted money on that?"

"I forget. In one test group, people prayed for actual sick patients to get better—but they got worse. More died than in the control group."

"You made that up. That doesn't make sense," she sniffed.

"Praying makes sense?" I asked.

"How could it hurt?"

"Maybe their minds weren't on their jobs."

"Okay. God helps those who help themselves," she concluded.

"Have it your way."

"Who's going to show up?" she asked.

"Probably the person who sent me that text."

"Aubrey Forsythe?" she asked.

"Could be. Maybe he wants to give himself up."

"You don't believe that," she said.

"No, I don't. And I still don't think he did this."

"Who else?"

"A copycat, maybe," I said. "But there are always other possibilities."

"Who?"

"Old friends, new friends? Guessing doesn't count. See you tonight."

Daydreaming at my desk, I watched a flock of pigeons, under reflected clouds, maybe the same flock, flying in tight formation between the skyscrapers. When no falcon attacked, I got bored. I grabbed my folded red necktie and my favorite letter opener and went home to feed and walk Skippy. He was happy to see me.

On our walk, the HR thugs were nowhere in sight. Neither were Ginny or her siblings. As Skippy took care of business, I had that itchy shoulder blade feeling, the caveman sense that a predator was eyeing me. I looked around carefully but couldn't see anyone I recognized—just strangers coming and going on foot and in cars, paying no attention to me. I scanned the rooftops, the windows. Nothing. Just the feeling. That feeling was an old friend.

Back in my apartment, I sat on the couch discussing possibilities with a disinterested Skippy.

"So, who got something from these killings?" I asked him. "Who benefits?"

Skippy cocked his head reflectively. He had no suggestions. I made fun of Izzy talking to corpses but here I was talking to a dog. At least Skippy was alive.

The next of kin would benefit from the killings. So Aubrey would get his husband's money. But Aubrey was the one *with* money. Cushing had several ex-wives and lots of kids but I doubted they banded together to bump him off. Who would get Pookie's fortune? But Izzy would be all over that stuff, inheritance, insurance, the routine cop stuff. If he had found anything, I'd know.

"I still can't see Aubrey being the Hacker," I told Skippy. "Unless Cash Cushing and Pookie Piccarelli killed Neil Leonardi together. Then Aubrey would be innocent of the first murder but guilty of the other two—for revenge. That works. But why would a greedy billionaire and a horny party girl team up to off a food critic's husband? No reason in the world. They had nothing in common. Except they all had money. And reality TV shows."

"Son of a bitch!" I yelled, startling Skippy. "Ratings!"

Neil's murder on the front page of the *Mail,* every front page, plus on TV, radio and the web. Millions in free publicity. I grabbed my phone and launched Google. Sure enough, the shows all had huge viewer spikes on TV, online, Netflix, everywhere, after each killing. Box sets of Aubrey's, Nolan's and Pookie's shows were topping the Amazon charts.

Somebody was making millions. I looked up the ownership. Three different networks. Damn. Aubrey's show, *Food Fight*, was on the FFY channel, Nolan's show, *You're Foreclosed*, was on the MMC channel, and Pookie's *Bitch Blanket Bimbos* was on TDC. They all had separate, competing ownership. Pookie's show was owned by billionaire Trevor Todd, the owner of the *New York Mail*, my ultimate boss. They were actually running promos for Pookie's show, using my front pages to draw viewers. They showed other cast members reacting to her death. A new season based around her murder was already being filmed. Tacky but not illegal.

Now it made no sense again. If it was a ratings scam, all the shows should have been on the same network or owned by the same people. Obviously Neil, Cash and Pookie were not willingly part of any plot that involved their own deaths. Maybe Aubrey *did* want to surrender and plead guilty with an explanation? But if not Aubrey, who? A stranger, a loony serial killer who hates rich reality TV jerks?

Stay tuned.

40.

What to wear to meet a serial killer?

I no longer owned body armor or an M5, or a SCAR assault rifle.

I only had my lucky red tie, the one with a dragon on it, and my black letter opener. The ancient Chinese sage Lao Tzu said "one who feels punctured must once have been a bubble," whatever that means. I changed back into my slightly dirty jeans and sneakers and put on a clean, long-sleeved white dress shirt. I donned my garish dragon tie, fiddled with it, and checked it out in the mirror. Felt a bit stiff but it worked.

I stood on the curb of Central Park Drive, close to where Pookie had been found. Stubs of yellow crime-scene tape still tied to a light pole and a tree fluttered in a vague breeze. Yellow cabs, cars and the occasional hansom cab, a black horse-pulled buggy used to separate tourists from their money, rolled by, ignoring me. Some sightseers cruised by in a black limo, taking pictures of the murder spot out the window. Twice a cab slowed to see if I was a fare but I waved them away.

It was already after midnight. I casually ran my eyes over the grass and trees and rocks all around me. I could not see any sign of Mary Catherine or her people hiding. Either they were very good or they were late. They certainly weren't close. Unless they were disguised as elms.

I took out my phone and checked for messages. Zip. Another yellow cab slowed to the curb right in front of me and I started to wave it off. Both windows on my side were open and the driver inside the dark vehicle—a short guy in black, wearing a light turban—asked me something I couldn't make out.

"No, I don't need a cab, thanks," I said, waving him away again.

"Drop the phone and get in. Fast, asshole," he said clearly. The voice coming from under the turban was Matt Molloy's.

"Hi, I'm Alec Baldwin," the little TV in the back seat said.

Before I could say no, another familiar voice from the back seat spoke up.

"Get in right now, Shepherd, or I shoot you where you stand. Drop your phone and get the fuck in—three seconds."

That would be Jack Leslie. I could barely see him, dressed all in black, lying on his back across the seat, propped up on the far door, both hands on his gun, which was pointed right at my chest. Eight feet from the gun to my heart. His automatic was cocked, ready to fire. He couldn't miss. Only in movies can people dodge bullets. We learned that the first day out. The round is through you and out before you hear the shot.

"If you see something, say something," Alec Baldwin said.

Jack Leslie began counting. I dropped my cell in the gutter, reached for the door and got in but I left the door open. Leslie moved his legs to make room for me and sat up.

"Close the door."

I ignored him and quickly took off my tie, wrapping it once around my left hand while palming the flat dark object hidden inside it with my right hand.

"Go!" Leslie yelled.

Molloy floored it. Leslie and I were shoved back into the seat, as I heard and felt the door slam behind me. Leslie's gun also went back, to my left. I sprang forward to the right and slapped at the pistol with my padded hand, grabbing it. It went off incredibly loudly, bright as a paparazzo's flash bulb, the expanding blast hurting my ears. I wedged the wrapped web of my left hand into the space in front of the cocked hammer as Leslie recovered, swinging the gun point-blank at my chest and pulling the trigger again.

I yelled in pain but held tight. I hit him in the chest, fast and underhanded, with my fisted right hand and held the grip of my letter opener against him. He gasped in astonishment.

"Abracadabra, motherfucker!" I yelled into his face, only inches away.

He spasmed and released the automatic, along with all the breath in his lungs. The pistol came away, attached to my left hand, the hammer still embedded in the silk of my tie and the skin between my thumb and forefinger. I safed the piece, freeing my hand, dropped the magazine and jacked the last round out of the chamber. Molloy's driving was tossing us around wildly. The pistol fell to the floor of the cab in three pieces. We were moving very fast, tires squealing. The cab banged off something and I fell backwards. Leslie crumpled into the foot well on his side.

I heard shouts and sirens. Several shots outside the vehicle. Molloy was yelling Leslie's name over and over but Leslie wasn't answering. I reached for my door handle. We fishtailed sideways, hit something else, bounced in the air and accelerated back the other way, fast as a bastard, clipping something with a bang. The rear window shattered and Molloy cursed and drove faster, still calling for his partner. I raised my head for a peek. Trees were flying drunkenly by. We had to be going more than a hundred, sliding all over the place. The sirens faded.

We sped onto another roadway, black trees flashing by. Then we left the road, thumping and bumping and scraping, slowing down as we hit several bushes and trees. I was tossed onto Leslie's body and took the chance to retrieve my high-density plastic letter opener from under his sternum. The composite graphite and phosphorus polymer was as sharp as a real knife and had ruptured his heart instantly.

Magic.

From his point of view, anyway. I dug a lighter out of my pants pocket and flicked it into flame. Once I cooked Leslie's blood off the dark blade, the weapon ignited. It was designed to cut and to burn like a flare, but much hotter. No messy evidence left behind. Another successful government product. Cost to taxpayers: $930. I shoved the lighter back in my pocket and fought to hold the burning blade steady as we banged all over the place, crawling back to my open window. In a quick shot, I hooked the flaming black blade, now one third consumed, and tossed it in the front window, into the front seat. Right onto Molloy's lap.

"Presto!" I shouted.

"Fuck!" he screamed. "Fuck! Fuck! Fuck!"

He swatted at it with his turban but it would not go out. He managed to knock the burning blade and the flaming turban onto the floor on the passenger side but it was still burning.

"Hi, I'm Sarah Jessica Parker," the TV said.

Time to go. I went for my door handle and shouldered open the door. It snapped shut like a steel jaw, as we hit a hillock. We were moving more slowly, rocking and rolling through a sparse wooded area in the dark. I tried again and dove out, hitting dirt and rolling. I heard shots. Molloy firing at me. I was sprawling through rocks and leaves and roots downhill. Fast. I had to get up and run but something hit me in the back of the head.

41.

It was still dark. I wasn't running. I was sitting on the ground, my back against the front tire on the driver's side of the cab, my legs straight out. The dented taxi, its lights and engine off, ticking, was parked in a woody spot, on an asphalt walking path, not a road. My head was pulsating with pain. I reached up to the back of my skull with my left hand and felt wetness on my palm. Blood. My Houdini from the moving cab had ended with me thumping my head into something hard. If Molloy had shot me, I wouldn't be waking up. But, unlike with Leslie, I had no element of surprise and no chance to move fast. I started to seriously re-evaluate my no-gun pledge, as I slowly drew my legs in and braced my left hand on the pavement.

"Don't fucking move, asswipe!" Molloy said in a hushed voice from the dark. "And keep your voice down."

I froze. I didn't remember saying anything, loud or otherwise. He had me. He was visible as an outline against the moonlight coming through the trees. In the distance a skyline of high-rise buildings glittered, a horizon of black teeth studded with diamonds.

Matt was scared and he was pointing his gun at me. For some reason, he was afraid of noise. With his other hand he held his crotch and jogged from one leg to another, obviously in pain.

"Sorry about toasting your balls but you'd do the same thing if somebody tried to kill you," I said loudly.

"I said keep your voice down or I'll fucking blow your brains out!"

"That would be even louder," I explained.

"Shut up. Who said we were going to kill you? We wanted to talk to you, get you to tell us what you're doing. Now you've screwed everything up. Everything. You got no fucking idea, asshole."

"Tell me."

"I'm asking the goddamn questions, dickwad. What are you up to? Tell me now or I'll fucking murder your ass."

I detected sniffling. Was he crying? For Leslie?

"Sorry I had to kill your friend Jack," I tried.

"You fucking bastard! How did you do it? You moved so fast I couldn't see what happened. He was good. How did you turn his own gun on him?"

"I didn't. I had a composite blade in my tie. I stabbed him once in the heart. It was quick. He didn't suffer. Sorry, self-defense."

"You had a knife? And a fucking firebomb? Where?"

"No. The knife burns. That's what I threw on your lap."

"A burning knife? I didn't find no fucking knife."

"Because it burned."

"They were right, you're not a dog dork. You're some kind of Special Forces killer, right?"

"Actually J-SOC. Not Delta. Working to keep America safe. Who are *they*—Badger and Edgar?"

"You didn't have to kill him," Molloy sniffed. "We weren't going to kill you."

"You mean not right away," I corrected him. "Not until after I talked."

He didn't deny it.

"Anyways, now I gotta kill you."

"That would be incredibly stupid, Matt."

"Don't call me stupid."

"Okay. Since you're not stupid, you know you were seen, Matt," I told him, improvising, hoping it was true. "You were caught on camera. Long lenses, night vision, the whole deal. They know who you are and are looking for you now. Remember the picture in the *Daily Press* of me with the fed? They're waiting outside your place right now. Maybe inside, too."

"Fuck," he groaned, massaging his groin.

He believed me. I wished it were true.

"You and Leslie sent the text to me, pretending to be Aubrey."

"Duh. And you called the cops? We didn't see them."

"I told the feds. Was NYPD there, too?"

"Yeah, I bounced off one marked blue-and-white car and one unmarked one. Fuckers shot at us. With a hostage. That's not right. This has been so sweet for so long, I can't believe it. I'm totally boned."

"What about the other ones, Molloy?"

He was silent.

"The smart move is to walk away. Take off or get a lawyer. Blame it on me."

"That's what I'm doing," he giggled. "This here's Jack's gun. I put it back together. He shot you, not me. I didn't know you guys was gonna kill each other."

"Molloy, you didn't kill anybody. You can say you thought the cops were drug dealers or something."

"I can still say that. Don't need you."

"But they will know you fired a gun. The forensics will be all screwed up and they'll come down on you. You can't kill an undercover and get away with it."

"I knew it. You're working for the cops."

"Yes I am," I lied. "Agent Shepherd. Put down the gun and we'll work this out."

His gun hand wavered and slowly lowered halfway, like it was very heavy.

"I'll make you a good deal, Matt."

"I can't go to jail again."

"No jail. You just lay out the whole thing and you're good to go," I told him, standing.

"The whole thing?" he asked, suddenly suspicious. "You mean all of them? Everywhere?" Damn.

"Forget that for now. Let's just start with the Joyce case and worry about anything else later," I assured him. "No problem, we'll just—"

"No fucking way! If I rat they'll kill me. He's got billions. You have no clue. These people are serious as a heart attack. NO!"

"The Witness Relocation Program is…"

The gun came up again. I rambled on but he wasn't listening. I reached into my left pocket and felt the lighter. My thumb moved the butane setting to high.

"On your feet." His weapon was centered on me. "Move to the back of the cab."

I saw he had the trunk open. I almost flicked the butane onto steady flame and tossed it into the open driver's window but I hesitated too long.

"Get in."

"No."

"Get in or I'll shoot you."

"That would be very loud, and a very big mistake."

"I just want to put you in there, so I can get away. I won't shoot, Agent Shepherd. Really. Get in and pull it closed. You'll see."

I didn't believe a word but my only choice was to rush him and that option would probably end with him putting at least one round into me before I could get to him. I left the lighter in my pocket, ducked into the open trunk, pulling it closed by the dangling glowing open-the-trunk cord. Even darker inside. No air. I fired up my lighter. I was in a deep box lined with dark felt-like material, the trunk rug. There was a horizontal ledge above me, under the rear window, that held a full-sized spare tire. I sat up and leaned toward it. The inflated tire was held in place by a steel rod secured by a steel plate, itself held over the metal center rim with a large wing nut. Excellent. I put the lighter away and worked in the dark. I spun the wing nut off and put it in my other pocket and put the metal plate aside on the shelf. I had to shift the tire to unhook the steel rod because it was hooked to the shelf underneath to hold the heavy steel belted radial in place. I hit my light again. The steel rod was about nine inches long and solid, a weapon.

The trunk thumped loudly. Molloy was kicking the outside of the trunk hard, over and over, laughing about how I should try to get out of that. He was deforming the area around the lock, so I couldn't open it. Why? I could think of at least one bad reason. I ignored his ranting and got busy. While he was denting the trunk shut, I pulled the tire off the shelf and curled into the fetal position in the main trunk well under it. Thank God for a full-size American spare tire, not some tiny donut spare. I got as much of my head under the center metal rim as possible and worked my way as far to one side as I could. I had to bow my head painfully to get it under the rim and I couldn't tell how much of me fit underneath. The thumping stopped. Then Molloy tried to open the trunk. It was jammed solid. I wondered how long I could stay this way.

"You hear me, Agent Asshole?"

I didn't answer. Why give him a better idea where my head was.

"Okay, play dead. First, I'm already in Witness Protection. Second, fuck your deal! Fuck you! This is for Jack."

I felt the first shot hit the tire and me like a hot hammer, the steel belted radial screaming and howling like a banshee as its air escaped. Or was that me? The shots came fast and loud. I could feel the rounds impacting, one after the other as they perforated the trunk more than a dozen times, half of them slamming me, some clanging the metal rim over my head like a bell, blowing me away.

42.

I was fuzzy all over, crushed in the dark, wet, dripping with pain. My head and arms and legs were slimy. I tasted blood coming out of my nose and mouth. My eyes burned, which is what happens when blood gets in your eyes. Not good. Some jerk was making noise, ranting, hooting, hurting my head. I wasn't supposed to talk to him.

"Still got ears, Agent Asshole?" the jerk demanded.

Shit. Molloy. Trunk. Jammed. Bullets.

"Who's stupid now? Who's dumb enough to bring a knife to a gunfight?"

Molloy waited for an answer but I kept my mouth shut. I began to choke on blood and I quietly opened my mouth to breathe. I began moving my body carefully under the dead, deflated tire. It was hard to separate me from the tire; it clung like a porcupine, quills dug into my flesh. Everything hurt. I was hit in both legs, one arm and the head and no medic in sight. I slowly shuffled off the treaded tire and rim with my good right hand. I felt it rip my skin, like it was part of me. I painfully pulled out the lighter and flicked it on. It was like a blowtorch in a casket. My pants from both knees down were shredded and bloody, as was the skin of my left arm below the elbow. I could feel new wounds on my face and head. I tried wiggling both toes, which resulted in surges of hot pain that took my breath away. My left arm had two holes with a spider pattern of cuts radiating outward for a few inches, all oozing blood. I tried touching it with my right fingers. It was wet, sticky, and ripped up, like a shrapnel wound. Damn. Maybe Matt was using exploding ammo. When I rolled my head for a closer look, everything spun, including my stomach. I smelled something sharp and familiar. Gasoline.

I stopped moving and shut off the flame but held tight to the lighter, waiting for the spinning to stop. I closed my eyes. The bullets had hit the gas tank under me. I was curled on top of fifteen gallons of flammable, dripping 87-octane gasoline. I could see it in my mind's eye, dribbling onto the asphalt, pooling under the car, ready to burn. If he was using exploding rounds, why didn't they ignite the tank? I opened my eyes in the dark. A ghostly green man swung back and forth in front of my eyes. I reached out and grabbed him. It was the florescent plastic tag hanging from the trunk release cable. Not a ghost. I wanted desperately to yank on it and open the trunk and get out but I remembered Molloy kicking in the trunk surface. It wouldn't work. Also I was playing possum. Bleeding possum. I let the green ghost go.

I took a deep breath and nothing got worse. I took another. The pain lessened when I didn't move. Okay. Concussion, wounds on lower legs, left arm, head. Still breathing, heart still pumping. The clock was running. I had to get out of this tomb and I had to get to a hospital. I held my breath as I flicked the lighter into flame again but I didn't blow up. The only way out was through the trunk wall and into the back seat. But not until Molloy was gone. Otherwise he'd just have a clear shot at me. How long could I wait until I bled to death? The vertical trunk wall was covered with a fake gray felt board and did not look too hard to break. But what was behind it? A steel frame and the back of the back seat, probably. I shut the lighter off and rested in the dark again. My green friend returned, floating still and silent. He seemed to be pointing at something. The way out of the trunk. I ripped my pants legs off and wrapped them around my bleeding leg wounds. I pulled off my shirt and did the same bandaging thing to my left arm.

That was when I smelled smoke.

"Still with me, asshole?" Molloy yelled outside, giddy. "Check it out, bro. You like fire so much, I used your fancy tie in the gas tank. Burns real good. Gonna toast *your* balls now, fuckwad. How you like that? Then I got more fun for you. Hold on, war hero!"

Smoke was seeping in. It was getting hot.

Time to go. I crawled up into the three-foot deep horizontal shelf that had held the tire. I used the metal rod to rip at the wall between the trunk and the back seat. It quickly came apart. Behind it was a framework of solid metal, steel beams. I ripped at it with the rod. Nothing. I banged the steel, used the rod like a crowbar to bend the bars of my cage. I punched it. Nothing. It was broiling and I began choking on the smoke. I could hear Molloy laughing beyond the flames and smoke. I kicked at the wall. Nothing. Then I sensed motion. The car was rolling, picking up speed. But I could still hear Molloy cackling behind me. He wasn't in the car, which was on fire and rolling downhill. Toward what? The speed fed the flames under me, the floor of the trunk as hot as a skillet. I wanted a fire extinguisher but I already knew there wasn't one in my trunk world. I continued my attack on the wall. Then I floated, like the car had taken flight. Everything flipped over upside down, banging me around in the trunk. It righted just before smashing into something. The hissing cab bobbed and began a gentle spin. It was cooler.

The fire was out.

Before I could celebrate, the front of the cab nosed lazily

down and I heard and felt cold water cascading in from all sides. The cab was floating in water but not for long. I was locked inside a steaming two-ton boat with a heavy engine and open windows. Titanic Taxi. I tried to think. Panic was bad. I tried my lighter. The cab headed down. I felt a shower on my head, extinguishing my lighter. Cold water was squirting in through Molloy's bullet holes. I felt blindly around the edges of the back seat wall, Houdini looking for a way out. I tried left and right and front and down. I was so tired. Think. What haven't I tried? I dove desperately for my glowing green man and pulled his trunk release cable for all I was worth.

Nothing.

I let him go. Now, my green buddy seemed to be pointing toward the back seat.

What else? There's always something else. Up. I didn't try up. I sloshed water up to my knees and crawled into the tire shelf again. This was it. I punched up, behind the rear seat, behind the rear window. Nothing gave. But it sounded different, hollow. I slammed my fist up into the rectangular panel. Was it giving or was I nuts? I had no leverage, no time. I painfully crawled my whole body into the small shelf space, bracing my back up against the top of the space. I pushed against the bottom with all the strength in my arms and legs, screaming with pain. The water was now lapping against me. Then I felt it on my back and I was drenched. I jumped up and was completely underwater. Something gave way and my head and shoulders popped up. I felt jagged glass and fought and kicked and twisted. My knees hit steel and I pushed off with my wounded legs.

I broke surface and grabbed air. I was out.

There was a ring of dark trees and fuzzy spots of light, tall buildings behind branches. A lake in Central Park. I tried to swim but my arm and legs hurt too much, the wet clothing bandages dragging me down. My shoes were gone. I dipped under the surface several times but kept going. Can't be far. A half-assed dogpaddle worked, until my shoulder hit a rock. I stood up in a muddy shallow and immediately fell down. I crawled until I was on solid ground. It stank of slimy duck droppings. Drowsy dark birds on either side of the shore muttered, edging away from me, gossiping about the large bleeding guy who had no bread. Slowly I sat up. On the hill above me, dark shapes. A predatory van with no lights on and a shadowy someone standing next to it.

Shit. Molloy was still there. My metal rod was gone. Maybe he couldn't see me in the dark. Why didn't he leave? All that shooting, cops should have come. But they didn't. Maybe this happens every night in Central Park. I froze. The figure did not move. If it wasn't Molloy I should yell for help. But if it *was* him, he'd come down and finish the job. I had nothing left. While I debated what to do, the figure got into the van and vanished into the dark. I waited for Molloy to take another crack at me but he didn't come. Run, motherfucker.

"I'm alive," I said out loud. I sounded strange. Overkill, that was Molloy's mistake, I decided. He could have just shot me or he could have burned me or drowned me but the jackass did them all together. Overkill led to underkill. Right.

I crawled achingly toward the light.

43.

My ghostly green buddy was gone and I was bathed in bright light in a hospital bed, pale faces hovering above me. I was bandaged and ached everywhere except my torso. Actually, that hurt, too. Mary Catherine moved closer on one side, Izzy on the other. Both began talking at once. They stopped and each apologized and invited the other to speak. I couldn't wait.

"Did you get him?" I asked Mary Catherine.

"Matt Molloy?" she asked.

"Who else?"

"No. Your friend Jack Leslie was behind the wheel of the cab at the bottom of the reservoir. Not surprising he drove off a cliff, him being so dead."

"Molloy is in the wind," Izzy continued. "We're looking."

I asked how long I had been out.

"A day and a half," Mary Catherine said. "They kept you doped up while they removed about ten pounds of metal from you, bullet fragments and shredded steel belting and rubber. You lost a lot of blood. You're a tetanus test case."

"I have to ask," Izzy interrupted. "Matt Molloy did this to you, right?"

"Fuck, yes," I answered. "He fired through the closed

trunk. Thank God for American-made steel belted radials."

"Not a very good bulletproof vest," Izzy observed. "Really ripped you up."

"Best I could do on short notice. Now the rest of me matches my face," I said to Mary Catherine, gesturing to my facial skid marks. "Tell me you got the bastards."

She hung her head.

"My boss, the U.S. Attorney, said you were probably a murderer and he saw nothing in our jurisdiction to investigate. He socializes with your boss, Lucky Tal Edgar."

"'Lucky' is right," I said.

"*I* got them," Izzy bragged. "I got search warrants for the *Mail* computers, records and phones before lunch. We interrupted them in the middle of large-scale file shredding and computer dumping. You know they have a whole room full of industrial-strength shredders? The NYPD computer people are trying to recover the data now."

"You hope," Mary Catherine told him. "Your District Attorney got a big chunk of her last re-election campaign war chest from the owner of the *New York Mail.*"

"If Mary Catherine couldn't get the U.S. Attorney to come in, how did you do it, Izzy?"

"I told the judge I was investigating the murder of one *New York Mail* employee and the mysterious disappearance of another. I said I had a witness unconscious in the hospital and that lives were in danger."

"My life?" I asked.

"We discussed several possibilities. You. Another serial killer victim. Maybe Matt Molloy. Gotta get the evidence."

"So we have evidence from the *Mail* on the serial killings and the Joyce case?" I asked hopefully.

"The recent stuff was the first shit they erased," Izzy said. "The computer guys are looking to recover whatever they can. Huge amount of stuff, it's going to take time. Fingers crossed."

I cursed Lucky Tal, his boss Trevor Todd, and all their minions and suggested they had sexual intercourse with their mothers and various barnyard animals. It didn't make me feel better.

Then I told them everything. Almost. I recounted dropping my phone, Leslie with the gun, the wild ride, my bailout, the trunk thing. I left out the part with my flaming knife and my ghostly green pal. Then the fire, the flying, the sinking, the swimming, the van, the ducks. Izzy said he would put out an alert for a black van. Maybe Molloy fled in one.

"So, Shepherd," Izzy asked, "did Molloy murder his partner or did you kill Jack Leslie in lawful self-defense, after he fired a gun at you and you were in fear for your life?"

"What are you comfortable with?" I asked.

Izzy and Mary Catherine chuckled.

"Well, we found one ejected shell casing on the back floor of the cab, along with the emptied nine millimeter, wiped clean of prints. The rest of the ejected brass was grouped near a burned spot on the rock above the reservoir, uphill from where the cab went airborne, consistent with Molloy firing at you inside the trunk. One deformed round was recovered from the right passenger door panel, consistent with someone firing level in the back seat. Your friend Mary Catherine here has night-vision video of you, apparently unarmed, getting into the cab, with your hands up. Looks like an abduction to me. The video recorded a flash and a bang as the cab sped away. Only one gun was recovered at the scene but no knife."

"A knife?" I asked.

"Didn't I tell you?" Izzy said. "Leslie was stabbed to death. Once. In the heart, by somebody who knew what they were doing."

"You mean like Matt Molloy?"

"I might be comfortable with that. He tried really hard to kill you. Several times."

"And maybe he and his buddy killed several people to boost newspaper circulation."

"Maybe. No evidence yet," Izzy said. "Do you remember your ordeal, sir?"

"Maybe. Not yet."

"Traumatic amnesia is a tricky thing," Izzy said.

"I hope so," I told him. "You bugged my phones."

"Could be," he replied.

"How else did you know to be hiding in the park at that moment? What happened? Your guys and Mary Catherine's people fell all over each other?"

They both looked at the floor.

"I'm sorry, Shepherd. I let you down," Mary Catherine said sadly. "We didn't know Lieutenant Negron and his men were going to be there. He didn't know *we* were there. They got away with you in the confusion. It's a miracle no one was killed. Well. Almost no one."

"I apologize for handcuffing you," Izzy said to her. "It's your fault, Shepherd."

"Go ahead, blame the victim. Who has my phone?" I asked.

"I do," said Izzy. "We're done copying it. I'll bring it next time."

"Thanks. I think."

"So…" Izzy continued, "your paper has put out a statement that it is cooperating fully with our investigation."

"Are they?"

"Hell no. Total stonewall of lawyers. We went to the Human Resources department and the woman in charge claimed she never heard of your pals. Leslie and Molloy had their own office in the basement, with lots of bugging equipment, burglary tools, cameras, radios, you name it. We were there all night, copying computer files, seizing paper ones, hauling everything out except the floor. We weren't the first ones there, though. Half the file cabinets were empty.

From the dust you could see two desktop computers had been removed."

I asked how I had got to the hospital and was told an anonymous caller reported a man had been hit by a car on Park Drive and was crawling in the roadway, bleeding and rambling about ducks.

"Ducks?" Mary Catherine asked. "What was that all about?"

"I don't remember. I have traumatic amnesia, remember?"

44.

I suddenly remembered Skippy.

"He's being taken care of by a friend," said Mary Catherine.

"Whose friend?" I asked.

"Yours," Mary Catherine replied. "Your girlfriend, the vet."

"Jane?"

"She called 911 and reported you missing. She was directed to me," Izzy recounted. "She said she was your girlfriend and she couldn't reach you and that you went to meet the Hacker. We told her you were alive and gave her your keys. Was that okay?"

"Yeah, of course."

"Jane seems very nice," Mary Catherine beamed. "She was very worried about you and relieved that you were alive. She was here while you were unconscious and said she would be here tonight, after work. So, tell me about her."

"I can't. Traumatic amnesia, remember?"

A doctor came in and checked me, then ran over the long menu of damage, including a mysterious funnel-shaped burn on my left forearm. Most of my wounds were the result of slugs that were broken up and shredded by the tire and exited the far side as a confetti of lead and steel that, fortunately, had lost most of its punch and ended up in my skin or the muscle underneath. Painful, ugly but not life threatening. I would never have a career as a pantyhose model. I thanked my doctor for saving me and was thankful for the *New York Mail* health insurance plan that paid for it.

Izzy and Mary Catherine spoke to the doctor in the hall before coming back in and just looking at me and each other for a while.

"What?" I finally asked them.

"The doctor said it's okay," Mary Catherine said, unfolding a *New York Mail*.

"Sorry. So much for the good news," Izzy muttered.

"This is today's paper," Mary Catherine explained.

"Don't believe everything you read in the papers," Izzy chuckled.

Mary Catherine held up the front page so I could see The Wood.

HACKER ATTACK?
Ace Reporter or Sly Slayer?

Uh-oh, the dreaded question mark, the one magic squiggle that made it possible for a newspaper to lie about anyone. Mary Catherine handed me the rag. My photograph, a head shot from my *Mail* ID, was inset onto a scene of cops examining Jack Leslie's wet body next to the banged-up cab. But they had done something to my picture, photoshopped it. My eyes were hollow and predatory. I looked evil. Under my picture were three words and one squiggle.

Cannibal Serial Killer?

This set me off on another jag, accusing my bosses at the *Mail* of incest and bestiality. As I read, I expanded my oaths to include various other perversions. The front page asked the question whether *New York Mail* reporter Francis X. Shepherd had murdered one and possibly two intrepid *Mail* security investigators, who had begun investigating him as the possible Hacker. Police, it said, had served a search warrant on the newspaper as part of its probe—of me. The byline was Don Badger and they had the gall to call it EXCLUSIVE. Turned out my favorite Human Resources executives were intrepid sleuths on the trail of an elusive killer—who had pretended to get exclusive stories on slayings he might have engineered. It quoted an anonymous law enforcement source, who said I might have killed Jack Leslie and Matt Molloy because their unofficial investigation came too close for comfort. Previously, cops had believed that famous foodie Aubrey Forsythe was the Hacker but investigators were now wondering if Forsythe had help in his horrific killing spree. What was clear was that Leslie and Molloy were heroes.

"They tried to lure him with a ruse but, sadly, it appears they seriously underestimated their quarry," the unnamed law enforcement source said.

It was strange that, when they spoke to the *Mail*, New York cops suddenly seemed to acquire British accents. The paper was cooperating with the police investigation, turning over records and computer data to help lock up the wily monster who had slain three—perhaps as many as five—if the courageous security men were counted. It went on like that for pages, re-hashing the hackings and speculating how I might have been in a perfect position to commit the killings and blame them on someone else. The only things missing were advertisements for torches and pitchforks. There was a particularly cute editorial by my fearless leader, Lucky Tal Edgar, an apology to his dear readers—for me. I was a viper at the breast of the First Amendment, a clever trickster who foisted myself off as an investigative reporter, after concealing past evil deeds that involved the death of helpless children. I was the worst person in the world, a suspected serial killer, lusting for the blood of innocents. Wow.

"Crap," I spat, throwing the paper to the foot of my bed.

"Don't worry," Izzy said. "I know it's bullshit."

"What about the DA?"

"He doesn't have the case yet. Not until I make an arrest."

"And my boss wants to stay out of it," Mary Catherine threw in.

"Not after he reads this," I said. "People with badges will be popping up everywhere. That was the idea. The *Mail* has taken over the investigation. They own the county prosecutors and the feds. The worst of this whole thing is… I have to… Oh, man…"

"What?" Mary Catherine asked, alarmed.

"This crap will be picked up everywhere. Even in Kansas, even on NPR," I explained. "Now I have to call my parents."

"That's the worst?" Izzy asked.

"You haven't met my parents."

45.

Jane arrived in my hospital room just as I was finishing up my call to my parents. She waited until I hung up then leaned in and kissed me.

"Who was that?"

I told her.

"It's funny, I can't picture you with a mother and a father. You seem like, I don't know, an orphan," she smiled. "Cute, lovable, maybe a little sad?"

"My parents think I'm an orphan, too."

She made a face and asked if I was kidding. I wasn't. "They rarely speak to me. They called me a serial killer before the *Mail* called me one. That was my mom I was talking to. My dad wouldn't get on the phone. When I left college to join the military after 9/11, they were horrified. When they found out I killed people, terrorists, they disowned me."

"But you were a soldier, fighting the evildoers."

"They don't see it that way. To them, I'm a killer, even if I kill killers. They're from the planet 1960s, pacifists. My dad spent Vietnam working as an orderly in a veterans' hospital, a conscientious objector. To Mom and Dad, I'm what's wrong with the world. I tried to tell my mother that the stuff in the *Mail* is all lies but I doubt it got through."

"Don't they believe in self-defense?"

"No. Non-violent direct action, you know, Gandhi, Martin Luther King Jr. They were Freedom Riders."

"What's a Freedom Rider?" she asked.

I changed the subject and we talked about Skippy. "That horrible girl from the *Daily Press* was hanging around outside your building," Jane said. "She and these two huge slugs demanded information. Of course I didn't tell her a thing."

"Sorry, she's just sucking around for a story, a day late and a dollar short."

After a nurse came in to take some blood, Jane began asking about my night in the park.

"You don't have to talk about it if you don't want," she said quickly.

I took a deep breath, which hurt, and told her everything.

"Wow," she said. "Aren't you worried I'll tell Lieutenant Negron?"

"He already knows. Not about the knife, probably, but he definitely knows I took Jack Leslie out. We're just waiting to see if Matt Molloy shows up and what kind of story he tells when he does. We'll take it from there."

"It must be nice to be so close to someone that you each know what the other is thinking," Jane said wistfully. "I'd like to have that with someone again."

"Don't be jealous of Izzy. We're just good friends. Look, Jane, look deep into my eyes and tell me what I'm thinking."

She looked. Then she moved closer and kissed me.

"This is a hospital," she laughed. "Someone could come in."

"See? That wasn't so tough."

She sat on the bed, took my hand and kissed me, better this time. It felt good.

A flash went off. Another. Ginny Mac was in the room, shooting pictures with a silver digital camera. Damn. Speak of the devil. She had probably followed Jane here. Ginny zipped around the bed for a better angle and took more shots. She stashed the camera and pulled out a pen and notebook and began peppering me with questions. Did I kill both Jack Leslie and Matt Molloy? Did I kill Neil Parmesan and all the other victims? Why did I do it? Did I get a sexual charge from it?

She was loving it. Now there was an explanation for how I beat her on everything. I was the Hacker. I tried to respond but she wouldn't shut up her ridiculous rapid-fire questions—I assumed so she could say I had refused to comment on whether I was a degenerate. She asked Jane her name and age and if she enjoyed sex with a serial killer.

"You are an idiot," Jane said. "Those goons from the *Mail* kidnapped Shepherd and tried to kill him, you moron. The police have video. Can't you see all these bandages? You think he shot himself?"

"Shot? That's not what his own paper says," Ginny countered. "They say you're the Hacker, Sheppie."

Sheppie?

"It's a cover-up because they're all involved. In this and a lot of other things," Jane protested. "They—"

"Don't, Jane," I warned her. "Ginny, I thought you got fired?"

"Only temporarily. You being a serial killer gave me an in. And this story will make me golden."

"Ginny, I'd be happy to comment if you'd stop talking for a second. Or don't you want me to respond? You just want me to say no comment, so you can run back to your office and write some stupid story. Like... let's see, what have you got? I know: 'Smiling Killer!' Or 'First Picture of the Hacker!' right?"

"Maybe, sweetie," she replied, sarcastically. "I was thinking 'Horny Hacker Humps in Hospital.' You know, 'Sex-Fest in Bed!—Serial Slayer Laughs at Cops,' something like that. We all know you're a gas in the sack."

I laughed. Jane was appalled and looked at me like Ginny and I had the same disease and she was wondering if it was contagious. She looked back and forth between Ginny and me, putting it together.

"You've got to be kidding," Jane said, pulling her hand away from mine. "You two?"

"Wait," I tried. "Let me explain."

"I don't believe it," Jane said, walking out of the room, with a frosty glare at Ginny. Ginny gave her a triumphant nasty girl smile. I tried to get up. No way. I asked Ginny for help but she just looked at me, and all my electronic and tubular attachments, like she was seeing my injuries for the first time. She took another shot with her camera. I gave up.

"Any comment, Hacker?" Ginny asked.

"That's crap," I told her. "You want to sneak around for this penny-ante shit, that's your choice. Or are you ready for a real story? A bigger story. Huge. One that will blow the *Mail* away?"

"You're just stalling me," Ginny said.

"You'll know soon enough. I get the feeling the *Mail* will not be publishing my story on the subject. I need an outlet, a job. If not you, then I'll give it to the *Tribune*. In fact, they were Aubrey's paper. They would love this and they're so much better at detail than you."

"The fuck they are," Ginny snapped, moving closer to me. "This story is mine."

"You keep saying that but it's not true. Not once. You just want it to be true and you have a big mouth. I can make it happen—if you shut your trap and listen."

"Let me guess," she said. "You'll give me a big story on Tuesday for a fuck today."

"You are an idiot," I concluded. "You pissed Jane off. Last chance—take it or leave it. Your bosses will go berserk and you will finally win. You want the story or not?"

"Maybe. I'm not agreeing until I hear it all."

"Fair enough. Off the record. For now."

She grudgingly agreed and I told her most of the story of my night in the park. Then I told her about Badger and the *Mail* on the Joyce case and that there were lots of others—leaving out names and specifics.

"Holy shit," she said, when I paused. "That's a fucking story. But we need proof."

She did not seem to notice that she had used the word "we."

"We'll have it soon," I said, hoping I was telling the truth. "More than we can fit in the paper. And this time take a better picture of me."

"We could do some nudes," she suggested.

"This is business, Ginny."

"Business?"

"Yes, business. You think I was going to give you guys the story for free? We have to talk to your boss. I'm your new partner—except I deserve a big signing bonus as the newest star at the *Daily Press*."

"What?"

"Don't freak out. You'll have a byline, too," I told her. Our story will be "By F.X. Shepherd and Virginia McElhone."

"In your dreams, Sheppie. My name goes first."

"Call me Sheppie one more time and the deal is off." Her mouth opened but shut without a word. I rang for the nurse. Time to go.

46.

It took another seventeen hours to sign discharge papers and escape from my hospital room the next morning. I was sore, limping, and exhausted—the painkillers wearing off.

Before she stormed out, Jane had brought my house keys and clothes: a loose-fitting short-sleeved sweatshirt and jeans because my bloody clothes had been taken as evidence. I took a shower and put on the outfit, along with a pair of brown cowhide Topsiders. Only the bandages on my left arm were visible, along with the cuts and bruises on my face, now added to my collection. My wallet was stained with blood but the credit cards were undamaged. The bills were mush from the lake.

I was unable to reach Izzy or Mary Catherine by phone from the hospital room so I took a cab home. Skippy wasn't there but a note from Jane, obviously old, informed me she had taken him to her place, which I already knew. My first order of business was a three-hour nap on the couch. It felt great.

Without a cell phone, I tried Izzy and Mary Catherine again on my landline and again got their voicemails. The clock was ticking so I took my antibiotic pill but not the painkiller. I needed to be sharp. I located my souvenir NEW

YORK MAIL baseball cap, went out and hailed another cab with my pitching arm.

Jane would not come out to the front desk at the animal hospital. Her assistant Xana said Skippy was at Jane's place and was okay for another day. Xana's t-shirt read FUR IS MURDER.

"Any message for Dr. Jane?" Xana asked me.

"Just tell her Shepherd needs to see her, thanks."

"Okay," Xana said, eyeing me suspiciously, the steel pin through one of her eyebrows twitching. "So, what's going on?"

Obviously my fan had read the lies about me in the *Mail*. I gave her the short version of what had happened.

"You're one lucky guy," she told me.

"Don't believe what you read in the *Mail*," I told her.

"I don't," she said, showing a nice smile and a flash of a silvery knob through her tongue. "Hey, if Dr. Jane isn't interested anymore, call me."

She handed me a card. I took it and muttered something pleasant as I left. The pincushion was hitting on me.

I got more cash from an ATM machine on the street and took another cab to Izzy's precinct. I had to wait half an hour before he came down and coldly ushered me out the front door.

"I'm sorry, Mr. Shepherd, but I am no longer on the case," he said in a loud voice. "Or, rather, I am still on the task force but I am no longer in charge. Someone else will be contacting you for an interview shortly. Here is your cell phone, which we already discussed."

He handed me my iPhone, which I took with my good hand and clipped onto my belt. He made me sign a receipt.

"You're kidding, right, Izzy?"

"No, sir, best of luck to you," Izzy said, like a real asshole.

He extended his hand. I didn't take it. His hand stayed in midair. I shook his hand. He gripped me firmly, making a show of a hearty handclasp, not letting go for several seconds. It hurt. When it was over, I put my hand in my pocket and dropped the small plastic object he had given me.

"Let me guess. Orders from headquarters. I'm now a suspect."

"Sorry, sir, I'm not authorized to discuss the case," Izzy replied, with a Joker smile. "Have a nice day."

He turned and walked back into the precinct. I glanced up at the building's surveillance camera that had captured the whole charade and smiled. Izzy was doing what he had to do.

I found a Web Crawler café, bought two memory sticks and used one of their machines to copy the data from the memory stick Izzy had given me onto them, sipping a latte. It was a good latte and time well spent. Then I took my phone from my belt. There was still half a charge on it. I called Mary Catherine's cell.

"Hello?"

"It's Shepherd."

"Oh, Mr. Shepherd, thanks for calling. I wanted to tell you that I'm no longer investigating anything that involves you and... the various cases. I've been reassigned."

"What a surprise," I said.

"Yes, isn't it?"

"There's a lot of this going around. So who is now assigned to investigate me?" I asked.

"I didn't say anyone was assigned to investigate you."

"Oh, okay. Have a nice day. I'm late for choir practice."

"Okay, Mr. Shepherd. God bless you."

One hour later, in a middle pew of the cavernous, echoing, gothic St. Patrick's Cathedral, a really pissed off Mary Catherine was waiting.

"I'm glad you remembered our emergency crash meeting protocol," she said. "Obviously the landscape has changed."

"That's why Lucky Tal and Badger nuked me before we

could nuke them," I observed.

"Well, he who nukes last nukes best," she said.

"Any weapons of mass destruction on you?" I wondered.

"Not one," she admitted.

"Mary Catherine, I need the loan of a little piece of equipment today. As soon as possible. Anonymously."

She asked me what I needed. I told her. She made a call and told me it would arrive in fifteen minutes. She asked what it was for.

"I'm going fishing."

In ten minutes, a young lady arrived with my item in a Starbucks bag and showed me how to use it before she left. She asked no questions.

"Thanks, Mary Catherine. Check this out and we can talk later," I said, handing her one of the memory sticks I had bought at the web café.

"What's on this?" she asked.

"Several nukes."

"Is this from the *New York Mail* computers? I thought the NYPD was closed down on this."

"Yes and yes," I replied. "I have to go. I have another meeting before I go back to work."

"How did you get it?" she demanded.

"In this town, it's all a matter of who you shake hands with," I explained.

"You can't tell me. Okay. Be careful. What am I supposed to do with this? I'm off the case."

"Don't look a gift nuke in the face," I told her.

47.

If they had voided my ID card, this would be a short mission.
I stopped in the bustling marble lobby of the *New York Mail*
building to pick up some mints at the newsstand, as the
lunch crowd hurried past me—buzzed but unwilling—back
to their desks. I did a recon and didn't spot any new goons
waiting to tackle me. My ID card opened the Plexiglas
starting gate at the turnstiles and I was in. That's the thing
about big organizations like a media company or an oil
tanker; it takes a while for orders to filter down from the
bridge to the engine room. I snugged my NEW YORK MAIL
baseball cap onto my aching head and strode to the elevators
before anybody stopped me. I used my ID card again on
the thirteenth floor to open the glass doors bearing the
NEW YORK MAIL logo and waved to the receptionist behind
the counter. She gave a friendly wave back; obviously not
someone who actually read the paper. I opened the second
door and walked into the City Room. Several people froze
when they saw me, literally stopped in their tracks, mouths
agape. Nigel what's-his-name—Bantock—was getting
yelled at by Badger at the City Desk. Badger's back was
to me and he was the last to turn. I gave him a big smile
and a thumbs-up and walked quickly toward Tal Edgar's

glass office. I could see his hulking shape hunched over his desk, slurring loudly into his phone. He saw me and stopped in mid-slur. He slammed down the phone and sat back in his chair, watching me approach, giving me that same I'm-going-to-kill-you glare. I ignored his assistant, shoved his glass door open and took a seat in front of him, scanning the room and desk, cataloguing the objects, rating them as possible weapons and ranking them according to utility.

"I'm back from sick leave, boss. Just thought I'd check in. I've got a juicy new exclusive for you I think is going to be big. Care for a mint?"

I held out a small metal tin of Altoids. I flipped it open to reveal scores of tiny, circular candies with a little letter 'A' impressed into one side.

"Sure you won't have one? Peppermint. Just the thing after a meal. That way, the boss can't tell you've been boozing at lunch."

Lucky Tal did not react.

"Get the fuck out of here!" Badger yelled behind me. "You must be barking mad."

"I work here," I protested. "How about you? Mint? You know you love Altoids."

"You're sacked. Fired, fuckwit," Badger countered.

"Really? No one told me that. My ID still works. I thought all was forgiven."

Tal just watched me and said nothing. You could tell Lucky Tal was pissed that I got in because no one had thought to cancel my ID. It probably never occurred to them I would drop by for an informal chat. I ignored Badger and addressed the Editor.

"Am I fired?"

"You know you are," he said quietly.

"Not until you tell me, Lucky Tal."

"You no longer work here. And I do not like that nickname."

"Why am I fired?" I asked, not breaking eye contact. "What nickname?"

"You know why you're fired," Badger sputtered, moving to my left. "You're a fucking serial killer!"

"Everyone in this room knows that is not true," I said. "You guys are the worst liars on the eastern seaboard. What's amazing to me is you guys have been lying so long you think if you can print it first, it's true. Don't you want to hear my big exclusive before you confiscate my coffee mug?"

"We don't want to hear anything you have to say—" said Badger.

"Yes," said Tal, his voice quiet. Badger stopped talking instantly.

I told them. I started with what Jack Leslie and Matt Molloy had done, what they had probably done—I guessed they at least killed poor Pookie, possibly Neil and Cash Cushing too—all sacrificed on the altar of circulation. Then I touched on the Joyce case, how they had browbeaten a desperate man into an exclusive interview by blackmail and caused his suicide. Tal sat there like a bullfrog, unmoving, unblinking, getting redder in the face. Then I began mentioning other cases, other deaths in New York and in California. I gave no details.

"Well, you boys get the idea. I'm going to hoist you by your own petards—is that the right word? No. Dicks. I'm going to hoist you both by your dicks. Thought you would like first crack at the cosmic exclusive. Least I can do. You guys just did a nice, big story about me. Time for me to do the same. Whataya say?"

"You have no proof, wanker," Badger said.

"So, it's true there is evidence but you don't think I have it?" I asked, still looking directly at Lucky Tal. "You think you've shut down the investigation but you're wrong, guys. I have proof."

Lucky Tal blinked. I took out a memory stick and tossed

it at the Editor. It landed in front of him. He shot a glance at Badger, who snatched it up and inserted it into a laptop on the desk. Tal never took his eyes from me and I never took my eyes off him.

"Fuck!" Badger spat. "How did he get this? That cunting chief promised me this would never see the light of day! Christ! He's got all the Sean Joyce memos and texts, the video of the threat about his kids. Somebody is going to hang for this! Shit! He's got the First Lady recordings, the mayor's videos, he's got everything! This can't be happening. If this gets out we're all going to jail," he moaned.

"Badger, shut your hole," Lucky Tal told him.

He shut his hole. The Editor stood up. I stood up. He smiled at me. I returned the smile.

"If any of this ever gets out, any of it, anywhere, you're a dead man," Lucky Tal told me. "We will have you killed and we'll sleep like babies. You are fucking with the wrong mob, mate. No cop in this town, no fed, is your friend. I warned them off. *You have no friends*. You think some other news organization will go against us? Think again. They know better."

"You're not denying any of it."

"What of it?"

"So you can libel people, blackmail them, kill them, and get away with it? What makes you think you can do that in this country?"

"Freedom of the press, mate. A license to print money and run governments. Also useful for squashing bugs. Now get the fuck out of here. I'm not done with you. Our exclusive for tomorrow is the fact that the NYPD and the feds are now investigating you. Apparently we hired a psycho who committed war crimes and is a serial killer."

"By the way, I think you need new Human Resources people," I said, heading for the door.

"It should come as no surprise that your parents are

sixties radicals, who raised you as a communist," Tal Edgar said.

"Democrat," I corrected him.

Three large, uniformed security guards were waiting for me outside the office, two in front, one behind, blocking my exit. They were all dark-skinned, in blue fake cop uniforms with square silver badges, and appeared to be from the Indian subcontinent. They all had their right hands on their hips, like they were about to pull pistols, but I didn't see any.

I looked around and took stock. I was stuck in an aisle, a flat table piled high with newspapers and magazines to my left, a row of heavy, waist-high metal filing cabinets on my right. The only thing on one of the cabinets was a black Hewlett Packard fax machine, screeching out a page. City Room staffers were peeking over and around their beige cubicle walls, like townspeople before a western gunfight.

"I am injured and just got out of the hospital," I told the guards, loudly. "I will give you no trouble, gentlemen. I'm walking to the elevator and out the front door. But, if you touch me, I'll have to hurt you. In self-defense."

They all smiled and pulled out matching telescoping black clubs and looked at Badger.

"He's a thief and he attacked us," Badger said. "Teach him a lesson."

I snugged my cap on tight. The security guys hesitated, so I made a decision. I grabbed the fax machine with both hands and yanked it hard, spinning in place and ripping out the cords. I spun a full circle and used the motion to launch the machine at one of the rent-a-cops in front of me, straight-arming the fax like a basketball at his upper chest.

"Here ya go!"

He fumbled with his baton and tried to catch the machine but went over with it backwards, hard, into a side aisle with a crash and a descending wail. His shaken partner took his eyes off me to watch his buddy go down, so I turned toward the one behind me, as that guy's club hit me across the back, burning like a bullwhip. Fortunately, he wasn't smart enough to hit me over the head. Yet. I spun, yelling like a motherfucker, and stomped his shin sideways, just below the knee, before he could wind up and do it again. He folded down onto the snapped kneecap, dropping his stick. I clipped his jaw with my right fist on his way to the floor. I turned back to the last man, as he rushed me from the front, his club high over his head. He brought it down hard, going for my skull. I met him and blocked with my left forearm, sliding my hand down his arm to grab his wrist. I stepped left, inside his swing, pivoting, locking my right elbow inside his right elbow. As he bumped into my hips, I used his momentum to lift and twist him with a shoulder throw.

He trashed a computer station with his back and head and didn't get up.

"You next?" I asked an astounded Badger.

He ran away. Fast. I heard a smattering of secret applause from the cubicles. I tipped my hat to the crowd and walked quickly from the area. I ducked into the stairwell and caught an elevator to the lobby from one floor down. As I hit the sidewalk, a blue-and-white screeched to the curb. I did not offer the two cops who got out any of my Altoid mints but I popped a few into my mouth. I turned the corner and kept walking west, toward my next appointment, my breath getting fresher with each step.

48.

I was cool with Ginny getting her name first on the byline but, after a brief negotiation with *Daily Press* editors over my signing bonus, they insisted my name go first on the front page. I had the goods—which I showed them on a laptop—not Ginny. Case closed. I apologized to her and fortunately she came up with her own exclusive to add to the package.

After a long night of work, with the help of many other new faces, I left my new job, went home, hit the arak, and collapsed on my bed, the aches from my injuries temporarily subdued. I set my alarm early, for another busy day.

In the morning, fresh copies of the *Daily Press* and the *New York Mail* were outside my door but this time delivered by a kid in a *Daily Press* t-shirt.

The *Mail* was a real collector's item. My former paper had more stories slamming me, claiming I forced my way onto the Hacker story with coverage "in hindsight, just too good to be true," an article smearing my parents as possible domestic terrorists, one predicting my arrest, and a real beauty calling for mob action and including my home address and apartment number. With the HR twins gone, Lucky Tal was openly recruiting thugs from among his readership. Time to go. I showered fast, grabbed the newspapers and left. I hailed a cab and scanned the *Daily Press* in the back seat.

The main story, "BAIL FOR THE MAIL?" featured a grainy color photo from my baseball cap videocam, provided anonymously by Mary Catherine and U.S. taxpayers, of a snarling Lucky Tal Edgar at his desk. The caption underneath was sweet. "We Will Have You Killed and We'll Sleep Like Babies. *Mail* editor 'Lucky' Tal Edgar threatens *Daily Press* reporter if he reveals alleged criminal activity by *New York Mail* employees now being investigated by police."

A little video camera logo directed readers to view the full video on the website. It even caught my little run-in with security and my flying fax machine. The main story said Lucky Tal, Badger and the HR thugs were under suspicion in the serial killings, partly because of the revelation of a cell phone video taken by a pedestrian of a sloshed Pookie being hustled into a car by two detective-looking guys less than an hour before I received the text sending me to Central Park the first time. This was Ginny's exclusive. Funny thing, the guy told Ginny he first sold his fuzzy video to the *Mail*'s photo desk for $5,000 but they never ran it. Buried. Luckily he had kept his original copy on his phone. Eventually, the guy pitched it to the *Daily Press* photo desk, hoping to double his money. The story said investigators had a dragnet out for Matt Molloy and would today try to question Lucky Tal and Badger but that was not the only news.

There was a full read on the Joyce case. Sean Joyce was the white city cop who had shot and killed a twelve-year-old black boy in the Williamsburg area of Brooklyn two years earlier. First, according to *Mail* records exclusively obtained by the *Daily Press*, two *New York Mail* "Human Resources" employees—actually security staff and former cops Leslie and Molloy—bugged the family and attributed the dirt they got to a source close to Joyce. In a cell-phone chat with another cop, a devastated Joyce, himself a dad, said the dead boy who fired a blank from a realistic-looking pistol was "a poor dumbass" for waving a toy gun at a uniformed cop. At the time, the *Mail* quoted Joyce as calling his young victim a "dumbass," sparking outrage. Somehow, a civil rights group known for threatening violence was given Joyce's home address and the *Mail* photographed the resulting ugly demonstration. There were death threats. Because Joyce would not talk, the paper took long lens photographs of the Joyce kids and blackmailed their father into an exclusive interview to prevent publication of the images. The cop cried and said he wished he could bring the dead kid back. The next morning, he checked into a local motel and blew his brains out.

There was also documentation for more blackmail in major cases, more hacking into phones and computers and emails. When the *Mail* couldn't get someone to give an interview, they opened their mail and burglarized their home. There was so much incriminating material that the *Daily Press* promised that today's coverage was just the first in a series.

I had the cab pull over at a bakery, then resumed my journey. Jane answered the door of her townhouse and I could hear Skippy barking, a good bark.

"Paperboy," I told her. "Collect."

"It's too early for emotional scenes," Jane said.

But she didn't close the door. She was barefoot, in red tartan PJ pants and a lacy t-shirt.

"So let's not have an emotional scene. Let's just talk. I brought the papers and breakfast," I smiled.

"I've had enough of newspapers and killings," she said.

Skippy appeared behind her, bouncing and yipping at me, eager to play.

"Somebody wants to see me."

She gave up and let me in. I had to spend ten minutes

catching up with Skippy before I could sit down at Jane's kitchen table, as she opened and served the bagels and fixings.

"I was with Ginny only once—before us," I blurted out.

She shrugged, a tough customer.

"It's not over because it never started. She seduced me so she could pump me for information," I protested.

"You poor thing."

"She practically raped me."

"Rape is not a funny subject," she said.

"No. But you overreacted."

"Maybe," she allowed.

She toasted the bagels, put on coffee and we ate. The room was filled with morning sun and her garden out back was green and full of flowers. Skippy begged. I showed her the *Mail* first.

"I don't want to see that thing again," she said, after seeing the piece on my parents, headlined "SOUR APPLE FALLS NOT FAR FROM TREE." "What are we going to do about it?" she asked. "You have to sue them."

"I prefer to settle out of court," I said, handing her the *Daily Press*.

She put down her bagel and lox and devoured the paper.

"That's more like it! I can't believe how fast you did this. Those bastards. So, the *Mail* has been hacking into people's phones and computers and bugging them for information? They basically killed that poor cop. They all should be locked up. So, you work for the *Daily Press* now?"

"For the moment," I said. "As long as it's fun."

"You are crazy," she told me.

"I'm crazy about you, baby."

"That didn't sound anything like Bogart," she giggled.

"I was trying for Bruce Willis."

"What happens next?" she asked.

"Sorry, that's confidential."

"I could seduce you for the information."

"That's what I was hoping."

Later, in bed, she cried again.

"Did you ever feel like you've thrown your life away?" she asked.

"You're talking to a guy who's spent the last ten years in deserts and mountains, killing people for $54,000 a year."

"My husband... after he died... I thought we were this amazing couple. But his girlfriends came to his wake. It was surreal. I only knew two of them. One was his secretary, another a neighbor. The others were strangers to me. Even my poor parents noticed. A few wanted to confess to me so they could feel better. Imagine. I wanted to kill them. I wanted to kill him but I just cried, like a silly woman."

"Jane, why do you have a shrine to him?"

"To remind me not to get fooled again."

"Wow," I said.

"Yeah, sorry. You should know what you're getting into."

"I'm getting you," I told her. "You're the best thing that has ever happened in my life."

"You poor dumb bastard," she laughed.

49.

Lucky Tal and Badger were like Wile E. Coyote in the old Roadrunner cartoons, walking over the cliff, defying gravity—until they noticed they were walking on air and fell. Badger no longer looked like his name or even a weasel. He looked like a whipped dog, his head down, as he was escorted from Central Booking at Police Headquarters, his hands cuffed behind his back. Lucky Tal did not hide. He lumbered between two cops and smiled as if this were all one big joke he was playing on us all, which, in a way, it was. When he spotted me among the reporters behind the blue barricades, his face changed to a feral stare of hatred and then quickly to one of joviality. He winked at me.

At their arraignment at the Manhattan Criminal Courts Building, in the same courtroom where Aubrey Forsythe had been arraigned, Lucky Tal looked bored and impatient, like he couldn't wait to get back to work. He reminded me of senior Taliban captives. They didn't fear us and knew they would be ransomed or broken out of prison. Why wasn't this guy worried? Both men were charged with illegal wiretapping, conspiracy to commit burglary and a few other items. No felonies. That was why. The charges were nothing. They would walk.

The judge set ridiculously high bail of $50,000 cash each but a company lawyer posted it instantly. He had wads of cash in his briefcase. Lucky Tal and Badger got into a waiting limousine and took off without talking to the press. Of course, they had their own press and hours until deadline.

Izzy, Mary Catherine and Jane were waiting at a back booth in a nearby pub, where we were supposed to celebrate. Nobody felt like it.

"Those were the heaviest charges we could bring until we can investigate all the other stuff," Izzy apologized. "If we find hard evidence linking Molloy and Leslie to Pookie's killing, we can indict Molloy as a prime mover and these two assholes as co-conspirators. We're just getting started."

"I got serious vibes from Lucky Tal today," I said. "They're not going to sit still and wait for us to come after them. If they killed three people for headlines, why wouldn't they kill us to make this go away?"

"But we're not witnesses against them or anything," Jane pointed out.

"I am," I corrected her. "Badger showed me illegally obtained messages from Aubrey's and Neil's phones. I can also testify about my little video from the other day."

"They will try character assassination in their newspaper and website, probably other outlets of the company, like the TV stations, but I can't see them getting physical now that this is in the open," Mary Catherine said. "It would backfire. I mean, they hacked the First Lady's phone."

"I agree with you, Shepherd," Izzy said, casually switching his chair so he had a good view of the door. "We have to assume that these scumbags will push back. Maybe hard. Mary Catherine and I carry guns but you don't. We should talk about that."

"Thanks, but I'll be fine," I said.

"Terrific," Jane said, as a waitress arrived to take our order.

50.

The smear campaign against me suddenly vanished from the pages of the *New York Mail*. The publisher, elderly billionaire Trevor Todd, was quoted in the paper saying he had ordered a full investigation of the affair and suspended, without pay, two possible rogue employees who were suspected of alleged illegality. Amazingly, he was referring to Jack Leslie and Matthew Molloy. Could they suspend a dead man? Not a word about Lucky Tal or Badger, who were out on bail. Todd said he had absolutely no knowledge of any wrongdoing and was confident that if any mistakes had been made in the exercise of journalism, they were unintentional. Any possible mistakes were perhaps committed by two misguided employees. End of story.

The *Daily Press*, with its new star reporter—me—continued to pummel the *Mail* with past cases, including the hacking of the mayor's car. The *Mail* had figured out how to access the phone, GPS and audio system of his SUV, so they could listen in to what was being said in the vehicle, eavesdrop on telephone conversations, and always locate Hizzonner.

Skippy and I tried to get back into our routine but I was working the same long hours, just for a different newspaper.

To complicate things, Izzy insisted on calling me all the time and made me promise to let him know where I was going at all times.

"What's new, Izzy?" I asked, when he called my cell at midnight.

"A few things. You leaving work?"

"Yeah."

"Can you keep a secret?"

"No. I'm a newspaper reporter."

"Forget it."

"Just joking. You know I can keep a secret. What is it?"

"Top secret. Your buddy, Don Badger, is going to roll on his boss. The DA is setting up the deal. He says Lucky Tal made him do it. And the big boss, the old man, Todd, he's in on the whole deal. He ordered it in the first place."

"That is excellent news."

"Yup. Don't tell anyone, even your girlfriend."

"Okay, no problem. This means we got them, Izzy."

"Yeah, I think it does, amigo. Talk to you in the morning."

I hooked a cab, hopped in behind the driver, and dozed off on the way. Car horns disturbed my nap a few blocks from home. I opened my window and let the warm air wake me up. I yawned and tried to figure out what Badger testifying for the prosecution would mean. It would bring down the *Mail,* maybe Todd's whole empire. Maybe. Robert Joyce, the dead cop's brother would appreciate that but nothing could bring back the dead.

When the cab stopped I paid in cash and asked for a receipt to hand in with my expenses. I slid across the seat and opened the right rear door, as the cabbie printed the receipt. I started to step out onto the sidewalk, when I realized the cabbie, as usual, had brought me to the wrong address. My apartment was two doors down the block, in the third of the identical buildings.

That was when I saw the guy. He was a watcher, about

a hundred feet away on the opposite side of Broome Street. He was casually leaning against a lamppost on the sidewalk, watching my doorway. I froze. My gut felt hollow. He was smoking a cigarette and wearing an open long coat, far too heavy for the warm night. A black tube poked out from under the coat, pointing toward the ground. Right side. Good enough for me. I jumped back in the cab just as the man calmly turned his head in my direction, calm, just checking us out.

"Just remembered something," I told the confused cabbie. "I need to go back to work. Fast. Do a U-turn, okay. Let's go."

"Can't. This is a one-way. One sec," he said, flipping on the interior light and picking up a clipboard from the seat.

Damn.

I didn't want to tell the clueless cabbie there was maybe a dangerous man up ahead because he might freak or refuse. I just needed him to drive away. Now.

Too late. The guy down the block turned and squinted at us. His whole demeanor changed, although he was trying to fake casual. He flicked his butt into the street and began to stroll down the sidewalk toward us. I couldn't see his hands anymore.

"Either take off now or I'll get out," I told the driver.

"What's the problem?" he asked, the light still on, still in PARK.

The guy down the block was looking right at my face, lit up inside the cab.

Time to go.

I popped the passenger door, ignoring the cabbie's questions and left it open. I ran fast and low on the sidewalk, back down the block, trying to keep the cab between me and my pursuer. He was right-handed, going in front of the cab onto the sidewalk, so I jogged right, catching a glimpse of him running after me, coat flapping, bringing the gun up. I sprinted across the narrow street toward a foot-thick tree trunk and crooked my arm out like a hook, as if I was a stripper aiming for a pole. I peeked back and saw that the man had stopped in the road, aiming from the shoulder. I spun around behind the tree and sat down hard, as the weapon rattled fast. Full auto. I couldn't see it but the sound was unmistakable. An AK. He stitched my hiding place, emptying a full thirty-round magazine into the tree, some bullets sparking off the pavement. Asshole. Maybe not—two or three rounds splintered all the way through the tree, inches over my head, showering me with hot, sappy splinters and bark. I couldn't see any other trees wider than my leg on my escape route. I heard shouting from the direction of my apartment building, then three quick shots, but the rounds weren't coming my way. Another shooter? I peered around the tree. The first attacker had hesitated and was turned toward the other gunfire, unsure. Time to go. I crouched like a runner at the starting line. Now he was getting much closer, walking towards me, eyes down. Reloading.

Mistake.

I sprang and went straight for him as fast as I could, hoping he didn't have a pistol. He saw his unarmed victim coming toward him, yelling his ass off, and it shook him. He had already dropped the empty magazine and slammed a new one home and was about to pull the bolt back just as I jumped him. I tackled the gun, not him, and slammed him onto the pavement with the rifle just below his chin. He was still trying to pull the bolt so he could waste me. I faked trying to pull the weapon away from him and when he pulled back on it with all his strength, I added mine and slammed it into his face, breaking his nose. I did it again and saw blood. I did it again. More blood. Some big guy yelling my name pulled me off the gunman before I could smash his ugly face again.

"Down, boy. We need him alive, Ace," Detective Phil D'Amico said.

Phil had his NYPD gold shield dangling from a chain around his neck and a black Glock in his hand.

51.

"You got him, Shepherd," Phil told me, taking the assault rifle off my bloody assailant. "Are you hit?"

He had to say it several times before I checked myself and told him I was okay. He sat me on the curb.

"That's his blood on your hands?" Phil asked.

I looked at my hands, pale, steady, bloody. My shooter started moaning.

"Yeah. His. Mostly. I'm okay, just some scrapes and bumps," I said.

"There were two of them. The other fucker with the shotgun was waiting on the other side of your entrance door. I had to take him out. Buddy, you are like a fucking shit magnet. I'm calling Izzy. Uniforms are on the way. Just sit there and keep your hands on your knees."

"Izzy asked you to babysit me?" I asked Phil.

"Damn straight. I've been sitting on your building for days."

"Thanks, Phil. I owe you. Wait. Tell Izzy to get on Badger. If they went after me, maybe they heard about Badger ratting them out."

"Oh, shit. We're not on him. That's the DA's show. I'll tell him."

A lot of nervous cops with guns arrived and I had to hold my hands up until Phil told them it was over. Then I called Mary Catherine, who said she was on her way.

"I was wrong, Shepherd," she said. "I should have known."

I called Jane to make sure she was okay. She said she was on her way home from an emergency and that she was fine. I told her I would be at her place after I wrapped it up with the cops and had picked up some clothes from my place.

"Be careful," I said.

"These people are insane, like mad dogs," Jane said.

"This is actually good," I told her. "This is conspiracy to commit murder. Someone hired them. My guy is alive. Maybe he'll talk."

I asked Phil to get uniforms over to Jane's place and he agreed. I phoned the *Daily Press* and got Ginny on the phone to warn her. Then I filed what happened for the website and the final edition.

"Let me get this straight," Ginny said incredulously. "He chased you, you ran, hid behind a tree, he blasted the tree, some bullets came through and then you came out and ran *towards* him?"

"Yeah. He was reloading and was walking in closer for a better shot. There was no way I could outrun him or the bullets and I was out of trees. My only chance was to close the distance before he could open up again."

"I could say his gun jammed," she suggested.

"You don't believe me?"

"No. Especially the part about the stripper pole."

"I don't care. Write what you want."

Izzy arrived in twenty minutes, walked through the scene and had me tell my story and then told me he had new information.

"This editor, Don Badger, is dead. He was the apparent victim of a mugger, who slit his throat open after he left the

New York Mail, about an hour before this went down. He was found a few blocks from the paper but the body had no ID. His wallet was gone. Some sergeant had a copy of the *Daily Press*, recognized Badger's face and called me."

"Holy shit. There goes your prosecution of Lucky Tal," I said.

"I don't think so," Izzy said. "We have you and we have all those emails, memos, recordings, whatever. I'll bet once we start charging other staffers with crimes, they'll line up to testify against their boss. And we have your shooter— the live one anyway. By the way, he said you were very unsporting. He's finding it hard to talk with so many teeth missing but so far he's cooperating. He's an illegal, Turkish, name of Erdem Bayrak. Has quite a habit, judging from his track marks. And from his shitty aim. His dead friend with the shotgun isn't talking, but apparently his name was Arhan Terzi."

"Great. Will Bayrak say who hired them to go after me?"

"Yup. Told us the whole thing. You were worth $5,000 in cash."

"Each?"

"50/50 split."

"I'm insulted," I said.

"He had a note in his pocket. He was supposed to leave it on your body."

That shut me up for a few seconds.

"What does the note say?"

"It claims to be a message from the Islamic Jihad something-or-other, saying you were executed in the name of Allah for your crimes against true believers."

"Cute. So, who hired him?"

"You won't like it," Izzy warned.

"Uh-oh."

"He didn't get a name but I showed Bayrak several pictures, some from today's paper, and he made a positive ID."

"Tell me."

"Donald Badger."

"No way."

"Way. Can't shake it. I think he's telling the truth."

"What the fuck?" I said.

"That's what I said."

"Don Badger hires this clown to kill me and somebody else hires another clown to kill Badger?"

"Or the Hacker got him. Sounds like a real circus," Izzy said. "I don't believe the robbery bullshit."

"It's got to be Lucky Tal," I said. "He said he would have somebody kill me."

"I'd bet on it but we don't have anybody in Badger's homicide. Waiting for autopsy and tests. Suspect at large."

"Think Trevor Todd will hire someone to kill Lucky Tal?" I asked.

"We can hope. Clean sweep. Then God takes out the Big Boy. I think we'll go see Mr. Lucky Tal now, see where he's been tonight and when. If he's alive. Maybe he's in danger."

"Mind if I tag along?" I asked Izzy.

"Only if you wash the blood off your hands, Shepherd."

52.

We soon arrived at the tacky gold and glass Cushing Tower building uptown, where Tal Edgar had a $3 million condo. It obviously hadn't bothered him to put the owner of his building's bloody murder all over the front page. The doorman was dressed in a ridiculous red fake palace-guard uniform, complete with gold braid. We entered the glittering lobby and approached the lobby desk. The man behind it was also dressed like the flunky of an Arab prince. When Izzy told him who we were there to see, he put down his large water bottle and looked at his computer.

"Mr. Edgar is not at home."

Izzy flashed his shield. The man shrugged.

"Mr. Edgar arrived home by car service at 9:16 p.m. According to our records he left about an hour later."

"Where'd he go?" Izzy demanded.

"I have no idea, sir."

"Yes you do," Izzy pressed.

"No. No idea. But he went to the right, north."

"What's in that direction?" I asked. "Off the record."

"Lots of places. Including a bar he goes to," the man admitted, in a whisper.

"How often?" Izzy asked.

"Every night, like clockwork," he confided. His eyes were darting around. "He walks. The Crystal Castle, two blocks up. Twenty-five-dollar Martinis, rich, famous drunks. Usually comes back about two, shitfaced."

"But not tonight?" Izzy said.

He glanced at a fancy gilt filigree clock on the wall near the elevator bank.

"It's 3:20 now? Nope, not yet. He's late. Don't tell anyone I told you anything, okay?"

"Our little secret," Izzy assured him, turning away to make a call on his cell.

An hour later, uniforms had checked the bar. No one else had seen Lucky Tal this evening. If he was heading to the Crystal Castle, he never made it through the drawbridge. Izzy called the *Mail* City Desk, on speakerphone, but a kid who answered the phone refused to call Lucky Tal's cell phone or home phone.

"He calls *us*. We can't call him unless it's a real big emergency," the kid explained, like Lucky Tal was the president.

"Has he called in this evening?"

"No, sir."

"But he usually does?"

"Every night."

"This is an emergency. We need a number."

"You don't understand. I can't do that. I'll call Mr. Badger and ask him to call *you*."

"That's not going to work," Izzy snapped.

"Why not?"

Izzy hesitated. Obviously, he was reluctant to give out information. And Badger's next of kin had not yet been notified.

"This may be life and death, young man. We need to locate Mr. Edgar as soon as possible."

"I'll get my boss."

A new voice on the line. One I recognized.

"Hello?"

I tapped Izzy on the shoulder, miming to hand over his phone. He did.

"Nigel, it's Shepherd. I'm with Detective Lieutenant Izzy Negron. We're trying to find Lucky Tal. The cops need to confirm he is safe."

"Why?" Nigel asked suspiciously.

I had already gotten Nigel Bantock fired and then rehired on a punishment shift. I looked at Izzy to see how much I could say. He held his thumb and forefinger slightly apart. Tell him just a little.

"Izzy," I said, "it'll all be on the *Daily Press* website by now."

Izzy gave a resigned shrug.

"What's on the *Daily Press* website?" Nigel asked anxiously.

"That Don Badger was murdered and I was attacked tonight. Cops are worried about Lucky Tal."

"Fuck!" Nigel said. "The *Daily Press* has this already?" He started asking questions. Lots of them.

"This is an emergency, pal," shouted Izzy, cutting him off. "We need phone numbers for Tal Edgar right now. If you know where he is you need to tell us!"

"He didn't call in earlier, which is very unusual," Nigel said. "But the last person to wake Tal Edgar up late at night without a damn good reason got fired and is now selling children's shoes in a New Jersey mall. I have no idea where he is. Hang on, I'll get you his numbers and *you* can call him. Don't tell him I gave them to you."

Lucky Tal didn't answer his home or cell numbers or return the voice messages Izzy left. Our new buddy refused to take us up to his condo, so Izzy called for backup.

"Listen, my friend. We are going into Mr. Edgar's apartment—with or without you. I have reason to fear for

Mr. Edgar's safety and he cannot be located."

"You can't do that. I told you, he's not here. He left."

"Maybe you missed him coming back."

"No way."

"No bathroom breaks between ten o'clock and now?"

"No... well... It's right here, I'm not gone for long," he admitted.

"But long enough for someone to walk in and into the waiting elevator?"

"No, well, maybe, but I don't think so."

"Are you willing to bet this man's life on maybe?" Izzy asked.

"And your job?" I added.

He actually gulped.

"Let's take a look at the security videos," Izzy said.

"My screens are live only, no playback. The camera room is locked until my boss gets here in the morning. I don't have a key. I swear."

Flashing red lights filled the lobby, as two cop cars arrived and the uniforms walked in. One of them was carrying a large, heavy metal cylinder with four handles—a door ram.

"Get on your phone and call whoever you have to notify but in three minutes you are either opening Mr. Edgar's door—or we are."

In the end the man caved and opened it with a key.

Lucky Tal's place was luxurious, a tacky clone of the lobby, Louis the Sixteenth's place in the city. But His Majesty was not at home. We backed out, closing the door. Two of the cops stayed to guard the door and Izzy called the DA's office as he drove me to Jane's.

"What's next?" I asked.

"We'll babysit the apartment until Lucky Tal shows up or I get a search warrant." He sighed. "Call me immediately if you hear from Edgar or Forsythe. Remember, the last time you went off for a secret meeting it didn't go so well."

"You'll be my first call if they get in touch."

"Remember what my grandmother used to say," Izzy continued, throwing a Spanish phrase at me.

"You know I don't speak Spanish or Yiddish, Izzy."

"It means 'never get into a tight spot with a crazy person.' Good advice."

I got out at Jane's, slowly, in pain, my arm and legs sore beyond belief. I woke Jane and Skippy up because I didn't have a key.

"I just fell asleep," she said, hugging me. "Thank God you're okay."

"You're not… religious, are you?"

"God no," she laughed. "It's just an expression. Like when you sneeze I say God bless you because, in the Dark Ages, people thought your soul left your body when you sneezed and you needed divine intercession to prevent demons from jumping down your throat. I don't believe that, either."

"You use a lot of big words for someone who just woke up," I observed.

"Tell me everything that happened," she said.

"Too tired. Short version now. Lucky Tal seems to be missing. He's not at home and he missed happy hour at his nightly watering hole."

"You think someone got him, too?" she asked.

"Maybe. Or maybe he took off."

"You mean jumped bail?"

"Possible. We don't know yet. Stay tuned. I've got to crash. We can talk in the morning, okay?"

"It is morning."

"Later morning," I mumbled, falling onto her lovely bed.

53.

In the afternoon I stopped by the double desk Izzy shared with Phil at the precinct. According to Izzy, Lucky Tal was in the wind. It was a difficult image to process—the bulky editor being blown about by a breeze. Outside, it was unseasonably warm and there was no breeze at all, just heat baking off the pavement. Lucky Tal did not come home, turn up dead, or go to work. I guessed the staff at the *Mail* were grateful for the temporary relief.

Izzy was unhappy. He had placed a call to the *New York Mail* demanding to speak to the publisher, Trevor Todd, only to be informed that the billionaire had jetted off to New Zealand in his private plane.

"As long as the only evidence I have on Don Badger points to a robbery homicide, we are stalled," Izzy complained.

"What's your guess?" I asked him.

"Izzy does not guess," Phil interjected. "He *theorizes*."

"Right," I said. "What's your theory?"

"I think the big bad guys bumped off the little bad guys, took off and left me holding an empty sack," Izzy said. "The DA says the prosecution of Badger is moot and they can't do a fucking thing to Lucky Tal—unless or until he fails to show up for his next court date, which is next month."

"Moot?" I asked.

"Lawyer word for 'pointless,'" Phil said.

"Oh, right."

"I have *some* news," Izzy said. "The CSI guys, always eager to live up to the high standard of their TV counterparts, have done a Sherlock. They matched the soles of the shoes Jack Leslie was wearing when he died with footprint casts taken from the scene of Pookie Piccarelli's murder in Central Park."

"That is good news," I said. "So you can tie them to at least one of the killings."

"Yep. They have another set that may be Matt Molloy's but he and his shoes are not available for comparison. Yet. That reminds me. You, your cameraman and your girlfriend need to give us the shoes you were wearing at the scene—so the techies can eliminate them."

"They need our shoes?"

"Yeah, easier that way. Ask your girlfriend and the *Mail* photographer."

"I don't work there anymore. He'll be the giant footprints."

"Okay, thanks for not making me get a warrant."

"No problem," I said, yawning. "You see Trevor Todd's printed statement in the *Mail* today?"

"He said he knows nothing about nothing," Izzy scoffed. "That's not what their own memos say. The lawsuits are already starting."

"It will be a tsunami," I predicted.

"That's probably why they've all fled the jurisdiction," said Phil.

"What have you got on Don Badger's murder?" I asked.

Izzy pulled out a file and spread several glossy eight-by-ten photographs across his desk. They showed Badger on his back on a dirty pavement, a yawning gap at the base of his throat. He was covered in blood. Everywhere, as if someone had poured buckets of it onto him. His usual smirk was fixed forever.

"It's sort of like Neil Leonardi and Nolan Cushing," I said. "But bloodier."

"Sort of. Different weapon, though," Izzy said.

"Who says?"

"The M.E. He says number one and number two—Leonardi and Cushing—were killed with identical edged blades but number three—Pookie Piccarelli—was different. And Don Badger was killed with yet another type of blade, but similar to that used on Piccarelli. That is, if you believe they can guess a weapon from the wound."

"Can they?" I asked.

Izzy and Phil both shrugged.

"Who knows?" Izzy said. "It's whatever you can get a jury to believe. The commissioner—who reads the papers and watches too many movies—wants us to psychologically profile the Hacker. He actually wants to invite the freaking FBI in to put the killer on the couch."

"You don't believe in profiling, I take it?"

"It's a crock of shit," Izzy snorted. "Fortune telling. Never caught a single fucking killer. Not one. Makes great TV, though."

"The killer is disturbed and resentful," Phil intoned in a goofy voice. "He is a male between the ages of twenty-one and ninety-nine, living in America, who likes to kill people. You can't miss him."

"I will believe profilers when they give me the name and address of a killer," Izzy declared. "Or winning Lotto numbers."

"So, what you're saying," I said, "is that profiling is moot."

We all laughed but not for long.

"I don't see any Altoid next to Badger in this shot," I said.

"Nope," said Izzy, "that's another difference. But they're small things. Maybe the CSIs on the scene missed it because they had no idea at the time that the death was linked to the

Hacker case. Badger wasn't identified until later."

"Is his blood work back yet?" I asked.

"Preliminary," Phil said. "No indication of drugs, but he had been drinking. His B.A.C. was point two nine. Drunk. Full tox will take longer."

"So," I ventured, "victims one and two were killed indoors and they were doped up. Either they took it themselves or someone drugged them, right?"

"Right," Izzy replied.

"But victims three and four were outside and not so drugged, just hacked," I said.

"Uh-huh. Maybe the later murders were rushed because it was in public," Izzy replied.

I thought about it. They thought about it. I looked at the pictures. Izzy told me he and Phil had places to go and people to see. We walked out of the precinct together. It was raining lightly and a steamy gray breeze was pushing dirt around. A pedal-cab rickshaw rolled by, pulled by a wiry guy in red, white and blue coveralls. Two Asian tourists in the back took our photos on separate cameras.

"Can I ask a dumb question?" I asked.

"That was a dumb question," Phil chuckled.

"Seriously," I continued, "just for the sake of argument, what if the last two killings, Pookie and Badger, were done by different people?"

Izzy and Phil looked at each other.

"That wasn't dumb, it was sadistic," Izzy moaned.

"Because it would mean three different killers, the Hacker, plus the Molloy/Leslie double act. Or five, counting the gunmen—Erdem Bayrak and Arhan Terzi—at my place. Maybe Badger wasn't killed by Molloy. What if what Bayrak said about Badger hiring him was a lie? Maybe he was hired by someone else higher up the tree to kill Badger first, then me? Do Badger and make people think I did it, then waste me and blame it on Islamic extremists, case closed?"

"You're complicating things," Phil said. "Jack Leslie and probably his partner, Matt Molloy, were at the Pookie Piccarelli scene, and there's a video that appears to show them taking her off the street. They killed Pookie in a manner similar to the previous two Hacker homicides, which they also committed. If we assume that the Human Resources crew killed three celebs to boost circulation, it fits. They then tried to do you, because you were onto them, but Leslie got dead and Molloy vanished. His disappearance after trying to snuff you demonstrates consciousness of guilt. The Hacker murders are over. The attempted hit on you was to shut you up and cover up the motivation behind the Hacker killings, as was the murder of Don Badger, which was probably Molloy. It didn't matter if Don Badger was killed in a different way—it was meant to look like a mugging, not fit in with the Hacker deaths. So the score is three dead Hacker victims, Leonardi, Cushing and Piccarelli, probably by Leslie and Molloy, two missing bad guys—Molloy and Edgar, and three dead bad guys—Arhan Terzi, Don Badger and Jack Leslie. And Erdem Bayrak in custody."

It was the most I had ever heard Phil talk at a stretch. "Does that mean the good guys are winning?" I asked.

"Right now, it looks like the game is just postponed because of rain," Izzy said.

"What if the DA called Tal Edgar back into court on Monday?" Phil asked. "You know, call an unscheduled bail hearing, try to get it revoked based on new evidence?"

"To find out where he is before a month goes by?" I asked.

"I like that idea," Izzy brightened. "We ask a judge to up his bail or revoke it because we uncovered new evidence."

"Yes," Phil agreed.

"What new evidence?" I wondered.

"We could RICO them," Phil suggested.

"I love it," Izzy grinned. "If he doesn't show up, we get a warrant. If he does, we can have the DA put him in front of a grand jury. He can either testify or plead the Fifth Amendment against self-incrimination. Beautiful."

My confused expression amused the detectives.

"RICO is the Racketeer Influenced and Corrupt Organizations Act," Izzy explained. "We use it to go after the mob."

"You're going to say in court that the *New York Mail* is like a Mafia family?" I asked.

"If the DA will agree," Phil said.

"Has this ever been done before?" I asked.

They both shook their heads and laughed.

"They are running an illegal scheme in which they are killing people for profit and to silence them. Sounds like wiseguys to me," Izzy concluded.

The pen is mightier than the sword.

54.

I spent the weekend with Jane and Skippy, just living. There were no more murders or breaking developments, much to the disappointment of my new editor at the *Daily Press*, a red-faced fireplug of a guy named Barney Blood. But Blood was content with the almost endless supply of scandal from the *Mail* files I had obtained, courtesy of the memory stick Izzy slipped me. Jane and I walked Skippy together, stayed up late, went out to eat. We drank too much, fooled around a lot and slept in.

"I'm a vet," Jane said, as we lounged in bed. "My diagnosis is we are eating like pigs, drinking like fish and fucking like bunnies."

She giggled at her own joke.

"How do you know fish drink?" I inquired. "Have you ever seen one with a glass?"

"They do nothing but drink. They are in the drink."

"You've got me there, Doc."

"No, I've got you here," she said, hoisting me by my own petard.

I looked up the expression online and discovered that it was about demolition men in the Middle Ages, who used gunpowder in big pots to blow open castle doors but sometimes used too much powder and became dead projectiles.

Later, as we got sleepy, we hugged and Jane asked me something so quietly I had to ask her to repeat it.

"I said 'is it over?'"

"You mean the case?"

"Yes."

"I don't know. No. Not yet."

"I wish it were," she said dreamily. "Neil was a slimeball. Cushing was a vile human being. I can understand why somebody wanted to kill them but that idiot girl, Porkie?"

"Pookie," I corrected her. "Relax, we're safe."

"That's only part of it," she said.

"What else?"

But she was asleep and breathing softly on my chest, the distant, pleasant aromas of her perfume and the Bordeaux from dinner scenting our bed. Wine and roses. I could get used to this.

On Monday, I tried to figure a way to end it, to figure it out. Barney Blood had assigned half the *Daily Press* reporters to work on leads from my documents and Ginny was zooming all over town, interviewing people who had been screwed over and spied upon by the *Mail*. To me, it was a pile-on, more of the same, just different names but the professionals didn't agree. When I got bored, I told them I was working on another part of it. They kept my name on the stories and left me alone. Ginny was happy to get more ink. There was no sign of Molloy or Lucky Tal.

On Tuesday, Lucky Tal failed to show up for his RICO court hearing. The District Attorney had told the judge that they were investigating the *New York Mail* as a possible Racketeer Influenced and Corrupt Organization and demanded that

Lucky Tal appear and respond to the charges. He didn't. The judge issued an arrest warrant—just like in Aubrey Forsythe's case.

I remembered my dumb question about whether several different people had committed the murders and thought of another dumb question. Why hadn't Aubrey come out of hiding? First, the *Mail* blamed the killings on me, then the *Daily Press*—with actual evidence—blamed them on the *Mail*. You would think Aubrey would have come forward and declared his innocence. But, with a text, he had called me to the second murder, the foreclosure on Cash Cushing, so he must have done at least that one. *If* he was the one using his phone to send the text. I still didn't think he had killed Neil and we knew Leslie and Molloy had probably killed Pookie. They had texted me on a new phone, pretending to be Aubrey. What if they had kidnapped Aubrey, like they tried to do to me, and used his phone to text me an invitation to Cushing's murder as well? That would mean they had Aubrey and were using him as a fall guy. Was he still alive? Maybe Matt Molloy and Lucky Tal Edgar were playing cards somewhere, with Aubrey tied up in a back room. But, if they would kill all these people, including me, why would they let Aubrey live?

Aubrey was probably dead, I decided. My HR pals must have committed Hacker murders two and three, Cushing and Pookie, pinning them on Aubrey, the fugitive. But it seemed unlikely they had killed Neil Leonardi. The *Mail* had had no exclusive—until I gave it to them, purely by chance. If you kill for circulation, obviously you have the exclusive. Maybe Neil's murder had been committed for more personal reasons and the *Mail* just jumped on the bandwagon to cash in on the story for the second and third killings? So who really killed Neil Parmesan?

I called Izzy with my new theory. He disagreed.

"The first one is like the second but not the third," he

said. "The first two seemed more... controlled. But I like the part about Leslie and Molloy using Aubrey Forsythe's phone to contact you. That's good, thanks. We can theorize that Molloy also killed Forsythe. The DA might like that. Maybe it was a big murder club, like the sex club on Pookie's show." He laughed.

"Sex club?" I asked.

"You never watched *Bitch Blanket Bimbos*?" Izzy asked.

"Never saw any of the victims' shows," I said proudly.

"You never saw *You're Foreclosed* or *Food Fight*?"

"Nope."

"You're kidding. Got Netflix?"

"Yep."

"You gotta treat yourself."

I did. I had nothing else to do.

55.

Jane did not have Netflix, so, when she went to work the next morning, Skippy and I went back to my place. I didn't have to look far to find what I was searching for. *Bitch Blanket Bimbos* was near the top, listed as "Popular on Netflix," and, as advertised, the show did have a "sex club." The show itself consisted mostly of drinking, loud arguments, sex and vomiting by high-school dropouts from New Jersey. It turned out Pookie wasn't quite Italian-American at all. She was a Balkan refugee who was adopted by an Italian family. The sex club involved Pookie playing a different version of beer pong and then asking some strange guy in a beach bar to show her his "club," after which they would have sex, usually in public, often with other "dudes" and "babes" joining in the fun, with body parts blacked out and discreet cutting. The drunken guy would then be added to an online interactive gallery of sex club members, on whom the audience could vote and rate their prowess and other qualities, like staying power—of his hair gel. Over eight long hours, I learned a great deal about the abilities of the late Miss Pookie Piccarelli, but little else. I did a lot of fast-forwarding but never saw Jack Leslie or Matt Molloy join her club, or anything else remotely resembling a clue to her killing. Fortunately, there was only one season made up of twenty half-hour episodes to watch or I would have committed suicide. The girl was a jerk with a drinking problem but she did not deserve to be butchered. I called it a day and Skippy and I went back to Jane's.

The next morning, after walking Skippy and eating breakfast, the self-inflicted torture continued. Right behind Pookie in the Netflix hit parade was *You're Foreclosed*, with his royal highness Cash Cushing sitting, literally, on a golden throne and deciding which unfortunate family to throw into the street next. They all pleaded their cases to him, as he made snarky comments about how it was their own fault and they were greedy and got in over their heads. Listening to a slimeball who was born into millions brag about how he was a self-made man was sickening. Especially since—as I discovered from Wikipedia—Cash himself went bankrupt in the 1990s while operating the world's tackiest casino in Atlantic City. He actually went broke in a business where morons bring you their money and throw it at you.

One woman with cancer, who had lost her job and her health insurance, pleaded with Cash to cut her monthly payment so she and her kids would not lose their home.

"It's not your home," Cash snapped. "It's the bank's home because you made the wrong decisions and now you want me to pay for them. This is the best thing that can happen to you. You're foreclosed."

When he said the catchphrase it was accompanied by a whooshing noise and "You're Foreclosed" lettering on the screen, along with special theme music. The woman sobbed. The woman killed herself three days later, so her life insurance settlement would pay off the mortgage. On the next episode Cash praised her for finally making a sound business decision.

The answer to the question "Who would want to kill Nolan Cushing?" was simple. Everybody. Including me.

But I still did not detect anything that would help solve his murder. The only direct link between Cushing and the *Mail* was the fact that Tal Edgar lived in one of Cash's buildings.

That killed my second day of reality-show surfing. I decided I wasn't getting paid enough.

I swore my third day would be my last. *Food Fight* was also getting serious play after the murders. It had begun airing the previous year and two seasons were available. Neil's murder had interrupted the filming of the third. It was pretty tame in comparison with the other shows. Aubrey was a bloated bastard, who lived to trash restaurants and humiliate people. Neil was sly but actually sort of charming. Each show had Aubrey pigging out on an industrial scale, while playing the gourmet. He would cook, with Neil assisting. It was obvious that Neil hated Skippy, from the way he would insult him in a fake-sweet voice. During the first such instance, Skippy came running in from my bedroom and barked at the screen. He watched the rest of the episodes with me.

The basic script was that Aubrey would go to a restaurant and make nasty notes on a tape recorder, the prelude to a trashing in the *Tribune*. In one episode, Cash Cushing made a two-second appearance at a gala dinner attended by Aubrey and Neil but the two men just waved and smiled at one another. Interesting. I fast-forwarded through a lot of the footage, looking for Skippy coverage, since that was what the last argument between Neil and Aubrey had been about—Neil kicking Skippy. The show was very repetitive. Only the names of the restaurants and the menus changed. In the second season, it was much the same. The housekeeper, Adela, made an appearance. I remembered talking to her on the phone when I'd been checking up on Skippy. I had read her voice right. She *was* an elderly Hispanic lady. Her screen time was limited, probably because she kept looking at the camera. Once she appeared with a young teenage boy behind her, who was leading Skippy on a leash. I rewound and hit PLAY.

It was strange to see the kitchen before the murder. The boy was the dog walker and his name was Bobby. He was shy and nervous on camera. Neil came over to try to put him at ease but the boy seemed to have stage fright. Neil tousled the lad's hair and Aubrey snapped at Neil. The boy left and Aubrey began to prepare a meal. I played the scene over. It was subtle but the kid shrank away from Neil's touch. It seemed just a friendly gesture but there was something odd in the way the boy recoiled. Also in Aubrey's overreaction. I watched it again, then fast-forwarded to find more footage of Bobby but he never reappeared.

I finished up the episodes and celebrated with a beer. I found one of my notebooks and called the number for the field producer of *Food Fight*. She did not remember the kid and tried to end the conversation.

"Doesn't everybody have to sign release forms to be on a TV show?" I asked her.

She sighed. "Yes, that's true. Hold on, I'll look it up." I heard the clicking of a computer keyboard. "He was only in that one episode, the dog walker, a minor, fourteen years old. We had to get his grandma to co-sign the release. She's the housekeeper. *Was*."

"Adela?"

"That's right. Adela and Bobby Enriquez."

She gave me an address on the Lower East Side, in an area called Alphabet City.

"What's this about?" she asked, smelling a story.

"I'm talking to all the people on the show. I'm doing a book," I lied.

"Cool. We should shoot you for the new season."

"New season?" I asked. "I thought the show was over?"

"With these numbers? Are you kidding? It's called *Food Fight III: The Investigation*. We have a detective, a psychic and a new chef, working together to solve the killings."

I suppressed a laugh. I told her it sounded great and we would get together soon—another fib. I called the library at the *Daily Press* and asked them to check Bobby and Adela Enriquez for past clippings but they found nothing. I googled the names. I got a huge number of hits but they were common names and none seemed to be the people I was looking for. I was done with fake reality shows. I wanted to be done with the whole case, so I decided to run over to Alphabet City before heading back to Jane's place. Talk about reality.

56.

It was a rough neighborhood named for Avenues A, B, C and D that ran north and south. The address was on the second floor of a beat-up tenement on a run-down block. The peephole window wobbled a bit.

I knocked. I heard movement but the door didn't open. "Mrs. Enriquez?" I asked in my best friendly voice. "Adela Enriquez? My name is Shepherd. Do you remember me? We spoke on the phone after Mr. Leonardi's murder, about Skippy. I've been investigating the murder."

The door opened a crack and her face appeared, barely, above the security chain. She looked tired.

"Can we talk?"

She shrugged, dropped the chain and let me in. The place was lemon-scented and immaculate, befitting her profession. Her purple sofa was glazed with plastic covers, under a large framed black velvet portrait of Jesus, his head shimmering with holiness, dripping crown of thorns in place. Her glass and brass coffee table had several greeting cards standing open on top. I tried to read them but they were in Spanish.

"Please sit down, officer. Can I make you some coffee?"

As I crinkled the plastic on the couch, I explained to her that I was a reporter, working with the police.

"Oh," she said, probably reconsidering her coffee offer. "You're the one who wrote those bad things about Mr. Aubrey?"

"I would say I wrote some bad, some good, just as he said it."

"Is he back?" she asked, brightening.

"No. Not yet. Have you heard from him?" I asked. She shook her head sadly. "You don't have a job right now, do you?"

"No. Mr. Neil is dead," she said, crossing herself. And Mr. Aubrey is gone. Nothing for me to do. Unless he comes back."

"Maybe your grandson Bobby has heard from Aubrey? Is he in school?"

She gaped at me for several seconds. Her sob was so explosive it scared the hell out of me. I jumped. She ran out of the room shrieking in Spanish. I stood up, unsure what to do. She was crying in the kitchen. I followed her and asked if I could help. She was blowing her nose.

"I'm sorry, sir... Bobby is in the hospital..."

"I'm so sorry. What happened? Is he sick?"

"Yes... My grandson is in God's hands." She blew her nose again.

I couldn't get anything more out of her. I gave her my number and asked her to call if I could help. She said yes, she would, but I knew she would never call.

Outside, an old lady was sweeping the front steps. I told her I just heard about poor Bobby Enriquez. The woman also crossed herself. It seemed to be contagious. I asked what hospital he was in. I wanted to send flowers. She told me he was in Ward's Island. The way she said it, it sounded like a death sentence. I asked when he was hospitalized and how he was doing. She shook her head like I was stupid and returned to her sweeping.

On the street, I got a listing and called the hospital, the

Ward's Island Rehabilitation Institute. I asked for Bobby Enriquez's room.

"The patient does not have a phone, sir," the operator told me.

"Really? Why not?"

"Sir, the patient is in the critical care unit."

"You mean, like he's in a coma or something?"

"I have no idea, sir, and we cannot discuss medical information over the phone. Are you a relative?"

"No, just a concerned friend, thanks."

I hung up. I considered calling back and pretending to be a doctor but I didn't know enough. I looked around the neighborhood. A bodega on the corner had three teens with droopy pants in front, drinking something out of paper bags and passing a joint around, like it was legal. Two had red t-shirts on and the third had a red bandana on his head. Gang colors? I went over.

"Afternoon, officer," the one in the bandana giggled.

They were high. Or low.

"I'm not a cop," I told them, perhaps unwisely. "I'm a reporter for the… for the *Daily Press*. You guys know Bobby Enriquez from the white building over there? He's in the hospital."

"An' he ain't comin' out, meng," Bandana said.

"Why?" I asked.

"Too much fun," Bandana said. "Got run over by a Mexican brown bus. Dumbass shoulda known better."

"An overdose?" I said, shocked, unable to connect the young, clean-cut kid from Netflix with heavy drugs.

"He and his *abuela* too good for everybody but not now. Bobby's brains guaca-fucking-mole," Bandana laughed, joined by his pals.

"Somebody do that to him?" I demanded. "Give him a hot shot?"

"He did it—who you think? One day he churchin', then

he wanna be outlaw. Not for long. Oh well."

They giggled. I tried to get a time frame out of them, when he had overdosed—before or after Neil was parmesaned—but they were in a different time zone. I walked away.

Why would a nice kid like that go bad? Of course, I didn't know he was a good kid. I just saw a few seconds of video. His grandmother wouldn't talk about it because she was ashamed. Or maybe something else... I could ask Izzy to check it out but that meant they would question the grandmother and rake it all up again. No kid, no case. Oh well.

57.

I went to visit Jane at work. She was busy, so I chatted up her assistant, Xana, at the front counter. Today, the message on the tight black t-shirt stretched over Xana's chest was SAVE A LIFE. ADOPT A HOMELESS PET. I couldn't tell if she had gotten new piercings or had just changed the jewelry in the holes. I wondered why such a pretty girl would go to such extremes to make herself look scary. I wondered why I was thinking like some old guy.

"Hey, it's Neil Parmesan," Xana giggled. "That headline still cracks me up. Still working on the Hacker case?"

"Yeah. Just following up a few things," I said vaguely, hoping she would drop it.

"I wish I had an exciting job like you," she gushed. "What's it like to be shot?" Her pretty eyes were wide under stainless-steel eyebrow hoops.

"At first you only feel electricity, heat," I told her. "Or nothing at all. Pretty quick, it hurts like a bastard. Your bones burn."

"Cool. So, you're, like, a detective, too. What's it like, you know, investigating murders? Like CSI?"

"No. They would have found the killers by now. Sometimes it's depressing," I told her truthfully, hoping to turn her off. "Like today, I thought I had a hot lead and it turned out to be nothing—just a kid called Bobby who overdosed on drugs and may be in a coma."

Xana's smile vanished.

"Oh my God, I know," Xana agreed. "Poor Bobby. It was so terrible when we heard. Such a sweet kid. I never thought he would get involved with dope."

I was quiet for about a minute, as she rambled on about what a good kid he was—until I realized I was holding my breath.

"You knew Bobby?" I asked, desperately hoping I sounded casual.

"Sure. He worked here part time. He walked dogs, helped out. Sometimes went out with me in the Catmobile. Really nice boy. Jane really loved him, too. We all did. His grandma is just devastated. I mean, brain damage? Terrible. And on top of that, she has no job now because..."

"I know. I just spoke to her."

A weird thing about people is if they think you know something they want to tell you all about it but if they think you don't know, they won't tell you. I calmly asked her about Bobby and let her talk, trying to steer the conversation around to Neil and Aubrey. She knew a little about Bobby but had only seen Neil and Aubrey a couple of times, when they brought Skippy in.

"Bobby also walked Mr. Cushing's dog, ya know?"

"He had a dog?" I thought back to the Cushing crime scene, remembered photographs of Cash embracing a ball of golden fur. "Wait, a corgi, right?"

"Yup. Named Bubbles. Mr. Cushing had joint custody with his last wife. Lucky Bubbles was in his own room in the back when it happened. He'd have been traumatized." She paused. "Funny how both of them got hacked—Mr. Leonardi and Cushing. 'Cashes out'—that headline killed me. How do you think of them?"

"Reporters don't do the headlines. Editors do that," I explained. "So, Bobby also walked Cash Cushing's dog, Bubbles? How did that work? Did he have a key and the alarm code for when no one was home?"

"Oh. What? Yeah, sure. Clients give Jane keys and codes if we need them. Why?"

"No reason. Do you remember if Bobby overdosed before or after Neil Leonardi was killed?"

She looked at me and licked her lips, thinking.

"Not sure. It was around that time," she said. "We didn't find out about Bobby until later, you know. Jane told us. Ask her. She might know."

I thanked her and turned to leave.

"You going?" Xana asked in a flirtatious mock-hurt tone. "Doctor Jane will be out in, like, three minutes."

"Tell her I just realized I have to go to the office and I'll call her later," I said, rushing out.

I went home, grabbed a snack, fed Skippy and took him for a walk. I found a friendly cabbie who took an extra ten bucks to let Skippy ride with me. It was a big deal to get Skippy into the *Daily Press* building. Security acted like I was bringing in a lion. Skippy was the center of attention. Everybody had to pet him and tell me how beautiful he was, like he was my kid. Skippy loved it, puffing out his white chest proudly. Even Ginny loved him. He seemed to like her too. Go figure. When Ginny asked me what I had for the paper, I said nothing yet.

I sat at my new cubicle and began thinking thoughts I did not want to think. I started at the beginning, before Neil's murder and tried to figure it out. Guessing did not count. Who. Why. How. I called Izzy and asked him about the drugs in Neil's body.

"Hold on," Izzy said. "Why?"

"I'm trying to reconstruct the killings in chronological order in my mind."

"More Sherlock stuff? Okay, *bubbulah*. Here it is. Autopsy on Leonardi says he had THC, grass, and halothane. I won't bore you with the associated metabolic breakdown by-products."

I asked him to spell it. Halothane.

"What the hell is it?"

"The M.E. says it's a general anesthetic."

"And the same shit was in Cash Cushing's system?"

"Yup."

"So Neil Leonardi and Mr. Foreclosure took or were given it before they were killed? Think it was at parties? Aubrey and Cash moved in the same social circles."

"Really? The M.E. says halothane can be inhaled, injected or taken in liquid form. He says it wasn't administered in a liquid form because it wasn't in the stomach, so I guess it was either injected or inhaled. Why?"

"Pookie had no halothane in her blood, right?"

"Um… Right."

"Same for Badger—no halothane?"

"Correct."

"Okay, thanks, Izzy."

"Wait, Shepherd, amigo. What are you up to? Please don't let me read something in the paper first."

"It's just me trying to work it out. I promise you I will tell you before I put anything in the paper."

"Okay."

I surfed the web, my stomach churning, as Skippy napped at my feet. I googled halothane. It was an anesthetic, as Izzy said. But not for people. Newer drugs with fewer side effects meant that doctors rarely used halothane, except in developing countries. But veterinarians used halothane. A lot. On animals. There were even portable gas delivery systems for vets to knock out animals, large and small, while making house calls. Vets also performed surgery. I thought back to what Jane had said just before she drifted off to sleep on Sunday. Maybe Neil and Cushing deserved it.

I thought back to the footage of Bobby, flinching back from Neil's touch. Abuse? Surely that might have been enough to turn a good kid into a self-destructive junkie. If Jane knew about the abuse, why didn't she tell the cops? Bobby walked Aubrey's dog and also Cash Cushing's. Her office had keys and alarm codes to the first two murder scenes. Why would she not tell anyone that? Was she seeking revenge on Neil? Did she serve up Neil Parmesan and try to pin it on Aubrey?

Fuck. Fuck. Fuck. Fuck. Fuck.

No.

Okay, Neil had a prior arrest for child molestation.

Maybe he molested Bobby. Let's assume that. The boy went on a suicidal drug binge and ended up brain-dead. Maybe Neil deserved to die, even if New York State law says he only deserved twelve to fifteen years behind bars. But Neil also kicked Skippy. The bastard was asking for it. What about Cash Cushing? He was also a slime who caused the death of another but who also faced no criminal consequences. I'm also cool with that. Fuck Cushing. He's foreclosed. Is Jane a serial killer? What if she is? So am I. I can forgive her, let it go. Mary Catherine and I can use her skills on our team. We could still be happy.

Bullshit.

Who would kill someone instead of calling the cops, cut off his ass, lightly sauté it in the fires of insanity and then slip the tasty dish to his husband, the food critic? Someone who was around the bend. A psycho-fucking-path, that's who. Last I checked, there was no cure. No psychopath pill, no operation. What would happily-ever-after look like with Jane? I would have to do all the cooking. I was thinking it all out, all the possibilities, the maybes and definites but I was interrupted.

"What's up, Brainiac?" Ginny asked, plopping down in the seat next to me. I quickly cleared my screen.

"Nothing," I lied.

"Bullshit. You've got that look," she said.

"What look?" I asked innocently.

"Like you're about to pull somebody's pants down," she laughed. "C'mon. We're on the same side now."

"Are we, Ginny? I thought you were only on your own side."

"Look, I'm sorry about... *some* stuff I did. I want to be friends like we were before, you know? That time I stayed at your place? I like you, Shepherd."

"Okay, Ginny. I like you too. I've got nothing solid yet. If I come up with something for the paper, I promise I will include you. Really."

"Okay, thanks, Shepherd. Want to grab some Thai food?"

"Maybe tomorrow. Got a date tonight."

"With that slinky vet?" she asked, on her way back to her desk.

"Yup."

"Too bad."

I called and made a reservation for two for dinner at Bistro du Bois. Then I called Jane. Dinner at our favorite place and then a quiet night at home? She said she was still working and suggested I pick her up there.

I needed to think. Skippy and I headed out, two bachelors on the town. As we walked uptown, Skippy spotted a bitch on another leash and was drawn to her like a furry magnet.

"No, Skippy," I warned him, pulling him back. "You don't know her. She may bite."

58.

I looked at my meal carefully.

"What's wrong with your Cherry Duck?"

"Nothing. Not a thing. It's yummy."

I decided I would not be like every amateur detective in a mystery novel and confront her with my suspicions. As soon as they did that they ended up shot or strapped to the railroad tracks, at the mercy of the fiend.

My fiend looked adorable in a clingy purple top and black tennis shorts.

I asked her if she played tennis. Of course she did. I decided to casually tell her what I had been doing. I started by recounting my marathon reality TV film festival, which she already knew about. Then I mentioned the sweet-looking teenaged boy who was walking Skippy. Funny thing, I said, gnawing on my duck drumstick. Neil tousled the kid's hair and the kid acted oddly. I told her I found out the kid's name. I said his name. I mentioned I had spoken to his grandma and that the poor kid had apparently suffered some kind of brain damage. Drugs. Around the time of Neil's murder. She did not react. Not at all. I asked her what she thought.

"About what?" she asked, sipping more wine.

"About this kid."

"Shame," she said.

I waited for her to tell me she knew Bobby and that he had walked the dogs of the first two murder victims. Nothing. She changed the subject, told me about her day. I changed the subject back.

"I think Aubrey is dead."

"Really?" she asked. "So somebody else texted you that night and sent us to find Cushing's body?" Now she seemed more interested.

"I don't know," I said. "But if Aubrey was already dead, it was the person who really killed Cushing. Probably Neil Leonardi, too."

"Wow. Have you told your friend Izzy about this yet?"

"No, I haven't told Izzy. I don't have any proof. Just speculation, possibilities."

"But I thought your crazy co-workers at the *Mail* were doing the killings to boost newspaper sales?"

"I think they just killed Pookie Piccarelli. That was why it was so different from the first two murders," I said. "But there's no way to prove any of this."

"That's a shame," Jane said.

She seemed lost in thought. At one point, she seemed about to speak but changed her mind and faked a cough.

"What?" I asked her.

"Nothing," Jane said.

Jane abruptly said she had to run back to the Arthur Animal Hospital after dinner and would talk to me later. I didn't ask why. During coffee and dessert, Jane became animated, chatting about her tennis team in college and then her veterinary internship, including a stint at the Central Park Zoo.

"How do you treat animals that are too big to bring into an animal hospital? Like tigers?"

"House calls," Jane smiled. "Den calls, burrow calls, pit stops."

"You really love animals," I observed.

"More than some people, sometimes," she agreed. That seemed to set her thinking again. Me too. I took a small red metal tin out of my pocket, opened the lid and offered it to Jane.

"Ah, my favorite," Jane said, reaching for an Altoid—but her hand froze mid-reach.

She gave me a puzzled look and took a peppermint. I had promised myself I would not try to confront her, or insult her, with suspicious questions.

"These are the same ones left by the killer, aren't they?"

"Yeah. I bought a box for fun," I replied, trying very hard to sound friendly.

"Maybe you're the killer," she said, grinning a friendly grin.

"I'm *a* killer but not *the* killer," I said.

"What about me?" Jane asked. "Could I be the killer?"

"You don't have any motive," I answered. "Do you?"

"No. I don't. But I do like Altoids."

"That's no crime," I said.

I told Jane I also had work to do and I kissed her goodbye on the sidewalk and said I would call her later. She stood there as I untied Skippy from the lamppost where he'd been hanging out and watched us walk away.

After Skippy took care of his business, we just kept walking and thinking. At least *I* was. I began talking to Skippy.

"Why do I suspect Jane might be involved? There are thousands of vets out there who would have access to halothane and scalpels. Why her?"

Skippy did not reply.

"Because Jane had keys to two of the properties. And because she never admitted knowing Bobby, much less that Neil might have been abusing him," I answered myself. "She should have come clean with the dirty little secret. But she pretended as if she had never heard of the boy. I went too far with the Altoid. But she was laughing about it, so maybe she doesn't suspect I suspect. Or maybe she does. She got a funny look and her internal gears were obviously spinning, although she said zip. Should I tell Izzy?"

Skippy sniffed a hydrant.

"Yes. But if there's no proof, he won't be able to arrest her. And there's no proof. And of course ratting out my new girlfriend as a possible serial killer might create some tension between us."

I thought back to the first killing. I didn't know Jane when Neil was killed. She sat next to me at the funeral. Was that a coincidence or did she choose to sit next to me? We found Cushing's body together. It couldn't have been her. But he was actually killed earlier. How much earlier? That was key. I had to ask Izzy the time of death. And she was with me when Pookie died. Actually she was with me hours earlier but we already know Jack Leslie and Matt Molloy did the murder. The timing on Cash Cushing's murder was it. Jane and I had dinner at that Asian restaurant. She wore that hot little black dress and diamonds and almost nothing else. What time was that? I had to nail it down. Two numbers. When Jane met me at the restaurant and when Cushing was hacked. Then I would know if Jane had time to kill Cushing and arrive for dinner. Two numbers, one answer. But, even if she had plenty of time to gas him into unconsciousness and open his throat, it would only be circumstantial. Not enough evidence to bust her.

"There has to be something else," I told Skippy, who turned to me expectantly.

My iPhone chirped twice. A text. I opened it. It was from Jane.

> We need to talk. I have something important to tell you. Meet me at work asap.

Interesting. This is the part where I blunder into the animal hospital and she kills me. I don't think so. Looks like the Altoid thing tipped her. Or just me mentioning that I knew about Bobby and had spoken to his grandma. She did ask if I had told Izzy about it and I said no. Perfect. This proves she did it. She's desperate to take me out before I tell Izzy. Maybe.

I could call Izzy but what could he do? I'll go. The hospital is on a busy corner but I won't go in if she's there alone. I will recon the place and call her out of her ambush, not walk into it. Yes. If she's the one, she has already gotten the better of two men who are now dead. Three, if Aubrey is among the departed. But they were soft civilians, not tough guys like me, and none of them knew it was coming. We will not be alone. And I have Skippy. Yeah.

What was it Izzy said, his Spanish expression? "Never get caught in a tight spot with a crazy person?"

Good advice.

59.

Skippy woke me, barking loudly from another room. I was freezing, shivering, cold tears dripping from my eyes. I felt tired. Who was I crying for? There was a chemical stench in the air, mixed with something bad. I opened my eyes.

I was in the hospital, a sterile treatment room. What the fuck? I was on a steel table, looking up at a florescent light on the ceiling. A counter nearby held equipment: a white plastic box smaller than a paperback book, with a clear plastic tube coming out of it, ending in something that looked like a small rubber mask. Blue lettering said it was an AERONEB. Of course, a nebulizer. A nice one. Like I'd seen on the web. Next to it, there was a steel box that looked like an old-fashioned computer modem, with wires coming out and a tube, ending in a short wand with bright yellow and red stickers on it. Black lettering, blurred through my tears, said VETRIX. Not helpful. There was also a stainless-steel surgical tool kit, and a large bone on the wall, smiling at me. A cartoon bone. What the fuck? Where the hell was I?

I couldn't remember how I got here. I tried to move but black straps held me tight on my ankles, knees, waist, chest, wrists and neck. Skippy kept barking. I was totally buzzed around the block. I could not recall when I last... it was weird. Every time I tried to remember it was like trying to use your finger to get a bug out of a glass of soda. Every time you went for it, by pressing your finger against the inside of the glass rim, it just slid away. Un-grabbable. I remembered I was at the grandmother's house. Whose grandma? She cried. Yes. How did I get here? Then the gang bangers on the corner. A cab, the office. Skippy and me. He was still barking. I tried to tell Skippy to stop barking but my voice didn't work. I remembered I spoke to somebody. Izzy. On the phone. He told me something about drugs. Now I'm on drugs. It was about the killings, it was something I'd seen on the web. Every time I tried to remember what had been on my screen, it disappeared. Very frustrating. Dinner. We went to dinner. Jane and I went to dinner, didn't we? Skippy suddenly stopped barking. It gave me a bad feeling. I blinked my tears and looked around. It was bright in the room but the hall was dark.

"Hello? Ish anybody there?" I yelled into the gloom. "Schkippy!"

My voice sounded damp as a sponge and slurry, shivering like the rest of me. I was whacked out of my gourd. Did I have a gourd? I was talking to Ginny Mac-and-Cheese. In the new office, but I was keeping a secret. What was the secret? I don't know it. Top Secret. About the drug? I don't know. Too cold, can't stop shaking. Can't stop thinking. I blinked tears out of my eyes again and tried looking around, as far as my neck strap would let me. Pretty pictures of pretty Jane with dogs and kids and cats. A Pepsi commercial. I was in Jane's animal hospital. Tied down. Drugged. Why? I remembered talking to Xana, Jane's assistant. About Bobby. Yes. Then I looked stuff up about vets and had dinner with Jane but she wouldn't tell me. Tell me what?

"Jane," I warbled.

Nothing happened.

Nothing could happen if I stayed outside the office. Jane

had sent me a text saying we had to talk. Yes. But I was too crafty. I would not go in unless other people were there. No crazy person in a tight spot. I'm bad. I had Skippy. But now I'm here. How? Maybe I should not yell. Maybe being alone and alive was good.

Too late. Someone appeared in the doorway and I had to crick my neck to see Jane.

It wasn't Jane.

60.

"Thank God, Xana," I said from my table.

Seeing her brought it back to me. Her SAVE A LIFE t-shirt, Xana, waving to me through the glass front door. She had unlocked it for me, so I knew I would not be alone with the killer, with Jane. Skippy growling at her. Helpful, whacky, sexy Xana, unlocking the door with her keys, telling me to tie Skippy up outside because there were cats inside. I looped and tied his leash around the railing and followed her in. Skippy barking his head off, snarling. Xana locking the door behind us. The sign flipped to CLOSED. That was the end of my rope. No more memory.

"Xana, get me out of thish. Untie me quick," I said, trying to keep my voice low.

Xana froze in the doorway, looking at me all trussed up. She must be stunned.

Then she laughed. It began as a tee-hee type of titter and blossomed into a long and lush laugh. Not a nice, wholesome 'for-goodness-sakes-what-are-you doing-tied-up?' kind of laugh but a chilling 'that's-hysterical-you're-so-high-you-think-I'm-here-to-help-you' kind of cackle. I was totally killing her.

"That is sick, Shepherd. You're a hoot. I forgot the drug

causes amnesia," Xana said. "Also, tearing, shivering and dizziness and, obviously, slurred speech. Your memory will come back... given enough time," she said, with a sad sigh.

I cleared my wet eyes again and looked at her.

"Neil moleshted Bobby."

"Yeah," Xana agreed. "His grandmother didn't know, or doesn't want to know. He wouldn't tell her. He never actually said the words to me but he nodded when Jane and I asked him outright. I saw how Bobby reacted when Leonardi came in here—it was odd. Neil was a total creep."

"Thash why you killed him," I told her, my accusation sounding ridiculous through my thick tongue.

"Of course," Xana said. "Bobby wouldn't tell his school or a priest or the cops. He was ashamed, didn't want anyone to know. Made us promise not to tell. I know what that's like."

"You were mol-ested," I said carefully, avoiding the slur.

"Yeah. I knew the signs. He was a good kid but he couldn't take it. Thought it was his fault, that he was gay or something. We found him unconscious out back, needle still in his arm. Jane tried to bring him back but he'd taken so much. It was a suicide attempt, really."

"Why didn't you tell the cops?"

"Because we knew he wouldn't talk, wouldn't rat out Adela's employers. He said his grandmother needed the money. Then he *couldn't* talk. I knew the cops wouldn't do anything even if I spoke up, not without a victim who could testify. Bobby has severe brain damage. Neil Leonardi basically murdered him." She paused. "Now, I sorta wish I *had* gone to the cops but, once I got started, I kinda couldn't stop."

"You tried to frame Aubrey becaush... because he knew about Bobby?"

Xana nodded. She looked at the clock on the wall, like she was late for something. It was 11:30. I needed to talk until my head cleared. How long would that take? Too long.

"You killed Cash Cush-ing and Aubrey but not Pookie," I said.

"Yes, Shepherd. Leonardi was scum. He hurt Bobby and he hurt Skippy," Xana spat. "And Forsythe liked eating flesh so much, I gave him something really special."

Meat is murder.

"You cooked up Neil's… flesh and served it to Aubrey at Bistro du Bois," I said.

"Amazing how all waitresses look the same to people like him. And I took precautions—wore glasses and a headscarf." She ran a hand through one of her pigtails of jet-black hair. "But the oinker never even looked up." My expression must have betrayed my feelings because her tone became scolding. "Okay, I went a little crazy but you wouldn't let me move on! It looked like you didn't believe Forsythe was the killer, even though he had—I love your headlines—Neil Parmesan in his stomach. Really—what do I have to do to nail the pig? You fucked everything up. My good deed. My justice. Forsythe knew about Bobby and did nothing. They both deserved everything they got. And Cushing was a greedy bastard. I needed someone else to die so I could pin it on Forsythe, and he fit the bill. All your fault. If you and the cops kept looking…"

"We might figure it out," I completed her sentence.

"But you didn't," she grinned. "You thought prissy Doctor Jane did it. Really? Hello!"

"And you used Aubrey's cell phone to lure me to Cushing's house, so I would think he was the killer after all," I said slowly, trying to keep her talking.

"And I just did it again tonight with Jane's phone," Xana smiled. "You're cute but you don't learn."

"You used her favorite mints."

"The mint was just fun," she said. "I had some from Jane, she leaves them around the office. It was a gag, after-dinner mint, you know? The second time, I thought I should continue and, you know, sign Forsythe's name to Cushing and maybe point to Jane if something went wrong."

"Instead of ending it, you created a franchise. Two men from the *Mail*—Jack Leslie and Matt Molloy—killed Pookie Piccarelli to raise circulation figures."

"Yeah. I really liked that show," she said sadly. "I know newspapers do anything for a story but this is, like, surreal."

"Yeah," I agreed with her. "How sick is it to kill someone for nothing."

Oops. Xana frowned and moved to the side table, where the halothane nebulizer and the other equipment sat waiting. Not good.

"Xana. You're right. Let Aubrey Forsythe and the goons from the *Mail* take the rap for Leonardi and Cushing. We can use someone resourceful like you on our team at the *Daily Press*. You'd make a great investigative reporter."

"Yeah? I like you too, Shepherd, but you would have to say that, wouldn't you?"

"It's true, Xana. I don't care if you killed Neil and Aubrey and Cushing."

"And Matt Molloy and Lucky-what's-his-face?" she added.

"Holy shit. That was you in the black van in Central Park." I remembered the shadowy figure standing on the hill above me as I had dragged myself out of the lake. I had thought it was Molloy.

"Of course. The Catmobile. Jane was worried about you. She told me you were crazy, going to meet the killer all alone. I cruised through the park but spotted your cops. Later, I heard the shots and saw a cop convention. I drove uptown, looking for you, and heard more shots. I was scared but by the time I got there, you were crawling out of the lake, alive but fucked up. I saw that dork Molloy. He had a gun. I hit him with the Catmobile. Just a good bump to knock him down."

"So Molloy brought a gun to a car fight."

"What?"

"Thanks for saving my life, Xana."

"You're welcome."

"This is how you killed them, isn't it? Forsythe and Molloy?"

"Yeah. Plus Leonardi and Cushing. A stun gun, then halothane. No one suffered. None of them felt a thing. I'm, like, humane. And your boss, that Edgar guy? He made up lies about you. I found him."

"But not Badger."

"I would never harm an animal."

"No. Don Badger, the editor."

"Who?"

"Okay. After you… put them down… what did you… I mean what did you do then?" I asked.

"Surgical laser," she said, looking at the modem and wand on the counter. "Disassembly. Final stage is the incinerator. You know, ashes to ashes?"

I began shivering again.

"Are you going to hurt Skippy?"

She looked wounded. Then she looked pissed.

"Skippy wasn't growling at any cats," I said. "He was growling at you. The person who killed Neil."

"He's smarter than you," Xana said. "You tied him up outside, remember? I'll gas him after I gas you."

"You still have time to get away before the cops…"

"Before the cops kick in the door and save you?"

"Yes."

There was that tittery laugh again.

"As if," Xana said. "Dude, I checked your phone. No calls, no texts, no tweets for hours and my text to you from Jane's phone was the last thing on your call log. I punked the big detective reporter twice. Deal with it."

"Xana, you're rich. If you hang around, you'll never get a

chance to spend all that money," I tried.

"That was, like, fate, man," Xana said. "Aubrey had this, like, treasure. A bag with stacks of cash and rings and watches. I can set up a whole animal rights thing in California."

"Exactly," I agreed. "Anything you want. Where's Jane?"

"Next door," Xana said. "Like you, but she's still out. Don't worry, you won't feel a thing. Neither will she."

Xana turned her back to me, opened a drawer and took something out. Time to go. I fought against the straps with everything I had. I wasn't proud. At the same time, I yelled my head off. I yelled "HELP!" loudly several hundred times. Then I tried screaming "POLICE!" I also shouted "FIRE!" because I had read that it was more likely to make New Yorkers respond. The straps cut into my neck, hands and legs painfully. I tried harder. Xana giggled. I stopped.

"Please don't hurt Jane," I said. "Maybe *I* can disappear but if your boss goes missing you're going to be suspect number one."

"No, Shepherd. You're gonna be suspect number one. You'll disappear but Jane will be found, tragically murdered—by you. I think you should, like, confess by text to that cop. Or maybe to your newspaper. The new one, I guess. More people will see it that way. So what do you think the headline will be?"

I thought about that for a moment.

"How about 'Dumb Reporter Killed by Psycho Goth Vet Aide?'"

"I'm not a Goth, dork. I'm Emo. And no, not the real deal—like, what people will think. See, you're going to totally admit all the killings."

"Okay. 'Crazy Pet Groomer Tries to Blame Serial Slayings on Dead Reporter.' You're going to get caught, Xana. Give it up. Walk away."

"Call me crazy one more time, paperboy, and I'll eat your

fucking face like a chimp," Xana warned.

I had no reason to disbelieve her.

61.

I heard a bang and a tinkle, like a drummer's rim shot and cymbal splash on a comedian's punchline. But I'm the joke. Xana's head snapped toward the dark hallway, her Pippi Longstocking pigtails whipping around. She heard it too, so it was real. Skippy began barking again. Xana did not look happy.

Good.

She grabbed something that flashed like a mirror in the bright light. It was Aubrey's fancy stainless-steel meat cleaver.

Bad.

She was indecisive. Hack my throat open now or postpone the fun? She smirked and dashed out. Then it was quiet. I tried to make my ears bigger but there was no noise. Then I thought I heard a crunching noise. Then nothing. I tried to get free again. No way. I tried screaming for help again. Nothing. Then, distant voices. Then nothing again. Normally, I wouldn't be able to stand the suspense but I realized I wanted as much suspense as I could get. Tons of it. I shut my mouth and waited. No hurry. No worry. Still alive.

Until I heard more crunching. And footsteps. Xana coming back. I sank back. I heard her coming into the room. I didn't look. I heard her laugh again. I hated Xana's laugh. But this sounded different. Familiar but different. I lifted my head.

"You comfy, Shepherd?" she asked. "Looks kinda kinky."

Ginny McElhone. She had the cleaver in one hand. She put it on the counter and took a notebook, pen and a silver digital camera out of her purse.

"Smile, Shepherd," Ginny grinned, flashing me on my table several times, before putting the camera down. "So why did that Goth bitch tie you up—and your girlfriend in the next room?"

"She's not Goth, she's Emo," I corrected her. "Is Jane…"

"She seems to be okay but really stoned, not making any sense," Ginny said, head buried in her notebook. "Also crying, lots of tears. What's going on? I thought the *Mail* guys did everything?"

"Ginny, thanks for coming but if you don't stop interviewing me and cut me loose in the next three seconds I will kill you when I *do* get loose."

She started toward me, then stopped and glanced up at the clock. She stopped.

"First, you tell me the whole thing and then I'll cut you loose. For all I know, you're the killer."

I knew it was bullshit but it *was* logical.

"Okay, Ginny, but first you tell me how you got here."

"Okay, Shepherd," Ginny said, grinning. "After you left, I called the guy from IT and told him my computer had crashed and I needed to recover some important notes. From your machine."

"You spied on me? Son of a bitch. I thought we were on the same team, Ginny?"

"Oh, please. I thought you were holding out on me and you were. So, the IT guy said there were no notes but there were web searches on some drug called halo-whatever and I looked it up. It said it was an animal doctor drug. You're dating a vet, so my brothers and I went to her house and staked it out for a while but you guys didn't come home. I found a listing for her office and we came here. We saw somebody was working in the back. I called but only got voicemail. Then I knocked and told the pigtailed freak I hit a dog with my car around the block and could she please come. She said no, I should go to somewhere else. She seemed real off. We struck out, so I thought a rock through the window might set off an alarm or something, stir things up. She came out with a friggin' meat cleaver and threatened to cut my throat, so my brothers grabbed her ass. Then I found you. Bingo!"

"Ginny," I told her. "You are the most sneaky, selfish, dishonest person I've ever met and I'm very glad you are. I owe you big-time."

"Yes you do. Tell me the story."

I told her. Everything. Ginny was writing it all down, like she was at a press conference about the city budget. It pissed me off but she *had* saved my life.

"Holy shit, that's great!" Ginny gushed like a kid on Christmas. "She confessed?"

"Yeah. Neil Leonardi, Aubrey Forsythe, Cash Cushing, Matt Molloy and even Lucky Tal," I said. "But not Badger or Pookie. Okay, that's it. All of it. Get me out of this," I said.

"No problem. Right after deadline," she laughed, moving to the door. "I've got just enough time to get my exclusive in for the final."

"It's not your exclusive if you steal it, Ginny. It's mine. You can't leave me here."

"Tough. My brothers are tying up the black-haired bitch on the third table. I'll call the cops after we get my exclusive up on the web and in the paper. With pictures of you, all tied up. You'll love it."

"Ginny, I don't care about the story. Let us go. What if Xana gets loose while you're filing the story? At least let Jane free."

"Nope. She'll call the cops and it will go out over the air. I'll call the cops in a few hours and they'll get you. You'll be fine."

"Ginny, don't screw around with this girl. She's seriously dangerous."

But she was gone. I cursed my head off until I heard another commotion outside the room. Damn. Shouting, thumping. More yelling. If Xana was loose, we were all dead.

Nothing happened for several lifetimes. I began shouting for help.

Nothing.

I caught a shadow on the wall outside the room, like an arm pointing. The hand held a gun shape. She had a pistol. At least it would be quick. The shadow got closer. A real gun and a real hand and arm appeared. It was attached to the most beautiful cop I ever saw.

"He's in here!" Officer Augie Gumbs shouted, holstering his weapon.

"Want to tell me what this circus is all about?" Izzy asked me, stepping into the room.

Fortunately, I was able to answer him.

"Sure," I told Izzy. "But I want it clear that I wasn't fucking the elephant."

62.

As he untied me, Izzy said he did his own web crawling after I asked about the halothane. He made the link between it and veterinarians, and a quick check of the Arthur Animal Hospital website showed they also provided dog-walking services. One call to Cash Cushing's house got a caretaker who had confirmed that Bubbles the corgi was walked by an Arthur Hospital employee, and that they had access to a key and knew the alarm code.

"I wanted to talk to your girlfriend, the one who messed up Cash Cushing's crime scene trying to revive him," Izzy said. "I couldn't get you on the phone. The uniforms at her place and your place told me nobody was home, so Phil and I cruised by here. We arrived the same time as a local sector RMP, responding to a 911 call about a broken window and an alarm. That's when we ran into your friend Virginia and her hulk brothers on the way out."

"Thanks, Izzy. Great minds think alike." I shook his hand and then rubbed my sore wrists.

"Great minds don't get hog-tied by a killer," Izzy pointed out.

"I knew it was her all along."

Izzy looked skeptical so I changed the subject and we

went to free Jane. I hugged her, not minding that she was leaking halothane tears all over me.

"Shepherd! I'm so sorry," Jane cried. "I promised Bobby's grandmother I would never say anything. She's very... old-fashioned. It didn't matter anyway, I thought. A week after Bobby overdosed, Neil Leonardi was dead and everyone was saying that Aubrey Forsythe had done it!"

I stroked her hair. "I get it. You thought that the bastard who hurt Bobby was dead and his killer, the one who knew about the abuse and said nothing, was on the run."

She nodded. "I thought it was over. I thought it was a kind of justice. I was wrong. When you told me Forsythe was innocent I worried that somebody in Bobby's family might be responsible but I didn't believe it was his grandmother."

"You have nothing to be sorry for," I told her. "I was an idiot. I... I thought..."

"You suspected me—I know," Jane said. "I was hurt and angry but it was all my fault. Xana... that monster... I can't believe she did all this and she was going to... She told me that she had already told you about Bobby working here. About the keys and the alarm codes and everything. She was clever and I must have looked very suspicious at dinner, pretending I never heard of him."

"It doesn't matter," I said. "None of it matters anymore. I want to take Skippy over to your place, have a drink and turn your husband's picture to the wall."

"Sounds good."

I reclaimed our phones, which Xana had left on a counter. Then I turned to Izzy.

"Xana killed Matt Molloy and Tal Edgar," I said. "Cut them up and put them in the incinerator."

Izzy grimaced. "Why?"

"To save me, apparently."

"Huh."

"At least it's some closure for Sean Joyce's family. That's

why I got into this business in the first place, to get closure. Mary Catherine and I will have to visit them, to let them know that the people who drove Officer Joyce to suicide are dead."

"First, we have some business to take care of," Izzy said.

Jane, Izzy and I adjourned to the waiting room. A furious Xana, Ginny and the McElhone brothers were cuffed to chairs, Ginny issuing threats about lawsuits and exposés that no one was listening to. Jane went outside to free Skippy and we gave him a lot of petting to stop him from growling and snapping at Xana.

"Next time, I will listen to you, Skippy," I told him. "Good boy."

"Breaking and entering," Izzy said loudly, pointing at Ginny and her brothers.

He turned to me and whispered. "We'll drop the charges and let her and her brothers go after you file your story, okay?"

"Thanks, Izzy, I appreciate that."

"I was rescuing them!" Ginny protested.

Izzy ignored her and turned to me. "So you got stuck in a tight spot with a crazy person? I told you not to do that."

"Fuck you!" Xana spat, squirming and kicking like a maniacal midget between two cops. "Don't call me crazy!"

"Seems to be the word, Xana," I told her. "Cheer up. Unlike you, New York State does not have the death penalty. Eventually, I'm sure you'll get your own reality show."

At that thought, a smile spread across Xana's mad face, becoming wider and weirder.

"Smile!" I said, snapping a picture with my phone. It would go nicely with my story.

I checked the shot. The horn-haired Hacker, putting on a bent smile for her public. The words SAVE A LIFE on her t-shirt stood out, nicely rounded on her chest, an intriguing mix of sex and irony.

I called the *Daily Press* to file my exclusive and emailed

the photograph of Xana, which I knew would be on the front page in the morning. I loudly told a rewrite reporter to put my name *and* Ginny's on the piece.

"Damn right!" Ginny said, rattling her handcuffs.

Then I quietly told the rewrite guy to hide Ginny's name in tiny type at the end of the story in a tagline as "additional reporting by Virginia McElhone." It would drive her batshit.

"You two are as crazy as Xana," Jane observed. "Do you know that?"

"Yes I do," I said.

"Foof," Skippy agreed.

F.X. SHEPHERD WILL RETURN IN

SHOOT

AVAILABLE OCTOBER 2016

ACKNOWLEDGEMENTS

With a quick tip of my press fedora to Evelyn Waugh, I want to thank my publicist, Katharine Trowbridge Carroll, for work above and beyond the call of duty. My thanks also go to my great editor at Titan Books, Miranda Jewess. I also thank my agent Jane Dystel for her help. My wife and first editor Riki made this book, and all of my books, possible and she has my eternal gratitude.

ABOUT THE AUTHOR

KIERAN CROWLEY is a *New York Times* bestselling author and award-winning investigative reporter, who has received communication from an actual serial killer and deciphered his secret code. He has covered hundreds of trials and thousands of murders and recovered evidence missed by police at numerous crime scenes, some of which helped bring killers to justice. He lives in New York with his family.

SHOOT

AN F.X. SHEPHERD NOVEL

KIERAN CROWLEY

F.X. Shepherd is juggling a new job as a PI, while keeping up with his strangely popular pet column. He is hired by a congressman who has received death threats, part of the escalating war between the Republican Party and Tea Party extremists. A series of murders of gun rights politicos at a presidential convention ratchets up the stakes, and Shepherd must fight off his liberal parents, do-anything-for-a-story reporter Ginny Mac, and a gang of mysterious gunmen.

PRAISE FOR THE AUTHOR

"An in-depth investigation… truly appalling all around: a story seemingly without goodness, except in the telling."
Kirkus Reviews

"A fast-paced account."
Publishers Weekly

AVAILABLE OCTOBER 2016

SONATA OF THE DEAD

A JOEL SORRELL NOVEL

CONRAD WILLIAMS

It's four months on from the events of *Dust and Desire*... Joel
Sorrell has recovered from the injuries he sustained in his fight with
The Four-Year-Old, but now a body has been found on a patch of
wasteland in Enfield, torn apart by a killer who comes to be known
as The Hack. More deaths will follow, linked to an unconventional
writers' group. Joel realises he has to infiltrate the group when he
makes the shocking discovery that his missing daughter is a member.
And she is next on The Hack's list.

PRAISE FOR THE AUTHOR

"A feat of dynamic equilibrium that seems more admirable the longer
I think about it." *Locus*

"A thriller of real distinction." *Crime Time*

AVAILABLE JULY 2016

TITANBOOKS.COM

DEAD LETTERS ANTHOLOGY

EDITED BY

CONRAD WILLIAMS

The Dead Letters Office: the final repository of the undelivered. Love missives unread, gifts unreceived, lost in postal limbo. *Dead Letters Anthology* features new stories from the masters of horror, fantasy and speculative fiction, each inspired by an inhabitant of the Dead Letters Office, including tales from Joanne Harris, China Miéville, Adam Nevill and Michael Marshall Smith.

PRAISE FOR THE AUTHOR

"Williams is so good at what he does that he probably shouldn't be allowed to do it anymore, for the sake of everyone's sanity."
Publishers Weekly (starred review)

"Conrad Williams writes dark and powerful prose balancing the poetic and elegant with needle-sharp incision." *Guardian*

AVAILABLE APRIL 2016

THE BLOOD STRAND

A FØROYAR NOVEL

CHRIS OULD

Having left the Faroes when he was three years old, Jan Reyna is now a British murder squad police detective, and the Islands are completely foreign to him. But he is drawn back when his estranged father is found unconscious in an isolated spot, a shotgun by his side and someone else's blood in his car. Then a man is found washed up on a beach, a shotgun wound in his side, but signs that suffocation were the cause of death. Is his father – who has suffered a massive stroke and is unable to speak – responsible for the man's death? What about his half-brothers, and the signs that one of them may have been blackmailed? Jan falls in with local detective Hjalti Hentze, a man after his own heart, but as the stakes get higher and Jan learns more about the truth behind his mother's flight from the Faroes, he must decide whether to stay and learn more, or forsake the strange, windswept Faroe Islands for good.

PRAISE FOR THE AUTHOR

"This is bound to be a highly successful series." *Hearthfire*

AVAILABLE FEBRUARY 2016

THE KILLING BAY

A FØROYAR NOVEL

CHRIS OULD

The arrival in Tórshavn of environmental activists campaigning against oil exploration in Faroese waters creates tension and conflict as islanders defend their rights to self-determination in the face of foreign ideology. Hours after a violent clash between islanders and protesters, a Danish woman from the activist group is found dead and apparently raped, for which a local man is arrested and charged. But as Hentze and Reyna look deeper into the case it gradually becomes clear that the killing has other motivations, and that both sides are being manipulated in a way which brings betrayal and another death before it's resolved.

PRAISE FOR THE AUTHOR

"Unmissable and thrilling fiction." *Lancashire Evening Post*

"This well researched story gives us an insight into the violent underbelly of London society." *Irish Examiner*

AVAILABLE FEBRUARY 2017

THE AGE OF TREACHERY
A DUNCAN FORRESTER NOVEL
GAVIN SCOTT

It is the winter of 1946, and after years of war, ex-Special Operations Executive agent Duncan Forrester is back at his Oxford college as a junior Ancient History Fellow. But his peace is shattered when a much-disliked Fellow is found dead in the quad, stabbed and pushed from an upper window. A don is suspected and arrested for the murder, but Forrester is not convinced of his friend's guilt. On the hunt for the true killer, he finds himself plunged into a mystery involving lost Viking sagas, Satanic rituals and wartime espionage.

The first novel is a brand new crime series by Hollywood screenwriter Gavin Scott.

AVAILABLE APRIL 2016

THE AGE OF OLYMPUS

A DUNCAN FORRESTER NOVEL

GAVIN SCOTT

Duncan Forrester's research on an Aegean island is interrupted first by the murder of a British archaeologist, and then by the outbreak of the Greek Civil War. The worship of ancient gods may provide a clue to the murderer, but in such a tumultuous time, little is what it seems...

AVAILABLE APRIL 2017

THE AGE OF EXODUS

A DUNCAN FORRESTER NOVEL

GAVIN SCOTT

Britain is still trying to exert control over Palestine and facing the terrorist threat of the Stern Gang. As a result of his activities in Greece, Forrester is asked by British Foreign Secretary Ernest Bevin to help avert a plot to assassinate the British Governor of Jerusalem.

AVAILABLE APRIL 2018

IMPURE BLOOD

A CAPTAIN DARAC NOVEL

PETER MORFOOT

In the heat of a French summer, Captain Paul Darac of the Nice Brigade Criminelle is called to a highly sensitive crime scene. A man has been found murdered in the midst of a Muslim prayer group, but no one saw how it was done. Then the organisers of the Nice leg of the Tour de France receive an unlikely terrorist threat. In what becomes a frantic race against time, Darac must try and unpick a complex knot in which racial hatred, sex and revenge are tightly intertwined.

A brand new crime series featuring Captain Paul Darac of the Brigade Criminelle.

AVAILABLE APRIL 2016

BABAZOUK BLUES

A CAPTAIN DARAC NOVEL

PETER MORFOOT

In the heart of the old town of Nice, the Babazouk, a woman's body is found. A quarter rich with the smell of Moorish coffee and fresh fish, the Babazouk is also Captain Paul Darac's own home, and he and his officers from the Brigade Criminelle are called to the scene. Then it is discovered that the woman suffered from a heart condition and her death is put down to natural causes, but Darac becomes fascinated by the woman's life and the anomalies of the case. He must put aside allegiances past and present to disentangle a story of greed and murder – and become a target himself.

AVAILABLE APRIL 2017

WRITTEN IN DEAD WAX

A VINYL DETECTIVE NOVEL

ANDREW CARTMEL

He is a record collector – a connoisseur of vinyl, hunting out rare and elusive LPs. His business card describes him as the 'Vinyl Detective' and some people take this more literally than others. Like the beautiful, mysterious woman who wants to pay him a large sum of money to find a priceless lost recording – on behalf of an extremely wealthy (and rather sinister) shadowy client.
Given that he's just about to run out of cat biscuits, this gets our hero's full attention. So begins a painful and dangerous odyssey in search of the rarest jazz record of them all...

"An irresistible blend of murder, mystery and music... our protagonist seeks to find the rarest of records – and incidentally solve a murder, right a great historical injustice and, if he's very lucky, avoid dying in the process."
Ben Aaronovitch, bestselling author of *Rivers of London*

"The Vinyl Detective is one of the sharpest and most original characters I've seen for a long time."
David Quantick

AVAILABLE MAY 2016

TITANBOOKS.COM

THE RUN-OUT GROOVE

A VINYL DETECTIVE NOVEL

ANDREW CARTMEL

His first adventure consisted of the search for a rare record; his second begins with the discovery of one. When a mint copy of the final album by Valerian – England's great lost rock band of the 1960s – surfaces in a charity shop, all hell breaks loose. Finding this record triggers a chain of events culminating in our hero learning the true fate of the singer Valerian, who died just after – or was it just before? – the abduction of her two-year-old son.

Along the way, the Vinyl Detective finds himself marked for death, at the wrong end of a shotgun, and unknowingly dosed with LSD as a prelude to being burned alive. And then there's the grave robbing…

"Like an old 45rpm record, this book crackles with brilliance."
David Quantick

"This tale of crime, cats and rock & roll unfolds with an authentic sense of the music scene then and now – and a mystery that will keep you guessing." **Stephen Gallagher**

AVAILABLE MAY 2017

LADY, GO DIE!

A MIKE HAMMER NOVEL

MICKEY SPILLANE & MAX ALLAN COLLINS

Hammer and Velda go on vacation to a small beach town on Long Island after wrapping up the Williams case (*I, the Jury*). Walking romantically along the boardwalk, they witness a brutal beating at the hands of some vicious local cops—Hammer wades in to defend the victim. When a woman turns up naked—and dead—astride the statue of a horse in the small-town city park, how she wound up this unlikely Lady Godiva is just one of the mysteries Hammer feels compelled to solve...

"Collins knows the pistol-packing PI inside and out, and Hammer's vigilante rage (and gruff way with the ladies) reads authentically."
Booklist

"A fun read that rings true to the way the character was originally written by Spillane." *Crimespree Magazine*

COMPLEX 90

A MIKE HAMMER NOVEL

MICKEY SPILLANE & MAX ALLAN COLLINS

Hammer accompanies a conservative politician to Moscow on a fact-finding mission. While there, he is arrested by the KGB on a bogus charge, and imprisoned; but he quickly escapes, creating an international incident by getting into a firefight with Russian agents. On his stateside return, the government is none too happy with Mr. Hammer. Russia is insisting upon his return to stand charges, and various government agencies are following him. A question dogs our hero: why him? Why does Russia want him back, and why (as evidence increasingly indicates) was he singled out to accompany the senator to Russia in the first place?

"It may be Spillane's hero throwing the punches in these stories, but make no mistake—it's the writer who knocks you out."
BarnesandNobleReview.com

"[Collins's] prose never lets up for a second... a slam-bang climax that had us needing a drink when it was over."
Pulp Fiction Reviews

For more fantastic fiction, author events, exclusive excerpts,
competitions, limited editions and more

Visit our website
titanbooks.com

Like us on Facebook
facebook.com/titanbooks

Follow us on Twitter
@TitanBooks

Email us
readerfeedback@titanemail.com